CITY
OF
SILK

GLENNIS VIRGO

Allison & Busby Limited
11 Wardour Mews
London W1F 8AN
allisonandbusby.com

First published in Great Britain by Allison & Busby in 2024.

Copyright © 2024 by GLENNIS VIRGO

The moral right of the author is hereby asserted in accordance with
the Copyright, Designs and Patents Act 1988.

*All characters and events in this publication,
other than those clearly in the public domain,
are fictitious and any resemblance to actual persons,
living or dead, is purely coincidental.*

All rights reserved. No part of this publication may be reproduced,
stored in a retrieval system, or transmitted, in any form or by
any means without the prior written permission of the publisher,
nor be otherwise circulated in any form of binding or cover
other than that in which it is published and without a similar
condition being imposed on the subsequent buyer.
A CIP catalogue record for this book is available from
the British Library.

First Edition

HB ISBN 978-0-7490-3184-8
TPB ISBN 978-0-7490-3199-2

Typeset in 11.5/16.5pt Adobe Garamond Pro by
Allison & Busby Ltd.

By choosing this product, you help take care of the world's forests.
Learn more: www.fsc.org

Printed and bound by
CPI Group (UK) Ltd, Croydon, CR0 4YY

For Izzie – my Persephone.
With love from your Demeter.

Report on an applicant for a place at the orphanage of Santa Maria del Baraccano, Bologna, in the year of our Lord, 1566

We are satisfied that the girl is a true orphan, lacking both father and mother, and is from a respectable artisan family. In the absence of any other living kinsman, she has been recommended by one of her father's journeymen. Her baptismal certificate has been examined and gives her age as ten years. Father and mother were citizens and she was born within the city walls. She has been neither begging nor working as a domestic servant nor tending animals in the fields since her parents passed from this life. This testifies to righteous conduct, but without the protection of the orphanage her honour could be in peril before much time has passed.

She has no deformities or disease – is neither blind, deaf, mute, hunchbacked, nor lame. Her eyesight is sharp. Though she speaks little, she is obedient and not considered lazy or a gossip. She has been verified as a virgin by a respected gentlewoman and shows no signs of an evil disposition. Though she is not especially fair, there is no impediment to her being placed in employment and married in due course, so long as she contracts no disfiguring ailment whilst under the care of the mistresses. In sum, there is nothing to indicate that she would weigh down the orphanage.

There is one further attribute to note. The girl has, it would appear, some knowledge of sewing which will be of benefit both to the orphanage and to herself.

Chapter One

Bologna, 1575

In those days, before we all took our revenge, a man in Signora Ruffo's workroom was as noteworthy as marten fur lining in a velvet cape – and a good deal less welcome.

The Signora had been widowed long before (her husband one of those tailors whose workshops stud the Via Drapperie) and her clients knew well that menfolk were not gladly received at their fittings. Fathers and husbands likely paid for the gowns and capes, the undershifts and overdresses, but neither their attendance nor their approval was required. The fittings took place in the afternoons and each working day was separated into two distinct parts. In the mornings there were but three of us in the workroom. The Signora and I spent our time cutting and sewing, and the loudest sound was that of shears sliding through silk or the soft thud when Sofia moved a bolt of fabric. The afternoons were a swirl of female chatter and gossip as each client swept in, accompanied by at least one sister or friend to give advice, together with a lady's maid to be loaded up with discarded clothing. Signora Ruffo had set up a corner of the workroom as a fitting area. There were tapestry chairs softened with cushions, a painted screen – its design of mulberry trees a constant reminder of the source of the city's wealth – and two small tables on which wine was served once the damasks and brocades had been safely put aside. As a rule, the two of us moved from one customer to the next, pinning and tweaking, reassuring and encouraging, until the last had flurried down the stairs.

That afternoon I was on my knees adjusting the hem of a blue silk gown (its owner far too short to do it justice, in my opinion) when a male voice, announcing its owner as Signor Martelli, rumbled under the usual chirruping and caused us all to look towards the door. I had expected the Signora to hustle the man away, but he wore the air of an expected visitor and she invited him to sit at her embroidery table, where they remained in conference for two strikes of the hour from the clock on the Accursio Tower. Signor Martelli was hard to place – his clothes were not those of a nobleman but they were well cut and the fabric of good quality. And he was neither old nor especially ugly. If I had thought a little harder, I would have tumbled to it, but I was too busy grappling with the swathes of silk.

I had spent all morning working on the gown, its colour mirrored in the early spring sky beyond the open windows. Only on the coldest days, when fingers became too stiff for sewing and chilblains threatened, would Signora Ruffo allow the shutters to be closed. She always said that working in the gloom is a certain road to crooked seams and clumsy pleating. Every so often, I had to stop and rub my hands together for warmth before picking up my needle again to continue the row of small and perfectly even stitches, but I did not mind. A room full of light, however cold, does not make me shiver – unlike shadows and flickering candles. The Signora's palazzo is tall and elegant, much like the mistress herself, and situated at the end of a block where the last buildings in the street surrender to smallholdings. From the top-floor workroom the view stretches as far as the solid walls which encircle the city and, in the other direction, to the jumble of buildings and towers which make up the church of San Francesco. He had been my favourite saint in my mother's bedtime stories, and I sent up a quick prayer for my next piece of work to consist of something other than sky-blue ruffles and flounces. A mourning dress in a sombre *monachino* would be perfect: collar standing sentinel around the neck, tightly fitted bodice and the only decoration a few tassels.

After making a neat finish to the final seam, I had gathered up the silk gown in my arms. The Signora was seated at her table embroidering a stomacher with gold thread which glittered in the sunlight, but she put it aside to scrutinise every finger's length of my work. Finally, she looked up and smiled.

'Excellent work, Elena. I could have made you the best seamstress in Bologna – given more time.'

I twisted my thimble ring round and round.

'Signora, is there any likelihood that this afternoon there may be a lady who requires a more . . . fitted gown?'

'There speaks a tailor's daughter! Always looking at shape rather than embellishment. Your mother should have birthed a boy.'

There was the rub. My skills may have rivalled those of any

pustule-faced apprentice, but my sex decreed that the door of every tailor's workshop in the city was closed to me. A gown may be as elaborate and well fashioned as any doublet and breeches but its making is women's work. There is no honour in it – or money either. Time and again, I had bludgeoned the mistress about my ambition but her response never wavered: that the closest a woman may get to being a tailor is to marry one. Her dismissal served to avoid further argument.

'Now, hurry along and help Sofia prepare for the clients.'

I bobbed a grudging curtsey before scooping up the completed gown and draping it over the hanging beam.

It was not the Signora who taught me to sew; I learnt those skills in my father's workshop, sitting on his knee. And later, inside the Baraccano, my talents were put to such good use that, on leaving, I was placed as a seamstress rather than some rich woman's drudge. But it was Signora Ruffo who taught me to measure and fit, to make adjustments which enhance a long neck or disguise a thickening waist. Most seamstresses do not venture beyond undershifts of fine white linen, while for outer garments there is Drapperie where many of the tailors are content to clothe women as well as gentlemen. But some ladies of good taste do not want to be measured and prodded by a man – and an artisan at that. Signora Ruffo made it her business to provide everything such clients may require, from a hooded cape to an undershift edged with decorative stitching. Not that I was required to make undershifts any longer.

The previous October, around the feast of San Petronio, Signora Ruffo had decided that there was too much work for just herself and me. Sofia sews a good, straight seam and can do so in haste when a customer decides for some reason that she has desperate need of new undergarments before the end of the week. It is also Sofia's job to keep the workroom tidy, which she does with great attentiveness; there is never a dropped needle or a speck of lint to be found on the floor. Sofia is not her real name, but no one is able to pronounce that, and I can no longer even recall it. When she arrived, her language was like an uneven seam, all stops and starts, with an accent even stranger than that of the Sicilians who haggle over the price of cocoons in the Pavaglione. In the afternoons she was kept busy at a distance from the clients. They were, for the most part, the wives and daughters of rich silk merchants, or aristocrats who had somehow clung on to the Holy Father's goodwill. If Sofia came too close, those ladies would affect a shudder. One even told the Signora that her new assistant needed to be scrubbed clean to get that horrible colour from her skin. But Sofia continued to sway a path around the edges of the room, her expression always serene.

Sofia and I each had a narrow bedroom, high up under the beams of the palazzo. One night I had been lying awake, fearing dreams of the Baraccano, when I heard sounds through the thin wall which divided the two rooms. Sofia was speaking aloud, but I could not work out what she was saying – even less who she could be talking to. I got up and pressed my ear to the wall: Sofia was repeating phrases she heard used in the workroom.

'Bring the crimson damask over here, please.'

'Feel the quality of this silk velvet, Signora.'

'Has anyone seen my needle?'

Sofia was trying to improve her Bolognese! From time to time, she would pause on a word and say it over and over again, struggling for the correct pronunciation.

The following evening, as soon as the murmuring began, I tapped on her door. For a few moments there was silence, then Sofia opened it a crack, her head lowered in apology.

'Sorry, Elena, sorry. I have disturbed.'

'I heard you practising. May I help?'

'No. Thank you. You sleep. I be quiet.'

It took me the length of a Mass to persuade her, but from that time onwards we spent every evening together. We began by chanting the names of fabrics and equipment, but Sofia was a quick learner and soon she was making up her own sentences. Gradually, the lessons turned into conversation and we would gossip about the clients. I even taught her some of the things I would like to say to them – on strict instructions that they must never be repeated:

'I am sorry, Signora, but you are far too old to be wearing that.'

'If you are rude to me again, I will stick pins in you.'

At first Sofia would trap a giggle behind her hand but soon we were both laughing out loud, glad that the mistress slept two floors below. We talked of clothes and handsome young men we had caught sight of in the street, but neither of us spoke of life before joining Signora Ruffo. For me, it would be like scratching an open wound, and I imagined that the same was true for Sofia. Even at that time, I thought it unlikely that she had arrived in Bologna of her own will. Though our talk in the workroom was of practical matters, sometimes we would catch each other's eye and have to turn away to hide our smiles.

It was about a week later that Signor Martelli stood on the threshold again, but this time there trailed behind him another, whose black robes and hat marked him out as a notary. Some of them, I knew, were learned men of means while others could scarcely afford their own quills; the depth of dye in this one's garments suggested that he fell somewhere between the two. He pulled from his bag a sheaf of papers as thick as half a Bible before joining Signor Martelli at the Signora's embroidery table. I tried to hear what was being said, but their discourse was held in an undertone and my customer would keep prating on about the exact fit of her bodice. Sofia was closer to the Signora's table and I hoped that she had been able to unravel some words.

After less than an hour of the clock the notary left, his robes flapping like the wings of a crow, while Signor Martelli remained seated, legs outstretched, and gazed around as though he owned us all. Each time his eyes lit on me, I repaid him with a scowl. Only when fitting had ended for the day did the Signora escort him downstairs along with the remaining customers. I immediately sidled over to Sofia.

'Did you manage to catch anything, Sof? Is Signora Ruffo making a will? Please tell me that man is not buying her business.'

Sofia continued stabbing pins into a pin pillow and would not meet my eye.

'It is about marriage, I think. They say "betrothal". That is marriage, yes?'

Though I felt as though a stone had settled inside me, I attempted a laugh.

'The mistress marry? She would never do that. She has

nothing to gain and would lose all her freedom. You must have misheard.'

'Not the mistress. They put names on papers. His name.' She looked up with a weak smile. 'And yours.'

I turned away, in need of re-winding a roll of damask. At that moment the Signora came back into the workroom and I strode across to her.

'Is it true?'

'Remember your manners please, miss.'

Sofia edged to the side of the room and looked like she wished to fade into a fabric bolt. I sketched an unwilling curtsey.

'I beg pardon, Signora. Is it true that I am to be married to Signor Martelli?'

Signora Ruffo gestured towards her table.

'Come and sit down with me.'

'No – I thank you. Please answer me, Signora.'

'I intended to tell you this evening, my dear, but I see that you have worked matters out for yourself. He is a good man, recently widowed, with no children. His wife died soon after their marriage.'

'I do not care about his wife! Nor do I wish to be his new one.' My voice was rising and I could feel the heat in my face. 'If I am not allowed to be a tailor, why may I not remain here? You are pleased with my work, are you not?'

'You know that I am, Elena, but you cannot pretend surprise.' Her voice was scratched with irritation. 'Three years of work and then a marriage – they are the Baraccano rules. I have done my best for you.'

All at once the cut of Signor Martelli's clothes made sense. I sighed.

'So he is a master tailor – but I surmise that he will not allow me to work.'

Signora Ruffo lowered her head and smoothed the gap between her brows.

'Some tidying of his workshop, perhaps, but that is all. I tried, Elena, but he was obdurate.'

She probably took my silence as submission, but I had already made my resolve: I was not going to marry Signor Martelli.

Chapter Two

I left no note: not because I was unable – the mistresses at the Baraccano slapped and cuffed our letters into us – but I was too angry to give any explanation or thanks. If the Signora thought me an ungrateful wretch, so be it; at least she would not come looking for me. As for Sofia – it pains me still that I did not take my proper leave of her and worse, that I unpicked our friendship in a few words.

'No lesson in Bolognese tonight, I beg you, Sofia. To tell truth, I have become wearied by them.'

That same night, I waited until it was certain that they would both be asleep before I took my bundle and crept down the flights of stone steps, pulling the front door shut behind me. In the courtyard I unbarred the gate and slipped round the side of the palazzo, heading towards the Reno Canal.

I spent the first part of the night ducking in and out of side streets, avoiding the main roads where the Legate's *sbirri* liked to roam in gangs, pretending to keep the peace. But soon after Matins a fine drizzle of rain which clung to my cloak and hood drove me to find shelter in the precinct of a tiny church, set back from the road. Its porch was in dark shadow and I tiptoed towards it, expecting to find at least one snoring vagrant stretched out on the stones. As I approached, a rat's tail flicked away into the surrounding bushes, but that and the lingering smell of stale piss were the only signs of life. I curled up behind a pillar, my bundle an unyielding lump beneath my head. Nearby a dog barked, setting off a chain of yapping and howling which faded into the distance, followed by silence.

I did not drowse for longer than an Ave Maria that night. Every footstep, every scuttling creature set my heart pounding and my thoughts weaving some shapeless danger. A lone girl lying on the ground in the dark invited violence, or so most would say – men and women both. And I had of my own will left a warm pallet and the safety of Signora Ruffo's palazzo. It was but one night, yet it gave a terrifying glimpse of what my life could become if I did not find work.

Finally, a grey dawn brought with it the first low rumblings from the massive mills which crouched along the canal banks, spewing out flour, paper and silk thread. The thrumming sound was ever-present during daylight and there was a saying in the city that you could tell a foreigner because he walked around with his hands over his ears. Here, so close to the mills, I felt like doing the same myself, but I had never before been so grateful for the pounding noise and the return to the daily round it marked. I peered round the pillar and saw men and women in heavy wool tunics already hurrying down the street in the direction of the canal. I fell in behind them, looking like just another silk-thrower on her way to work.

Hard against the canal was a mesh of streets, already narrow but further straitened by porticoes on either side where households had extended their upper floors to make space for a paying lodger. I knew that if I could afford a room anywhere it would be here. At the first house I tried, a weary-looking mother with children tugging at her skirts suggested I share a room with two infants. I smiled a refusal and walked a little further on. This time the door was opened by an elderly widow who, it seemed, had become wary of letting out to students from the university after one almost burnt the place down. Consequently, the rent would be low for a quiet and respectable seamstress. It took only moments before I was unwrapping my bundle in a tiny room which teetered over the street below. I had, of course, forfeited my dowry by running away, but I'd managed to save most of the purse money the Signora was contracted to give me, as well as my earnings from piecework at the Baraccano. It was enough to live on for a few months but I needed a tailor to give me work soon – if I was to avoid lifting my skirts in order to eat.

I was bawled out of most of the tailors' workshops which jostle for attention along the Via Drapperie, and in others the welcome was more physical. I could feel where bruises would soon ripen on my arms because eager journeymen wanted to be certain that I found the door. As for the workshop of Signor Martelli, I hurried past its counter – that meeting would be a humiliation too far. Now there was but one left to try. It occupied a position of prestige on the corner where, no doubt, light coming in from two sides was reflected in the rent. Nevertheless, I smoothed down my apron once again and stepped through the gap in the counter into the back room. This workshop, though larger and brighter than the others, shared with them the smells of new fabrics and waxed thread and was laid out much the same, with rolls of cloth propped around the edges and half-finished garments hanging from a beam suspended along the back wall.

In the lightest corner of the room four tailors sat cross-legged on a long table. One was grizzled with age and held his work close to his eyes, but all were older than their master, who stood at his own bench within sight of the street. He wore his hair and beard neatly trimmed and his clothes were in the highest fashion: ivory silk doublet and crimson breeches, both with just enough slashing to let a richer fabric show through while avoiding a penalty under the sumptuary laws. I curtseyed.

'Good day, Signore.'

There was a long silence, sliced through by the sound of his shears on a fine blue serge. Finally, he cocked his head and waited.

'I come to ask if you have need of an apprentice.'

He sighed.

'Is your brother, husband . . . or pimp unable to ask for work?'

'I ask for myself, Signore.'

There were stifled guffaws from the journeymen, which he quelled with a glare, and I pressed on.

'I have worked for three years as assistant to a seamstress. My stitches are so small as to be almost invisible and my seams hold firm. I am also an experienced fitter.'

This was usually when the shouting or manhandling began, but he waved in the direction of a small basket under the table.

'There are fabric scraps in the *cavolo*. Join two of them with stitches of exactly equal length.'

I was so taken by surprise at this chance to show my skills that it took me some time to select my pieces. I knew he would expect me to pick some linen, an obvious choice for a seamstress who had worked only on undershifts. Instead, I chose a heavy, embossed damask which required particular care with matching of the pattern across the sewed seam. I had to search around for the haberdashery I needed, since the journeymen had buried their noses in their work and showed no sign of offering help. Set along the side wall was a small set of drawers and inside I found thread of the right colour as well as needle and thimble. I considered hoisting up my skirts to join the others on the table, but thought it more prudent to settle on a cushion on the floor. There was silence inside the room – the only sound the muffled chatter of matrons in the street beyond. At first, my hands shook, but I took in a deep breath of the familiar workshop smells – beeswax, wool, silk, a wisp of woodsmoke from the stove – and was soon lulled into the rhythmic repetition of stitching.

I was once again that small child back in my father's workshop, where I learnt to thread a needle after running a thread across a lump of wax; to use a bodkin to make eyelet holes; to mark fabric with a sliver of leftover chalk. Mine was the best-dressed wooden doll in the street, with a collection of outfits which I sewed from scraps too small to be of use to the tailors. But my doll did not wear flowing gowns and capes of linen and silk, because I had long since decided that it was a boy. Father had split the doll's stump, usually hidden under skirts, to create separate legs so that I could clothe them in little damask breeches, and I added matching doublets and even tiny ruffs.

If the journeymen were working, I kept myself tucked in a warm corner out of the way, my hair tousled from time to time as one of them passed by. But once they had left for the day, Father would dart around the room with me trotting behind.

'Feel this *perpignano*, Elena. Isn't it soft?'

'Look at the gold thread glittering in this brocade, Elena.'

I learnt the name of every fabric and how to use it to best effect as well as the tricks and ruses used to enhance a man's figure. Mother always knew where to find me and she would patter down the stairs from our living quarters to bring me a piece of bread or remind me to use the privy; when I was in the workshop with Father, I was like to forget everything else.

'Signore.'

I held out my completed work. The tailor did not take it straightaway but continued cutting along his chalked line until he reached the end. Then he snatched the fabric from my outstretched hand and walked to the doorway where he held it up to the thin March light and peered at it, pulling at the seam, tugging it this way and that. At last, he spoke.

'You sew a tight seam, girl. The stitches are even too, and that is better pattern-matching than I have seen from some journeymen.'

I caught him glancing in the direction of the youngest assistant, whose neck flushed. Then he turned and tossed the fabric back into the scraps basket.

'But I have no need of an apprentice. We do not even dress women here. I cannot abide frills and flounces.'

'Exactly, Signore . . .'

But I knew that it was useless to argue; he had already turned back to his work, as had the gawping journeymen. I left the shop, blinking away angry tears, and pushed my way through the labyrinth of streets until one spilt out onto Piazza Maggiore. It was not a market day so the square appeared vast, bounded only by the civic buildings which loudly announced Bologna's self-regard. To my left loomed the massive bulk of the basilica of San Petronio, its façade still only half-clad in marble, though the rest of the building had been completed before I was born, so they say. I climbed its shallow steps and sat down near the top just behind a pair of chattering women, baskets on arms, whose children scampered up and down around them. They offered a good screen against any man who might think I needed company.

I adjusted the cape around my shoulders, hands still trembling with anger, my thoughts as tightly wound as a skein of yarn. What had I done to deserve such contempt? My skills had impressed the tailor, I had no doubt of that, yet he must have found amusement in offering me a morsel and then snatching it away, as though I were a hungry bird tethered by its leg. At least the other tailors had not tortured me with hope. But he had pretended the test was a real one when he had no intention of taking me on; his arrogance was a very good fit for the city.

A dark cloud covered the sun and the women began gathering up their children to return home. I shivered and pulled my cloak tighter. There were no tailors' workshops left to try in Drapperie and I had no other plan. Perhaps the married women on the steps had made the right choice, after all; at least they could rely on a roof and a full stomach, even if their husbands were brutes and the lyings-in endless. Without work or a man's protection, my life would likely be a hard church porch, my hand stretched out for alms. And the only alternative would soon beckon: earning a living flat on my back on a pallet, forced to trust a pimp to frighten off the worst of the abusers.

I stood up to shake off the thought and glanced towards the darkening alleys of shops leading away from the piazza. Tucked away among them was the tailor's warm workshop, lined with bolts of fine fabric. Though I had been there for less than an hour, it had felt like home – and what was more, my tormentor had no interest in clothing women, so he was the very person to teach me how to become a gentlemen's tailor. And, though he had thrown me out like all the others, he was the only one who asked to see my work, the only one who allowed me to show what I could do. I had no other recourse; he may have claimed that there was no place for a girl apprentice, but the tailor was not going to rid himself of me that easily.

Chapter Three

On the following morning, before the tailor's shop had even opened, I was leaning against a pillar on the opposite side of the alley, watching the journeymen arrive one by one and duck under the half-open shutters. Shortly afterwards, the youngest of them came out and lifted the shutters to their full height, but not before throwing me a glare. I remained at my post all morning while gentlemen, already fine in silk and wool, came to choose fabric from the bales piled high on the counter, or slipped inside the workshop for a fitting. The tailor certainly did not want for customers. I whiled away the time imagining the sleeves I would fashion to make one look as though he had broad shoulders, or the breeches to disguise another's paunch. Every so often, the tailor himself would appear at the counter, nodding at passers-by and sometimes engaging a likely client in conversation. He must have seen me, though he pretended he had not.

By the time the shutters came down for the lunchtime pause,

my aching back was demanding a seat. The bell signalling the end of the market in Piazza Maggiore had just rung and Drapperie was bustling with matrons, each carrying a basket of produce on her arm. I dodged my way through them until, not many paces along the street, I reached the tiny church of San Matteo which nestled between two tailors' workshops. I crossed its narrow churchyard and gave a gentle push on the wooden door.

Inside, the only light came from a few candles burning down in front of a statue of the saint, and I stood for the length of an Ave Maria while my eyes became accustomed to the gloom. I was glad that I would not need to feign prayer as an excuse for my presence; the church was empty, though the lingering aroma of incense suggested that a Mass had only recently ended. My first impression was that I had stumbled into an especially fine draper's shop for, as well as the usual statues and paintings, the church was richly adorned with fabrics. In addition to the altar cloth, which hung in extravagant gold and scarlet folds, lengths of embroidered silk were draped from the low beams. The statue of San Matteo himself was dressed in a robe of sage green and the chair on which he sat to write his gospel was upholstered in a dark damask: brown, perhaps – it was hard to tell in the half-light. Even the crucified Christ who hung above the altar wore a real loincloth of what looked like ivory silk. I sank into a pew, which was softened with a thin cushion of patterned damask, and stretched my back and shoulders this way and that. To one side of me, there were tombs set flush into the wall, none of them elaborate, yet the occupants were named and there was some simple decoration. One made me smile. Some master tailor was clearly so proud of his profession that he had made sure all knew it; embedded within the vertical surface of the gravestone was a pair of real cutting shears, slightly open and pointing downwards. They took me back to Father's workshop where I had watched him mark up a linen toile for a doublet. I must have been about eight summers and I was standing close beside him at the cutting-table, following every stroke of the chalk. When he had finished, he picked up the shears and held them out to me.

'Here, Elena. You try. Nice, smooth slices using the whole length of the blade. No snipping or clipping.'

I took the shears – they were so heavy it was all I could do to hold them in one hand – and began sliding them through the fabric along the cutting-line which marked the side of the doublet. Father gave no advice but watched every cut as I followed the curve of the armhole, the neckline, then down the sweep of the front. I now suspect that the linen was of low value and that any mistakes I made would have been of little consequence, but I took as much care as though it were costly cloth of gold. As soon as I had finished and set down the shears, he wrapped me in his arms and twirled me around the workshop, while Mother clapped from the bottom of the stairs where she had been looking on. Father's old workshop was still there, a few doors down from where I sat, but it had a new owner now and I had recognised not one journeyman when I had gone there asking for work.

I settled against the back of the pew, amazed at how the textiles in this 'tailors' church' muffled the sounds from the street and made it feel almost warm on a chill spring morning. My eyes wanted to close and I allowed the lids to droop for a moment.

I was startled awake by the sound of the door scraping open and immediately slid to my knees, hands palm to palm. Using a church for sleep was the act of a vagrant and I had no wish to be taken for one; but I need not have feared. By the time the door banged shut a young priest was already bustling down the nave before disappearing round a corner, without even noticing my presence. I slipped from my pew and crept out of the church.

When I arrived back at my place opposite the workshop, the young journeyman was already raising the shutters once again but this time did not even bother to look at me. A determined drizzle was setting in and I stepped back under the portico, at the risk of rousing the ire of another artisan. I remained there until the end of the working day when the craftsmen joked and ragged their way down the street. Then I turned in the opposite direction and trudged off home.

I returned to my post the following day, and the days after that, never missing. Once I tried to speak to the tailor. I waited until he was at the counter, nodding greetings as usual, before I walked over and made my most respectful curtsey. He looked me up and down.

'I have already told you that there is no vacancy for an apprentice – and certainly not one in skirts.'

I was tempted to offer to wear a codpiece, if that was all I lacked, but thought better of it.

'I am willing to do whatever work is required, Signore.'

But he was gone before I had finished speaking.

It was one morning about a week later when only three journeymen stooped under the shutters; the eldest was missing. There was a disorganised air around the workshop all day, with customers having to bang on the counter repeatedly to gain attention. *The old man must have been afflicted by some malady*, I thought. *No doubt he will soon be back to earn his wage, even if not fully recovered.* But the days passed and he did not return. The workshop moved from disorganised to frantic and the other journeymen were now grumbling their way down the street at the end of the day.

Though it was not long till Holy Week, the weather had turned bitterly cold. A northerly wind sliced down Via Drapperie all day, and at night it rattled and buffeted my narrow room. Every evening when I left my post opposite the workshop, it seemed less likely that the tailor would change his mind. And I was so lonely; I shared not a word with a living soul, unless handing over rent to my landlady counted as conversation. How I missed Sofia and our bedtime gossip. One morning, after little sleep and that broken by Baraccano nightmares, I was tempted to forgo my vigil and remain under the coverlet. But then I imagined the tailor's shrug of indifference and set off as usual, my cloak wrapped tight.

Though I was a little late arriving, the journeymen were still shivering outside the workshop, waiting to be let in, until eventually the youngest banged on the shutters and the tailor appeared, hair uncombed and his doublet wrongly buttoned, and with heavy eyes that suggested he had been working all night. Once the men were inside, he looked across at me and beckoned with one finger.

'I will give you a trial – a few weeks. My name is Francesco

Rondinelli, but you will call me Maestro. Your job will be to make our work easier – fetching what we need, sweeping up, waxing thread. That sort of thing. Do not think that you will be doing any tailoring. Is that understood?'

'Yes, Maestro.'

He raised the shutters a little higher and I followed him in, hoping that the old man's illness would be of long duration.

The Maestro had not lied; I was more of a servant than an apprentice. But not the sort of servant who is given clear orders. Instead, I was expected to anticipate the individual needs of each tailor in the room. One would require a roll of cloth to be brought to the table, another a ribboned bodkin or a selection of threads from which to choose. I learnt to judge, by the sound, when a pair of shears was in need of sharpening. I worked out how long to leave 'the goose' on the stove so that each garment received the correct amount of heat for pressing. I had to wax thread or find a slashing tool of the right width, and all of this without disturbing the men at their work. My first task every day was to arrange the heavy bales of cloth on the counter, ready for opening time, and my last was to sweep the floor and remove every trace of lint from the tables. The only words ever spoken to me were 'Now!' or 'Make haste!'

The three journeymen, I learnt, were called Filippo, Stefano and Ulisse. Filippo was a widower with grown children who did not visit as often as he would have liked. He got little sympathy from Stefano who kept a wife and five youngsters on his artificer's wage, supplemented, if I understood the hints correctly, with a little fencing of stolen property. Ulisse, though in his early thirties at least, saw no reason to swap the kind offices of his mother for those of a wife. At the midday break, the Maestro would go upstairs to his quarters, while his assistants huddled round the stove eating bread and raw onion and lamenting the sausages denied them by Lent. I was never asked to join them, so I would take the floor cushion to the far corner of the room or perch on the wooden chest under the window and pretend that I was not listening to their grumbles. That was how I found out that their elderly fellow-worker, who was called Prospero, had been gradually losing his sight for the last few years. The apothecary's drops of eyebright had not cleared the clouds and finally the Maestro had sent him home for the last time. I expected the others to be spitting rancour and yet they expressed no anger on the old man's behalf. *They probably do not dare*, I thought, but I could not help rejoicing that he had gone for good and all. The artificer also gossiped about customers: which followed the newest fashion and wanted their breeches puffed out like pig's bladder balloons; which preferred a prominent codpiece, or a little space around the middle for a good meal. I started to make a list of the names and preferences in my mind, ready for the unlikely opportunity to tailor for them.

One morning all the tailors were bent over their sewing and I was stacking rolls of cloth when two girls peered around the counter entrance. The younger was perhaps twelve or thirteen years old, scrawny, with straight hair of an unexceptional brown and an anxious furrow between her brows. I might have been looking into the face of my childhood self. A few steps behind came the slightly older chaperone, her expression wary. I knew that their roles would have been explained with fierce clarity: the young one simpers her request for alms while the elder ensures that they are not lured into a cupboard or, worse still, the shop-owner's rooms. They both wore the familiar sky-blue uniform, and I could have joined in with the young girl's words.

'Can you spare alms today for the Conservatorio del Baraccano, Signore? You will be remembered in our prayers.'

The Maestro pulled a coin from his purse and thrust it at the girl without even raising his eyes. She bobbed her thanks and both girls scuttled out. I found myself touching my neck, remembering the place where my uniform had always scratched.

My parents' funerals had taken place within an hour of each other – or so I was told. One of my father's journeymen had straightaway taken me, stiff with grief, into his household. But the place was jumping with children and it was clear even to me, at only ten years old, that there was no room for another. A few days later I sat, hands in lap, and watched his wife pacing up and down, stopping every so often to crane her head out of the window. Finally, there had been a knock on the door and a woman whose drab garments resembled those of a nun swept into the room.

'Is this the girl?'

'Yes, ma'am. She is called Elena. Elena Morandi.'

'Her family name is of no consequence. After all, she has no family. Thank you, Signora. We will take care of her now.' She grabbed me by the upper arm, sharp fingers digging in. 'Come with me, girl.'

I had often in the years since blamed myself for allowing the woman to lead me away, as docile as a sheep outside the butcher's shop just before its throat is cut. I should have kicked and screamed the length of Via Santo Stefano. Instead, I had done my best to keep step as I was marched almost as far as the city gate, where a long row of looping arches fronted the orphanage. In moments, I was inside and the heavy door banged shut behind me.

It was the silence I remembered most from that first day, together with the rough hands pushing and pulling my body this way and that. No one spoke to me – not even to tell me what to do. I was immediately undressed by two of the older girls, my own clothes bundled off somewhere. Then they dragged the uniform over my head and tied it tightly at the waist. They continued to flank me for the whole day, pressing my head into a position of meek obedience if I dared to look around, crushing my hands together in my lap while we waited for the evening meal. Even in chapel they had tugged me from kneeling to sitting to standing and back again. It was as though they felt some malice towards me, though I could not imagine why that might be.

By the time I and the rest of the younger girls were finally led to the dormitory, I was swaying with exhaustion. I was directed to the far corner of the room where a bed was pushed hard against the wall, another less than an arm's length away. As I curled up under my blanket a whisper came from the nearby bed.

'Hello. My name is Laura.'

I went to the doorway and watched as the two girls bobbed in and out of the tailors' workshops along Via Drapperie.

Theirs would be a long morning. After going from shop to shop begging for money or food, they would be expected to visit the homes of some who, unlike me, had accepted the husbands chosen for them, hoping for a happy marriage – or at least one without too many black eyes. The new wives, it was believed, would want to support the institution which had saved them from penury. Even on the walk back to the Santo Stefano Gate the girls would be expected to importune passers-by for a small coin or a cabbage from their shopping basket. All would be collected and counted as soon as they were through the orphanage door, and a hungry night would follow if it was deemed that they had not collected enough. I had served my years of alms collection but the needs of the conservatory at least saved me from the job of chaperone. Nor, as the orphan of a respectable tailor, was I doomed to wear the permanent stink of silk-reeling. That was the fate of those born to the wives of pigmen or street-cleaners and, because of it, the rest of us skirted around them.

The two orphans had just turned the corner when I was wrenched back to the present by a shout.

'Girl! I do not pay you to stand at the door daydreaming. I need some wadding to line this doublet – got to give the man some shape.'

I hurried back in and spent the rest of the morning rushing from one tailor to the next, keeping them supplied with everything they needed. By lunchtime I was afraid that I might fall asleep on my cushion, so I left the shop to feel chill air on my face. I squeezed through the crush of people milling around the shoemakers in Via Calzolerie and turned right into the broad Via Mercato di Mezzo where the Two Towers reared up in front of me – the shorter of the two, the Garisenda, leaning drunkenly towards the Asinelli as though for support. Crowds ebbed and flowed around the fabric market at the foot of the towers and I strolled from stall to stall, discreetly rubbing between my fingers a silk brocade here, a woollen serge there. I had already learnt that Maestro Rondinelli despised any customer who appeared with a few *braccia* of his own cloth bought from the market and asked for a doublet or a shirt to be made. He never refused, but made it clear that he could not be expected to produce the same high-quality work 'with this inferior fabric' as with that from his own counter. At that, the client usually gave in and chose anew, their first purchase now destined for the wife's linen chest. I had thought it just the master's ploy to sell more of his own goods, but my brief investigation proved him right. His fabrics had a texture and richness which could not be matched by the stalls of the Ravegnana market.

I was just about to turn back towards the workshop when I sensed a change in the crowd's mood. There was always some sort of trouble when the Bolognesi gathered in numbers: a cutpurse caught in the act, or a scuffle between rival stall-holders. But this was different; the crowd parted, like the Red Sea in the story of Moses, and conversation hushed. Then I saw the reason. Treading a path through the shoppers, head held high, ignoring the startled glances and turned backs, was Sofia. I ran up to her.

'Sof, I am so pleased to see you! Are you well? And the mistress?'

Sofia raised her eyebrows and did not return my smile.

'Very well. Thank you. We have new girl.'

She went to walk away and I called out.

'Please wait.'

Sofia turned back to face me.

'We friends, I think.' She shook her head in frustration. 'I thought. But you just go. You say nothing. Friends do not do that.'

The words were intended to wound – and they did. I lowered my head in apology.

'I am so sorry. I should have explained. I should have said farewell.'

'Yes. You should. But now I will say it. Farewell, Elena.'

Before I could reply, Sofia had set off along Mercato di Mezzo, cutting a new swathe through the crowd as she went. I rubbed my eyes with the heel of my hand and plodded back to work.

That afternoon the workshop was busier than ever. The next day was Holy Thursday and customers would want their new clothes ready in plenty of time to show them off at Easter Masses, even if they were strangers to their parish priest for the rest of the year. Stefano, Ulisse and Filippo were finishing off one garment after another and I was rushing around the workshop finding buttons, waxing thread, offering selections of ribbons for matching and all the time checking that 'the goose' was ready – now for linen, now for wool, now for silk.

The Maestro did no new cutting but stood at his table waiting for each garment to be brought to him. He scrutinised every seam and slash, sometimes thrusting it back at the journeyman with a command to 'Do that again!'

From Piazza Maggiore came the constant sound of banging and sawing where a stage was being erected for the Easter Passion Play. My head ached with the noise but, like the others, I did not pause until the wooden beam was crowded with completed garments ready for collection. When every last stitch had been sewn, the three assistants slid off their table and clapped each other on the back, laughing. Even the Maestro joined in. I fetched the broom from the corner.

'Come here, girl.'

Clearly, I had performed some task ill and I went to stand before him, awaiting my reprimand.

'Maestro.'

'You have done well today.'

I curtseyed my thanks and waited in case he had not finished. But he turned away and I returned to my sweeping, hiding a smile.

Chapter Four

No new work was started the following day. Instead, the Maestro led in one customer after another to try on their new breeches or doublets. Since I had no part to play, I made myself busy tidying equipment, for in the tailors' haste the drawers had become a complete jumble: slashing tools had ended up where thread should be stored, needles had not been replaced in their fabric holders and thimbles had rolled onto the floor. The task was a good excuse to keep my back turned; no client would want a young woman watching him undress.

As each gentleman was brought into the room, the Maestro announced his name so that one of the journeymen could immediately bring the correct garment or, in some cases, a whole outfit. Nothing was hurried. Once the client was dressed, the Maestro walked round and round him, looking closely. He would smooth sleeves or tweak fastenings, tug at a shoulder fitting or examine a button. Meanwhile, Filippo, Stefano and Ulisse stood very still, waiting for the judgement. In most cases, the Maestro was content, but sometimes a frown would bring the guilty one rushing forward to adjust a few stitches or neaten a finishing.

It was late morning when there came a loud rap of knuckles on the counter followed by a booming laugh.

'Come on out, Signor Rondinelli, you sluggard! I know you are just paring your nails in there.'

The Maestro hurried outside to greet his customer, while a smile of recognition passed between the three craftsmen. This client was plainly someone they knew – as did I. My first instinct was to run away, never mind what the Maestro thought, but the two men were now blocking the entrance so instead I crouched on the floor, as if in search of dropped needles. A few moments later, a distinctive smell of hair oil filled the room, causing me to retch, and the customer's greeting to the journeymen was as jovial as any he'd given us at the Baraccano.

'Good day, my fine fellows. I trust my breeches and shirt are ready – and that you haven't put in three armholes by mistake.' He laughed loudly again and I heard him clap the Maestro on the back. 'Just jesting.'

'I should hope so, Signore.'

I had never heard the Maestro sound uncomfortable before and he seemed eager to get on with the task in hand. I remained motionless on the floor, hand over my nose to avoid smelling that familiar odour.

'Ulisse, bring the Signore's garments.'

Out of the corner of my eye I saw Ulisse go to the beam and lift down a huge cream linen shirt and a pair of breeches in the brightest yellow that *herba roccia* could produce. They met with instant approval.

'Oh, they look very fine. But you and I know, Rondinelli, that the fit is everything.'

When I heard the rustle of fabric as the man removed his clothes, I thought I was about to faint. I put my head down between my knees and the conversation in the workshop became muffled, as though it were taking place behind a heavy curtain. Then a voice cut through.

'Girl! I asked for pins.'

At that I stood up and scrabbled in the drawer to find a set of pins, while Ulisse watched and smirked. I walked across to the Maestro and held them out, keeping my head lowered. But his client would not let such an opportunity go by. He placed a stubby finger under my chin and lifted it so that I was forced to look into his face.

'A girl apprentice, Maestro. That is most unusual.'

'Not an apprentice, Signore. She is an assistant – and on a period of trial.'

The man raked his eyes over me.

'I am certain she will do extremely well. Delighted to meet you, my dear. My name is Antonio della Fontana.'

He clearly thought that he was telling me something new. Then that habitual rictus smile before he bobbed his head, and I realised that concealment had been unnecessary; there was absolutely no sign of recognition.

Only a small adjustment to the waistband of Fontana's absurd breeches was needed, so it was not too long before he had paid his bill, adding a handful of coins for the journeymen. As soon as he was gone I began to tremble, fists tightly clenched by my sides.

Ulisse gave me a sly look.

'I like Fontana. He's more amusing than some of the old sticks we get in here. Don't you agree, Elena?'

I had no idea how to reply but the Maestro took away the need.

'Enough of your chatter, Ulisse. The cutting-table is in disarray – tidy it. Just because we have an assistant doesn't mean you can slack.'

The journeyman turned to the task, but not before he had thrown me a look of pure dislike.

I spent that evening sitting on the floor of my room, wrapped in a blanket. My stomach turned every time I remembered Fontana's touch on my chin or the sound of his laugh, and I could not bring myself to eat anything. I had thought there was sanctuary from the past amongst the Maestro's bolts of fabric, but I was mistaken; Fontana owned every corner of the city and could take possession of a room simply by walking into it. He would be welcome anywhere, for most people thought like the Maestro's journeymen, and praise for Antonio della Fontana could be heard on any street corner.

'Always so friendly to everyone, whatever their station.'

'And so charitable.'

'The work he does for those poor girls at the Baraccano.'

'Did you know that he visits constantly to check that they are well looked after and content?'

'He even has personal interviews with them so that they can speak freely about their treatment.'

Ah yes – the personal interviews. Every few weeks a

message would come to all the workrooms that Mistress Serafina required the older girls to go to the refectory. There were only two reasons why a girl was excused: either she was in the sanatorium or having her menses. Both felt like a gift from heaven. Even the silk-reelers were included, despite the stench that hung around them, though they had to hand over at the door the pouches of hatching silkworms which they hung between their breasts to keep warm. I could only assume that Fontana drew the line at coming upon those. Once in the room, we took our places on the benches at the refectory table, as if we were about to eat. Laura and I always sat side by side at mealtimes, and on those occasions we drew closer together.

As *portinara*, Mistress Serafina controlled all the comings and goings of the conservatory, ensuring that the orphans remained confined and outsiders could not get in. But she did not apply the rule to Fontana. Like him, she must have been in her fifth decade – far too old to arouse his interest – but that did not stop her simpering around him like a girl. Her face flushed with pleasure as she escorted him into the refectory, where he greeted those assembled with loud enthusiasm, telling us what fine young women we were. All the time he was pacing up and down the room, his eyes lighting on each in turn. Every girl kept her hands clasped in her lap, eyes downcast, hoping she would not be chosen. Finally, his heavy hand would land on a shoulder.

'Come and talk to me, my dear. I am eager to find out what you have been learning.'

And one poor girl would have to trail behind him along a narrow corridor which led from a corner of the refectory, then up the stairs to the boardroom of the confraternity, while the rest of us exhaled and we were dismissed back to our workrooms by a smiling Mistress Serafina.

I was not often the unfortunate one and every time I escaped that hand, I thanked God for my uneven features and scrawny figure. I used to think Fontana saw me more as a penance than anything else. But Laura had grown into a beauty until every girl in the conservatory envied her lustrous dark hair, deep-brown eyes and lips like a Cupid's bow – not to mention the shapely figure her baggy uniform tried hard to conceal. Laura had soon found out that good looks were no advantage in the Baraccano, for she became Fontana's favourite and was always gone longer than the rest. Every time she stood up to follow him I gave her hand a tight squeeze. Such a useless thing to do but it was all I could offer. As for Fontana, I had never wanted to injure a person so much as on those days when Laura was his chosen one.

The boardroom was up a dark winding staircase, far removed from any workrooms or living quarters. Once he had turned the key, no one would ever come. In the centre was a large table, surrounded by high-backed chairs. The room was always very dimly lit – the windows small and high – and in winter he would only light a candle or two, which made flickering shadows but failed to illuminate the dark corners.

The conversation began as though it truly were an interview with no other purpose in mind; perhaps that salved his soul. He would invite the chosen girl to sit, and take a seat himself alongside, the smell of his hair oil growing stronger as he edged closer. There were a few questions about work at the conservatory or whether the food was palatable, but all the time his breathing was becoming heavier until finally he was panting. Then the hands would start to wander over one's body, until he could restrain himself no longer and his breeches were round his knees. What happened next varied: I had been straddled across his lap, thrust backwards over the table and even pushed to the floor while he gasped and bucked on top of me. But although his fingers squeezed and penetrated, Fontana always stopped short of violation. Every girl told the same story: though she might be forced to hold his member while it spurted, it always remained outside her body. Even in the throes of his lust, Fontana knew better than to damage the conservatory's goods, for the Baraccano's motto was 'preserving purity' and those men who agreed to marry one of its products expected a virgin.

I dragged my blanket over to the bed and curled up under it, certain that my time at the workshop was over. Fontana's easy manner and the presence of his measurements strip were both the marks of a regular customer and, though I had endured being in the same room with him that day, I did not think I could bear it again.

Chapter Five

As usual, no shops or businesses were allowed to open on Good Friday, and the Maestro had told the whole workshop to stay away on Saturday too, as nothing now hung from the beam and no man would be thinking of new garments until Bologna had been reassured that Christ was risen. I was awake at dawn, my thoughts tumbling this way and that; only movement would calm them and, once dressed, I crept down the stairs and out onto the street.

The air was soft and warm and there was an unaccustomed silence along the Reno without the throbbing of the mills. Rather than taking my usual route towards the centre of town, I turned north along the street which ended at the Porta Lame. Very soon the tightly packed houses began to part and I caught glimpses of green life through gaps and over walls: grape vines in first bud trailed from blossoming apple trees and woodbine crept over tiles; water bubbled and splashed in hidden fountains and hives buzzed just out of sight. It reminded me of the gardens at the Baraccano where, very rarely, we girls would be allowed to thread our way along the paths before being reeled in once again. Laura and I loved to stroll there arm in arm, saying little, faces lifted to the sun.

I walked on until I was close to the gate, then stepped off the road onto rough grass before I could be challenged by the two guards playing a desultory game of dice in the shade of the gateway. I approached the city wall and stood on tiptoe to peer down at the sluggish moat which fringed the city. Beyond it were lines of mulberry trees in all directions as far as I could see, but it was many years ago that I had last walked among them and my whole life since had been enclosed within Bologna's walls. It had never concerned me before but now I felt trapped, unable to escape Fontana's long reach. How could I return to the workshop when the doorway might at any moment be filled by his flabby body? I did not think anyone had noticed my distress the previous day, but what about the next time, and the one after that? Could I be certain that I would not disgrace myself and the Maestro when Fontana turned up at the workshop again? The only answer seemed to be to revisit every tailor in Drapperie, but I would likely be even less welcome on a second occasion.

The two guards had started to look me up and down, so I turned around and went back the way I had come. By the time I crossed the Reno I was one of many, all funnelling towards Piazza Maggiore for the Passion Play. The stage was set up just in front of the Palazzo dei Notai where three crosses had been erected, and black-robed notaries were hanging out of the windows, keen to get a privileged view of the preparations. In the piazza, crowds had already gathered and pedlars wove in and out selling Lenten vegetable stew with hunks of bread. I bought myself some food and hovered at the edge of the throng – things could get violent at the Passion. Finally, the leader of the confraternity charged with the performance that year stepped up onto the stage and called for quiet.

'Citizens of Bologna, we – the confraternity of Santa Maria – are most proud to present the last days of Our Saviour's life on earth.'

At that, a line of sheepish-looking men, more at home in a workshop or mill, stomped up the steps to form a row behind him. There was a murmur of applause but it was what they were wearing that made the crowd chatter and point. Instead of the usual cast-off outfits, mended and adorned, the actors were decked out in costumes made of the finest fabrics and in the highest fashion. It was as though the divine order had been turned upside down, and the heavy-set young man cast as Pontius Pilate could almost have passed for one of Bologna's most noble citizens. The *confratello* named each character in the line and then, after a short delay and some hissed instructions, the play began.

The members of the confraternity had learnt their lines well but the citizens knew their part too. When Judas kissed Christ on the cheek, the crowd became one, baying the traitor's name until it bounced off the high buildings on all sides. The actors shouting to free Barabbas were drowned out by the people of Bologna calling for Christ to be saved. Each stroke of the whip on Christ's back was accompanied by a groan from the audience. Only when the actor playing Christ mimed His crucifixion in front of the central cross did the people fall silent, awaiting their Saviour's final words. When the 'body' was finally lifted down, those at the front set up a ululation which swept through the crowd, as though the plague had returned to ravage the city. The final scene was the suicide of Judas, and the cheers and catcalls seemed to fill the square. There were no Jews left in Bologna to suffer the usual consequences of the Passion Play, but the leader of the confraternity was taking no chances. Once the players had taken their bows, he brought the actor who played Judas to the front of the stage and waved away the boos.

'Citizens of Bologna, do not be mistaken – this is not Judas. It is Marcello the butcher. You all know him well. He has a shop in Via Caprarie, where he tells me the meat is the best in the city.'

Laughter.

'He is a good Christian soul, as are you all.'

Most clapped and cheered at that, and I hoped for Marcello's sake that those who did not at least understood the difference between real life and the stage. The *confratello* waited for quiet before continuing.

'And we give thanks to the noble citizen who supports, with his customary generosity, the widows and fatherless children of our confraternity and who has provided us with such fine costumes for our play.' He spread out a welcoming arm towards the side of the stage. 'Signor Antonio della Fontana.' There was no escaping the man.

Fontana, wearing those bright yellow breeches, lumbered up the steps and performed absurdly low bows in all directions as the audience whooped and shouted. I shuddered and screwed up my eyes for a moment, trying to block the sight. My first thought was to get out of the square immediately, but such an exit would only draw Fontana's gaze in my direction and I felt safer in the crowd. He was now patting the air with his hands for quiet and, once it was achieved, he boomed his good humour at the audience.

'Good citizens of Bologna, it has been my great honour to provide the fine men of Santa Maria with their costumes for today's excellent performance. Even if I did have to raid the wardrobes of all my good friends.' Laughter. 'Just jesting. But I urge you all, most seriously, to open your money pouches today for God's poor. Members of the confraternity will come among you with alms bags. Please give what you can spare and I pledge to double the final sum.' More applause, this time accompanied by whistling. The *confratelli*, some still in costume, lost no time before weaving in and out of the crowd with velvet alms bags attached to sticks. I shook my head at the man who thrust one under my nose, earning his hissed rebuke.

The mood of the crowd was changing now, like a clew of yarn which had begun to unravel. Family groups, eager to leave the piazza and get home, were jostled down the nearest side street by young thugs who ran between them yelling and shrieking. A group of *sbirri* had already formed in the centre of the square, swinging their cudgels casually to and fro, no doubt waiting for an excuse to use them. A single, mournful bell was tolling from the campanile of San Petronio and I decided that fulfilling my Easter duty would be safer than walking home straightaway.

As I skirted round the edge of the square I noticed a figure, also alone, standing at the corner of Via Clavature. From the expression on his face, the Maestro did not appear to have taken much joy in the morning's entertainment and I wondered why he had bothered to come at all. But then the same could be said of me. I dipped a curtsey to which he nodded in reply, then I followed a woman, tottering with age, up the steps of San Petronio to the entrance. There I gave my name to the priest's pimply assistant, who tutted his annoyance that I was not attending in my own parish.

There was a time when I attended Mass at least twice a week – there had been no choice at the Baraccano – and once my sewing skills were judged competent, I had sewn vestments for the palsied priest. When I was very young, I envied him the bright colours he got to wear, now green, now red, now purple depending on the time of year. The only change in my blue uniform was the size. My envy subsided when I was old enough for him to insist that confession included any 'impure thoughts' – at length and in detail. I could hear him panting through the grille. Since the Baraccano door shut behind me, I had fulfilled only the minimum attendance required by the Church authorities: Easter Mass. The same women who had compelled me to worship Our Lord with enthusiasm had also compelled me to accept Fontana's groping. The one had tainted the other.

I slid into a pew and gazed around. I had only been inside the basilica once before but it was just as I remembered it – vast and gloomy with side chapels like dungeons along each side. To mark the day of mourning, every statue and painting was draped in black, as though there was no colour left in the world. But in my memory, it was filled with colour and light and I was standing in the front row of pews alongside Laura.

It had been some years after my arrival at the Baraccano when the confraternity had, for the first time, allowed all the girls to visit the city's favourite church to mark the Saint's feast day. Most of my time at the orphanage resembled a piece of fabric without seams, each day a continuation of the last. Those days which did remain in my memory were generally there for the worst of reasons. But that festival of San Petronio was one of the best days I could remember.

We had filed down the long aisle two by two, Laura my companion as always, until the huge gold crucifix above the altar was so close that it seemed to loom over us. We had been ordered not to move from our places in the front pews, on pain of . . . I could not remember the exact penalty but was certain there would have been one. The rest of Bologna's citizens milled around, greeting each other and chatting, while the Baraccano girls stared straight ahead with no choice but to study the fine embroidery on the back of the bishop's chasuble, as he muttered his way through the Mass and tasted God for everyone. When the bell tinkled, the silence was immediate and complete. The bishop had turned and, struggling a little under the weight, raised above his head the gold casket which contained the Saint's earthly remains. A communal sigh rose from the people and hands moved in self-blessing. The ceremony was over.

Drawn no doubt by the smell of roasting pig already drifting in through the doorway, the rest of the congregation were already hurrying outside to watch the jugglers and mountebanks, and stuff themselves with pork and bread, fruitcake and oranges. We had all turned towards the aisle, expecting a swift march back to the Baraccano, but Mistress Giovanna stepped out from her place at the end of the pew. It was surprising that the *guardiana* was there at all; she scarcely knew our names and ran the orphanage from an office which resembled the inside of a padded jewel-box. Her announcement was even more unexpected.

'The leader of the confraternity has given permission for the older girls to spend some time in the piazza. You will remain at all times in pairs and be back at the *conservatorio* by Nones. Without fail.'

It was one of the happiest times I ever spent. Laura and I looped in and out of the crowd in Piazza Maggiore, as drunk on freedom as the mulberry farmers were on wine. At each corner of the square a group of musicians played fiddles and tin whistles, the lively tunes blending into each other as we moved from one to the next. It had been so long since I had heard anything other than religious music – always sombre and stately – and I wanted to dance for joy. In a marked-out area in the centre of the square young men in bicoloured hose threw heavy flagpoles into the air and elegantly caught them time after time, the flags fluttering in the breeze. Laura caught the eye of more than one of the performers and she blushed under the knowing winks and smiles, then scurried away with me in her wake.

Nearby was a mountebank who sliced his arm with a knife and, while blood dripped onto the ground, anointed the cut with 'a very particular oil' which not only staunched the flow but appeared to heal the wound immediately. There was even a fortune-teller, a woman, who wore a turban and a robe more colourful and exotic than anything I had ever seen. I longed to have a coin in my pocket so that I could have my fortune told, but Laura pretended to shudder and said she would rather not know hers. It was only when Laura checked the Accursio clock that we realised how late it was. We ended up running (strictly forbidden) down side streets to arrive back just as the bell of the San Baraccano church tolled Nones. It had been a wonderful day but only now could I see the unwonted treat for what it was – a guilt offering.

A choir, invisible from where I was sitting, burst out with the Sanctus, cutting the thread of my memories. I must have been standing and kneeling at all the right times during the service out of habit – a habit deeply marked within me like the pattern on a figured damask. Now the thoughts of that San Petronio Day reminded me of all that I had lost – and not just Laura. Sofia no longer wished to know me, a new girl now earned the Signora's praise for her stitches, and even Signor Martelli would, no doubt, have found a more biddable young woman to become his wife. My choice was simple: to go back to the workshop after the Holy Days and endure Fontana's overpowering presence from time to time; or to run away once again, this time with even less expectation of finding a tailor to take me on.

I knew that only desperate need had driven the Maestro to offer me work but, since then, he had praised me, had recognised my ability. What was more, despite the turned backs of the journeymen, I felt at home in the workshop and had even begun to hope he might let me remain. By the time the priest delivered the final blessing to announce the end of Mass, I had made my decision: Fontana had taken enough from me already, and I would not let him take that too.

Chapter Six

It was Filippo who spoke to me first: a 'good morning', or a 'good night' at the end of the working day – greetings which I returned. Then one lunchtime, as I was settling on my cushion, he called me over.

'Why don't you come and join us, my dear?'

Stefano had just started a story, which proved to be very long, about a friend who was nearly caught fishing a silver salver with a rod through an open window. Though he did not exactly say, it seemed likely that the salver was now stashed under the bed at Stefano's house, awaiting a likely buyer. Filippo and Ulisse laughed in all the right places while I chewed on last night's leftover bread, occasionally fixing a smile on my face when I thought it was required. At the end of his tale Stefano earned a clap on the back from Filippo.

'Prospero would have enjoyed that one. I can just see him rocking backwards and forwards on his stool, wheezing with laughter.'

'I miss the old boy. How does he fare?'

'Happy as Easter! He never stops singing the Maestro's praises. That pension keeps him in bread and wine and a lot more besides.'

The question was out of my mouth before I could stop it.

'The Maestro supports him?'

Filippo nodded.

'He does, girl – and I would not need many fingers to count the masters who do the same.'

I smiled to cover my surprise. I would never have believed such charity possible of our surly Maestro.

Though I would have much preferred my solitary cushion, to be accepted by the journeymen was important, so after that day I regularly joined their circle of stools, which edged further from the brazier as summer warmth crept into the workshop. Soon we would all be cursing the need to keep it lit, but the Maestro left us in no doubt that well-pressed seams were more important than our comfort. Little by little, Filippo and Stefano began to include me in their conversation and I learnt all the names of Stefano's children and their astonishing abilities. Their only fault, it seemed, was how much they could eat. Filippo complained about his daughter-in-law, who, he was convinced, had dripped poison about him into his son's ear. Only Ulisse seemed determined to make me uncomfortable, often turning his back or making some bawdy remark. On those occasions Filippo would change the subject, asking me questions about myself. Ulisse only became interested in my replies when I mentioned the Baraccano.

'You must know Antonio della Fontana then?'

I nodded.

'Fine fellow, isn't he?'

I did not trust myself to reply.

'Do you not think so, girl? Would have thought you had some gratitude for the man. After all, he saved you from the streets.'

I knew Ulisse wouldn't let up until I said something.

'I am grateful to the Baraccano for some things, sir.'

'And Fontana *is* the Baraccano, so I hear.'

'Leave the girl alone, Ulisse.' Filippo brushed crumbs from his tunic. 'What can you know of life at an orphanage, when your mother still ties your shoes?'

Ulisse flushed but Stefano laughed and stood up.

'I expect we'll be seeing the man again soon. It must be time for his summer wardrobe.'

Ulisse rubbed his hands.

'Can't wait to see what ridiculous colours he wants this year.'

I slipped away to sharpen the Maestro's shears, stomach clenching already at the thought of Fontana's next visit.

Though I had often stepped out to visit the Ravegnana market during the midday pause in hope of seeing Sofia again, our paths had never crossed and I realised that I would have to seek my friend out – if I still had any right to use the word 'friend'. On the next Lord's Day I rose early and crept down the stairs so as not to waken the widow. The city seemed unnaturally silent without the rumbling of the mills, and there was not a Christian soul to be seen as I crossed the Reno Canal at the point where it slid under the street. It had rained during the night and, although the sun was beginning its climb into a blue sky, I had to dodge puddles in muddy alleys which stank of every kind of fetid waste. By the time I entered the street which ran alongside Signora Ruffo's palazzo the silence had been replaced with a cacophony of bells, as every church in the city announced the Lord's Day to its parishioners.

The air was fresher here, and I settled on a low wall which gave a good view of the front door and waited. There were few people abroad: a devout matron busy with her rosary passed by, no doubt on her way to Mass, and a beggar hobbled in the same direction. But it was the sight of a careworn couple shepherding their children for some recreation beyond the city gate that swept me back to an equally warm and sun-bright day some nine years since.

Mother had persuaded Father that the workshop would not fall down without him in it, and we left the city by the San Vitale Gate for a walk in the mulberry orchards outside the city walls. I scampered among the trees while they strolled behind swinging a basket of food between them, sometimes in conversation, sometimes sharing the silence. When the morning stillness was replaced by the rhythmic humming of cicadas and the sound of lizards scuttling away from our approaching feet, we settled under a weeping willow by the river Savena where it bends close to the city. Mother had packed bread, olives and some preserved figs together with a flask of well-watered wine – all of it so much tastier in the open air than in our cramped rooms above the shop.

After we had eaten, they both dozed in the sun while I gathered leaves and flowers from the riverbank and made patterns with them on the grass. On the walk home, I had begged Father to carry me on his shoulders but he said I was too old, and instead we all three walked arm in arm singing a silly song.

Within a few days, both were coughing and shivering on their pallets, their nightshifts drenched in sweat, victims of whatever malady had Bologna in its clutches that spring. After that, there is a hole in my memory which I have never been able to darn, and I do not know who took care of me until I landed at the journeyman's lodgings. What I do know is that all happiness had been torn from within me, leaving an open wound. But an open wound needs to be cauterised and I have become an adept surgeon, worthy of the medical school at the city's university. Recollections serve no purpose and I shook my head to chase them away.

The sun had risen over the Signora's palazzo now and the bells had fallen silent. The only sound came from a buzzing hive in a nearby allotment and I feared that, lulled by its sound and the warm sunshine, I would fall asleep. I stood up and paced backwards and forwards alongside the wall, rehearsing what I would say, until the sound of a door banging shut made me turn around and I saw Sofia striding in the direction of the church of San Francesco.

'Sofia!'

She looked over her shoulder briefly but did not lessen her pace, and I was forced to trot to catch up with her.

'Please slow down. My legs are not as long as yours and I so much want to speak to you.'

Finally, she slowed a little and I drew alongside.

'May we sit?' I pointed at a large stone slab which marked

the boundary of the church precinct.

Sofia nodded without meeting my eye and we perched awkwardly side by side. I cleared my throat.

'How are you?'

'Well. Thank you.'

'Sof —'

'My name is Sofia.'

'Sofia. I am so sorry that I left without saying goodbye. I was thinking only of myself and that I must leave straightaway.'

'You do not tell the truth. You pretend to yourself. You did think of me but it was too hard.'

She was right, of course.

'I should have told you, but I knew that you would be hurt and I did not want to see your face or hear your words. It was cowardly. I was a coward.'

'It is true.'

I took a deep breath.

'I did it all wrong, Sof, I mean Sofia, but I could not bear to marry Martelli. I would have spent my life scuttling around in the background, cooking his meals, pushing out his babies, lucky if I got to sweep up the workshop.'

'And what you doing now?'

My smile was rueful.

'Sweeping up a tailor's workshop. But I am certain that it will not always be like that. One day he will have to let me cut and sew, maybe even fit the clothes.'

Sofia exhaled a laugh.

'Have to? And how you make him do that?'

'I will just work very hard. He will wonder how the workshop managed without me.' I put out a tentative hand

and touched Sofia on the shoulder. 'Will you forgive me?'

Sofia turned to look me full in the face.

'I need to walk now. You come?'

The church of San Francesco marked the edge of the tight, built-up streets, and beyond it were smallholdings where ripening melons drooped towards the ground and chickens scrabbled in the dirt. As soon as the paved street turned into an earth-beaten path, Sofia's shoulders lowered and the usual wary look went from her eyes. I thought at first it was because there were no strangers greeting her with forked fingers to ward off the Devil, but there was a purpose to Sofia's stroll, as though it were a kind of pilgrimage. As we weaved in and out of the paths which separated the allotments, she would stop every so often and approach a tree, touch its trunk with the flat of her hand and murmur into its bark. She gathered wildflowers from the verges as we walked – anemones and daisies. Then, where Via San Felice crossed over the Reno, she laid them by the side of the road, again muttering some words. Then she turned to me and smiled.

'Now I have forgiven you – and I am Sof again.'

I took her arm and squeezed it.

'I am so glad. But what were you doing?'

'I pray.'

'To God?'

'To the spirits – of the trees, of the crossroads.' Her expression became defiant. 'I do nothing wrong.'

We started to walk on again, arms still linked.

'Of course not. But . . . are you not a Christian?'

'I am baptised. He made sure of that. And I go to church with the Signora sometimes.'

'Who is "he"?'

'The one who – what is the word? – buyed me.'

I stopped and looked at Sofia, my eyes wide.

'Someone bought you?'

'"Bought" – that is the word I should say. I was small – six years, perhaps, or seven. Mother and I captured, came on ship from our land. He bought us both but Mother died soon.' She was gabbling now. 'I am like a . . . pet, a thing to show people. But then I grow up. He does not want black girl in house. I go to Signora Ruffo.'

That explained Sofia's presence in the city, but I still did not understand where Signora Ruffo came into it. It was hard to think badly of my mistress – my former mistress.

'She did not buy you too?'

'No, no. She say she will not buy person, but she will give me job. He was glad I go.'

I breathed out my relief and we resumed our walk.

'It seems Signora Ruffo saved us both, Sof. How long will you stay with her?'

Sofia looked surprised.

'Always, I hope. I am safe. I have room. I like to sew. What more I need?'

I squeezed Sofia's arm. Although I could not share my friend's contentment, I almost envied it – and her religious belief. My own faith was once pure and uncomplicated, while my mother and father were still alive. I said my prayers every night, learnt my Bible and the stories of the saints, and went to Mass when I was told. There were times when Mother's prayers became frequent and heartfelt (usually when yet another pregnancy had come to naught before the baby quickened), but God was more like an occasional guest than a constant presence in our home. Not so at the Baraccano, where we were drenched in religion, day and night. Every action demanded a prayer, every mistake a penance, and eternal damnation was always hovering close by. When I was young, I asked no questions, and it was only once I was included among the 'older girls', who were required to gather in the refectory and await Fontana's attentions, that I began to doubt both the usefulness of prayer and God's power over the Devil. Even now, I find it hard to begin a meal without mumbling a grace, but my prayers are perfunctory and I expect little from them.

I shook my thoughts away and began to pump Sofia for all the gossip from Signora Ruffo's workroom; we spent the rest of our walk giggling over the Signora's efforts to impose some measure of taste on her more stubborn clients.

Chapter Seven

It was a week or so later when the Maestro gathered us all together before the workshop opened.

'We will be very busy this afternoon, lads.' He looked at me. 'You too, girl.' We all nodded. 'Antonio della Fontana comes to be fitted for his summer wardrobe – breeches, doublets, undershirts, everything. Now I know he makes some unusual choices . . .'

'I'll say!' Ulisse coloured. 'Sorry, Maestro.'

'As I was saying – the man makes unusual choices but he always pays on time and, more important, he tells everyone when he receives good service.'

I could not help thinking that it depended on the sort of service.

'So,' the Maestro went on. 'We will dance attendance on him till closing time and beyond, if necessary. Filippo, you will need to check his measurements against his paper strip first of all. He could easily have added to that paunch since

Easter. Be tactful! Oh, and nip over to The Sun and get a jug of the best wine they have. Stefano and Ulisse, pick out bolts of fabrics he will like – bright colours, big patterns, you know the sort of thing. Pile them up on your table. I will need mine for sketching designs. And Ulisse . . .'

'Maestro?'

'If I see so much as a smirk on your face . . .'

Ulisse gave an obedient nod. I was still waiting to be told what my job would be, when the Maestro beckoned me and I followed him to the front counter, where we could not be overheard by the others. He looked out towards the street, avoiding my eyes.

'I need you to be as charming as you can to our client, Elena – serve him wine, smile at him, that sort of thing. I'm afraid he has a bit of a reputation with young girls.' He turned back to me with an awkward smile. 'But that's just Fontana. There's nothing to concern yourself about. I promise that you will not be left alone with him.'

I curtseyed, not trusting myself to speak.

Antonio della Fontana announced his arrival as before with loud knocking on the counter.

'I am here, Rondinelli!'

The Maestro smoothed down his hair and stepped out of the workshop.

'Signor Fontana, please step inside.'

I lined up alongside the craftsmen – a smile fixed to my face – and waited for Fontana to edge through the counter gap and burst into the room.

'Greetings, my good fellows!' His eyes raked over me. 'Ah, I see you still have your young "not apprentice", Rondinelli. I hope she is not one of those misses who freezes at the sight of a man in his undershirt. Better if they are a bit pliant, know what I mean?'

The Maestro lifted his chin at me.

'Some wine for Signor Fontana, girl.'

Fontana rubbed his hands and laughed.

'I trust you have something decent, Rondinelli, rather than the lees you served me last time. Just jesting, just jesting.'

The Maestro and Fontana settled side by side on stools at the cutting-table and I brought over the jug and cups. I placed a cup in front of each man and poured, trying hard to stop my hands from shaking. The Maestro nodded his thanks but before I could step away from the table, Fontana slid his hand around my waist and pulled me towards him.

'Thank you . . . what is your name?'

The familiar smell of his hair oil made bile rise in my throat; I swallowed.

'Elena, sir.'

'A pretty name for a pretty girl.' He squeezed me tight, the hand creeping imperceptibly higher up my ribs. 'But you could do with feeding up. Pay her more, Rondinelli! I am sure she is worth it' – he leered into my face – 'and her figure needs, what shall I say? Filling out a little.'

As soon as he let me go, I scurried back to join the journeymen behind the pile of cloth bolts. Filippo gave me a sympathetic smile.

For the rest of the afternoon, the tailors and I dodged this way and that, trying to avoid bumping into each other as we answered the Maestro's calls for crimson damask, purple velvet, 'the softest rose silk you can find' or just 'more pins!'. Fontana took the pose of a classical statue while cloth was draped over him, or strode around the edge of the room, testing the fall of a particular linen. But whenever I came close, he found some excuse to stroke my arm or brush against my breast. Each time I summoned up a smile and longed for the day to end.

Finally, the Maestro's table was covered in sheets of sketches, all annotated with instructions on fabric, colour and design details – right down to the size of button to be used. Fontana was back wearing the clothes he had arrived in and was taking his leave, accompanied by ostentatious bows, but not before he had placed a generous pile of coins on the journeymen's table.

'My dear lads – Filippo, Stefano, Ulisse – thank you so much for all your work today. You are a fine group of men. A fine group of craftsmen. Rondinelli – I am all agog to see what wonders you perform for this poor figure of a man. As for you, Elena.' He lingered over my name as though it were a fruit to be savoured. 'I hope that Rondinelli retains you at his workshop. You could perform so many useful services for his customers.' And he winked, slowly.

Then he was gone, escorted out by the Maestro. The three journeymen slumped on their stools and puffed out their sighs of relief. All I could do was stand rigid in the middle of the room, but as soon as the Maestro walked back in, all smiles, I pushed past him and out into the street, bending over to vomit my lunch into the gutter. My actions earned disapproving looks and clicking tongues from some of those who passed by – but no offer of help. I wiped my mouth on my apron and walked back in, head lowered. No one spoke to me and I busied myself collecting up discarded pins and re-winding fabric rolls. The others were gathered round the brazier, clapping each other on the back and laughing at nothing.

'Made a bit of a scene, didn't you?'

Ulisse was talking to me.

'Sir?'

'Throwing up your guts just because a man gives you a compliment or two.'

I felt heat rise to my face and was in danger of making an impertinent reply, but the Maestro cut in first.

'Close your beak, Ulisse, and do something useful. I need all those sketches sorted into piles: breeches, capes, doublets. Get to it!'

I went back to tidying the workshop, my actions mechanical and my thoughts once again back at the Baraccano.

It had been the day of one of Fontana's visits and he had chosen Laura, as so often before, to usher up the dark staircase. But this time she was gone all afternoon. I was in the sewing-room making a partlet for one of the orphanage's female benefactors. It was of fine silk organza, no more than a wisp of fabric, designed to provide a light covering of modesty to neck and shoulders. I should have completed it already but instead I was staring into space, twisting my thimble ring round and round. What had kept my friend this long?

When Laura finally slipped into her place beside me, she was still retying her belt and tucking dishevelled hair under her cap. It was only when she raised her head that it was clear something terrible had happened; her face was as pale as milk, her eyes wide. I dared not speak until the sewing-mistress was distracted by some disaster involving lost buttons at the far end of the room, and I touched my friend on the arm.

'He did not . . . ? Tell me he did not.'

'There was no violation. Though it was all but. I thought he would never be finished with me.' Laura gasped a sob. 'It is worse than that.'

'What could be worse?'

'He has persuaded Mistress Giovanna that when we leave here my work contract should be at his home. He has told her that his wife needs more help in the kitchen.' She hesitated. 'He promised – that was the word he used – many more afternoons like this.'

Laura scarcely spoke for the rest of the day, carrying out her tasks like one of the mechanical figures on the Accursio clock. That night we had gone to sleep holding hands across the narrow divide between our beds – and I would that I had never loosened that handclasp. When I woke to wintry light, Laura was gone.

The clatter of the shutters being pulled halfway down brought me back to the workshop and I noticed that the journeymen had already left. The Maestro was sitting at his cutting-table shuffling through the sketches and he looked up as I began sweeping the floor.

'Thank you, Elena.'

'It is my job, Maestro.'

'I mean Fontana. You suffered for us all today. For the workshop.'

My memories made me bold.

'I will not say it was a pleasure, Maestro. That would be a lie.'

He nodded. 'I need to ask your help again. I have a customer due in this evening for a new doublet – a Signor Malatesta.'

I flinched, eyes wide.

'No, no! I have not made myself clear. He is an honourable man, I assure you. I would like you to assist me with his fitting.'

It was late when our customer arrived and as soon as the Maestro heard his gentle tap, he hurried to the front of the shop. I heard: 'Giorgio, come in, please, come in.'

'It is good to see you, Cecco.' The shutters clattered shut and a brief silence followed. Then the two men entered the workshop and I curtseyed.

'Giorgio, may I introduce Elena. She will be my assistant this evening. Elena, this is Signor Malatesta and today I am measuring him for a new doublet – and hoping to persuade him to have it in something other than black.'

Signor Malatesta raised his eyes to the ceiling and laughed. He was a good head taller than the Maestro, with a full beard and a huge, beaming smile. He made me an extravagant bow, but there was no mockery in it, more a joy in the movement itself. While he removed his cape and doublet, both black, I searched through the rolls of fabric propped against the walls. First, I lifted onto the Maestro's table a roll of damask in a deep blue with a repeated pattern of pomegranates, then placed alongside it a soft linen with a bluish tinge. Though

Signor Malatesta had not come for an undershirt, there was no harm in giving him the idea. I also remembered a deep maroon velvet, with acanthus leaves figured from a combination of cut and uncut loops. It had been deemed too sober for Fontana and had been pushed to the back of the standing pile, but I thought it might just appeal to Signor Malatesta. I hefted it onto the table. Alongside it I placed a roll of silk *brocatello*, beautifully embossed but perhaps a little too soft to hold the shape of a doublet. I would risk the telling-off. My final choice was a damask in forest green with a leaf design in a lighter shade. I also sorted through the measuring strips which dangled from one end of the beam and unhooked the one with Malatesta's name on it, but the Maestro waved it away. It seemed there was to be no checking of measurements or creation of a linen toile; the expensive fabrics would be put to the shears with little preparation. Signor Malatesta must be in a great hurry for his doublet.

He rubbed each of the fabrics between his long fingers.

'Excellent choices, Elena. Sober colours, yet such quality!'

The Maestro nodded at me.

'Not bad at all, girl, though of course the *brocatello* has not sufficient strength for the task.' He passed the roll back to me and I put it away. Signor Malatesta had still made no decision between the other three, so the Maestro held up each roll in turn and let the fabric fall across the Signore's chest, shaping it against him with his hands to give the illusion of fit. After two rounds of this, Malatesta snapped his fingers.

'I have decided! It is to be the blue damask. And, yes, I will have an undershirt in the linen to go with it. You have a clever young assistant here, Francesco. I know her little trick to get me to buy more.' He gave me a broad smile.

The Maestro immediately got to work entirely freehand with his shears while Signor Malatesta perched on a stool nearby and they chatted about Bologna's politics. I understood little about such matters, beyond the common knowledge that the Holy Father was determined to smother the city's independent spark before it fanned back into a flame, and I was too busy taking note of every cut the Maestro made to bother with their conversation. Once all the sections of the doublet were ready, I stood by to assist with the fitting. Signor Malatesta's narrow, sloping shoulders would have proved a challenge for any tailor, but as I handed pins, one by one, to the Maestro, I watched him transform his client's shape with every pleat and tweak. I had used similar tricks at Signora Ruffo's to enhance small breasts or disguise thick arms – though try telling a tailor that a bodice demands as much skill as a doublet! But I must confess that, when the Maestro had finished, Signor Malatesta looked as if he could hold his own in a particularly rough game of *pallone* – and I had memorised every adjustment the Maestro made.

Chapter Eight

When I arrived at the workshop the following morning the journeymen were already sitting on their table, surrounded by sections of poppy-red brocade. Filippo had one leg dangled over the edge and was using the thigh of the other to shape a shoulder; Stefano stabbed a bodkin repeatedly into the doublet's left front; while Ulisse was taking obvious pleasure in making slashes along the length of a detachable sleeve. Fontana's summer wardrobe was underway. The Maestro was taking no part; his attention was fixed on matching the pattern in Signor Malatesta's doublet, but as soon as he saw me, he gestured with his head at the pieces of pale blue linen piled up at the end of his table.

'Invisible stitches, Elena – and some embroidery round neck and cuffs. I leave the design to you. Giorgio – Signor Malatesta – seems to trust your taste.'

Out of the corner of my eye, I saw Stefano nudge Ulisse in the ribs and it took me a moment to realise what the Maestro was asking me to do. Granted, it was only an undershirt, but it meant so much more than that; he was recognising my skills – and my loyalty. I bobbed my thanks and went to choose my equipment. As I passed Ulisse, he bent his head towards me, voice too low to be heard by the others.

'Don't get any ideas, girl, just because you are making something for the Maestro's "special friend". The guild doesn't go handing out apprenticeships to those with tits – however small they are.'

I ignored him. His jibes were becoming like the hum of a mosquito: irritating but of no consequence, unless the insect lighted on a patch of bare skin. But he was right about the uncompromising tailors' guild. The whole city knew that it had responded with a curl of the lip to flirtatious approaches from the cloth merchants hoping for an alliance. The likelihood of the tailors scribbling an addition to their ancient statutes for a Baraccano girl was as tiny as a needle's point. And yet the Maestro treated me in every way as if I were an apprentice. I had gone from tidying to watching, from watching to assisting. And now he had given me a sewing task.

I picked up the bundle of soft linen pieces and placed them on my cushion before looking for a matching thread. White would be far too stark against that palest of pale blue – there would be no chance of my stitches being invisible. Then I noticed a dove grey. At least, it appeared grey when lined up in the drawer with other colours, but when I laid a strand across the linen it almost became part of the warp and weft of the delicate cloth. Once waxed, its colour would melt into the seams. My needle threaded, I tried to settle onto the cushion as usual, legs tucked to one side. But soon I was wriggling to find a comfortable position, my back already aching from the awkward twist in my body. I glanced around the room but the tailors were too busy with their work to notice me. Under the guise of adjusting the cloth on my lap I shifted my legs until I was sitting tailor-style, legs crossed, skirts arranged to cover them fully. It was a pose I had never held before, one which would have earned a slap at the Baraccano, and yet it felt so very comfortable, almost as though my body had been designed to sit that way.

The long seams of the undershirt were simple but brought with them the danger of tedium, which I knew could result in rushed and uneven stitches. To keep myself slow, I imagined the more interesting parts of the work. Both the high neck and cuffs would be gathered with decorative stitching and I pictured a pattern of tiny, interlinked pomegranates in dark blue thread to echo those in the doublet. Altogether stylish, but not too flamboyant for Signor Malatesta. I scarcely noticed the morning unwind until the Maestro put down his needle and thimble and walked towards the stairs.

'Pause for lunch when you reach a suitable place, lads. And you, Elena.'

It was then that Stefano looked across and noticed how I was seated on my cushion. He pointed.

'Look out, boys. She'll be up here on the table with us next.'

It was not intended unkindly and I joined in the laughter with Stefano and Filippo. Ulisse just leered.

'Can't imagine anyone wanting to have her on a table.'

The others chose to ignore the remark but I was in no doubt of its meaning. I pulled myself up from the floor and stared at Ulisse in silence until he shrugged before returning to his seam.

I had arranged to meet Sofia at the Ravegnana market where she was picking up a regular order of ribbons and threads from one of the more reliable stalls. Our meeting would have to be a short one – the festival of Calendimaggio was only a few days away, when summer would be welcomed in and prayers sent up for good harvests. For ladies whose fathers or husbands had the money, this required a new dress or, at the very least, new trimmings for an old one. Signora Ruffo's workroom would be as full of chirruping and display as any starling roost, and Sofia would soon be missed. I saw her as soon as I turned the corner onto the main road. She was standing, straight-backed, bundle under her arm, next to a portico pillar at the edge of the market, and a small space had formed around her where people had stepped aside so as not to get too close. The only person nearby was a young man, not much more than a boy, with a full face and an attempt at a wispy moustache. He was leaning against a wall and sketching the scene in front of them with silverpoint, his hand flicking across the page. I caught him glancing across at Sofia and flashed him a glare before rushing up to greet her.

'Sof! I have such good news. I am sewing again! It is only an undershirt but . . .' I stopped, suddenly aware of what I had said. 'I'm so sorry, I did not mean that. Undershirts and undershifts are very important. You make beautiful undershifts . . .' My voice trailed away. Sofia tried to assume a look of deep offence but was betrayed by a giggle.

'Yes. Undergarments *very* important.'

I laughed and we set off in step.

'I'll walk back with you so Signora Ruffo does not become desperate for her haberdashery.'

Via Mercato di Mezzo is straight and wide, like a ribbon pinned down at one end by the Two Towers. Early in the morning mule carts, loaded with animal carcasses dripping blood or sacks bursting with mulberry leaves, roll along it and then rattle back empty. At that time of day, though, it belonged to pedestrians who used it as the quickest way to get from one end of the city to the other, and it was so crowded that no one noticed Sofia until they came face to face with her, when a startled expression was all that she had to fear.

I chattered on about the beautiful damask I had chosen for Signor Malatesta and how I would capture its design in the undershirt's embroidered edging, and soon we were at the crossroads where the Signora's palazzo threw a dark splash of shadow. Sofia resettled her bundle on her hip.

'You come in? See the Signora?'

I shook my head.

'I do not think she would want to see me. Not yet. But . . . give her my greetings.'

I squeezed Sofia's arm and turned to leave before calling back, 'Calendimaggio! Don't forget!'

A few days later I awoke not to the usual sound of mills cranking into movement but to distant singing, which came from the direction of the canal. There were several voices, both male and female, and they were accompanied by familiar instruments: whistle, tambourine and a buzzing crumhorn. The singers were more enthusiastic than tuneful; there was a bass rumbling below and a rather squeaky soprano, with a collection of unidentifiable tones in between. It took me a moment to divine what was happening but then I remembered – the sun had scarcely risen but the young singers were already welcoming the May morning.

The singing grew closer in a stop-start progress as the small chorus wished each group of households prosperity in the coming year. I rushed to the window and pushed open the shutters. At the Baraccano only faint wisps of Calendimaggio music had slipped past the thick walls and we girls were never allowed to look out, let alone take part in the celebrations. But on that day I leant right out over the sill and clapped my hands in delight when the straggling little procession turned the corner into my street.

The singers were young, about my own age, and their drab everyday clothes were completely covered in trailing ribbons of all colours. Both girls and boys had flowers twined in their hair – anemones, poppies, daisies – and those not playing instruments carried baskets of fruit over their arms. They moved down the street with little dancing steps, jigging from side to side until, to my delight, they stopped immediately below my window and started up a new song, wishing for good harvests. Even a grumbling shout from across the street to 'be quiet and let a man sleep!' did not deter them, and after a few more verses they set off again, the music becoming fainter as they followed the route of the canal towards the city centre.

Soon afterwards I set off to join the crowds milling around Piazza Maggiore and to find Sofia among them. In the centre of the square a pine trunk, naked of branches, rose tall against the sky, with three cartwheels encircling it at top, middle and bottom. From the highest wheel flags fluttered and long ribbons dangled to the ground. The other two were covered in elaborate twists of leaves and flowers, forming platforms for eggs and fruits. At the foot of the decorated pine was a chair, made to look like a throne with offcuts of red and gold brocade no doubt begged from the nearby tailors' shops. The throne was currently empty and an officer of the Quaranta, dressed in his formal breeches and cloak, was making sure it stayed that way. Others dressed just like him were clearing a large area around the pine by pushing the crowds roughly back. I looked around for Sofia and caught sight of her, stranded on the other side of the square. We waved at each other but just then a trumpet sounded and everyone turned towards the fountain of Neptune, set in its own little piazza adjoining Maggiore.

Two lines of young women were passing round the fountain like channels of water diverted by a rock. The girls formed pairs, each dressed in identical gowns in the same colour: first rose, then pale blue, lemon yellow, violet and finally soft green. The trumpet had been joined by pipes and lutes to accompany their progress, a tambour providing a quiet beat on which their steps rose and fell. Behind them, driven on a small mule cart which was almost invisible under cascades of flowers, came the Countess of May, a young woman whose dark good looks reminded me of Laura. Not that Laura had ever had the chance to wear her black hair loosely knotted at the nape of her neck and threaded through with daisies. The girl's silk gown was the same colour as the flowers and round her neck she wore a simple garland of bay. I did not know how she had been chosen for the role, but her expression was a mixture of pride and nervousness. Once she had been handed down from the cart and was seated on her throne, the small orchestra joined her under the decorated tree. While they played lilting tunes, her ten attendants danced elegant patterns, holding the ribbons of the pine and weaving in and out, like a human loom. There were some catcalls and whistles from the crowd but they were silenced by the pointing finger of an official; it was never wise to be noticed by either the Quaranta's or the Papal Legate's men. Not far from me stood a priest who was clicking his tongue repeatedly in disgust at the sight of young women with loose hair cavorting in public. But this was a day when city trumped Church, and he soon scuttled off up the steps of San Petronio.

Once the dancing was over, the Countess was helped back onto the cart and her attendants lined up beside it. Behind them formed a long queue of young people which ribboned its way around three sides of the piazza. I ran across the empty space to Sofia.

'Shall we follow?'

'Where they go?'

'Outside the city, to a church on a hilltop.'

Sofia bit her lip.

'I have never been outside walls.'

'I have. But only once – and that long ago. Would you not like to?'

There was a pause and then she nodded. I grabbed her hand and we joined the line, just as the cart creaked off towards the rear of the basilica.

As soon as the procession started moving, the music changed to raucous singing which rippled down the line and back again, one song sometimes crashing into another in the middle. Many of the songs were bawdy and contained words neither of us had heard before, but we grinned at each other in delight and hummed along. The crowd sang its way down Via Tagliapietre, voices raised even louder as we passed the Convent of Corpus Domini, then straight on towards the towering arch of the San Mamolo Gate. When we passed through the gate and crossed the lowered drawbridge over the moat, I felt like a child out on their own for the first time. I squeezed Sofia's hand and we both threw back our heads to take in the sunshine and soft breeze. Soon the singing became quieter and then stopped altogether as the column puffed its way up the steep path out of the city and into the trees.

The last part of the track up to San Michele in Bosco doubled back on itself once, twice, three times, like a thread securing a button, until finally the monastery and its church appeared, perched on top of the hill. The cart rumbled onto a paved area in front of the buildings and came to a stop. Immediately, most of the young followers surged forward to watch whatever ceremony it was that went on between the monks and the Countess of May. Sofia and I made an unspoken decision to stay where we were and soon found ourselves at the back of the crowd. While swallows swooped and darted above us, we moved to the edge of the hilltop and looked down upon the city. From there it was a muddle of terracotta rooftops, a view which was impossible to imagine from within its maze of streets. Sofia gasped and pointed.

'Look, Elena! I see the Two Towers – and San Petronio.'

I traced round the city walls with my finger and jabbed the air.

'And that must be the Baraccano, just inside the Santo Stefano Gate. It looks so small and unimportant.'

'What is this Baraccano?'

'The orphanage where I grew up. It seemed as big as God's earth, a place you could never escape from.' I smiled. 'But from here it is nothing.'

Sensing the presence of someone else on the outcrop, I glanced sideways and saw the young artist I had noticed at the Ravegnana. He was sitting on a boulder, one leg folded across the other to form a surface for his sketches. From where I was standing, I could see a page of disconnected faces and figures, but in the centre was a head-and-shoulders portrait which was unmistakeable. It was Sofia. I strode across to the boy.

'Who gave you permission to draw my friend?'

'E . . . Ex . . . Excuse me, Signora.' The young man leapt to his feet, a blush already spreading up from his neck. 'I meant no offence. I wished to capture the young lady's unusual . . .'

He stopped, not sure where his sentence should be going. Sofia had now joined us and touched my arm.

'It is of no matter.' She turned to the boy. 'May I see?'

He held out his sketch and made an awkward little bow.

'I like to draw and paint ordinary people.' His hand shot to his mouth. 'That is to say, people who are not rich. Or powerful.'

We bent our heads together to examine the sketch, which was of fine quality, especially for one so young. I had not forgiven his impertinence but could not deny that he had somehow managed to convey the serene composure of his subject.

'How long have you been an artist?' I asked.

He smiled and, in doing so, appeared even younger.

'Always. My elder brother is too, and my cousin.'

'Did you learn the skill from your father?'

'No. He was a tailor.' He paused. 'I have forgot myself. I am Annibale Carracci and I am pleased to make your acquaintance.' This time the bow was a low sweep as though he were greeting a pair of duchesses at the very least. I hid my smile and we offered our best curtseys in return.

At that moment a bell tolled from the campanile of San Michele, signalling the end of the ritual, and the young people behind us began to jostle and push their way to the top of the path. I glanced round and by the time I turned back, Master Carracci had disappeared into the crowd which was scampering back down the hill, once again singing and shouting. Sofia and I chose to stroll along at the rear and were among the last to return to the city.

Piazza Maggiore was now lined with stalls selling wine and cake, and Bolognesi of every age, dressed in their best to welcome the summer, chatted with friends or took part in impromptu dances. The whole city seemed to be gathered in one place. We wove in and out of the crowd arm in arm, commenting to each other on the cut of the sleeves on one woman's gown, the fur trimming on another and, in my case, the success or otherwise of a doublet's padding. We were giggling together over a particularly extravagant neckline when someone dressed in the finest poppy-red brocade blocked our progress. I looked up into the face of Antonio della Fontana, who made an extravagant bow, the feather in his hat brushing the ground, and boomed his greeting.

'Good morning, ladies.'

Anyone watching would have thought he was showing respect for two young women of humble background, but then he lowered his voice so that only we could hear and his next words told a different story.

'A tailor's sweeper-up and a swarthy slave – what perfect companions. A man could take his pleasure with both of you at once. As long as he kept his eyes shut, of course.'

He threw back his head and guffawed – and then was gone. My own body had gone rigid and it took me a moment to realise that Sofia's was the same.

'You know him?'

Sofia took a deep breath.

'He is the one who own me. Show me off to his friends as his "little black girl". Make me scrub my skin in front of them to show it is not paint.'

I hesitated but needed to ask.

'Did he . . . did he use your body?'

'No. I remember when I am about twelve years he tell me that he cannot bring himself to fondle me. "Wrong colour" he say.'

'I am glad of it.'

'And you know him from the tailor's?'

'Yes, from there and before. At the Baraccano.' I paused. 'I was not the wrong colour.'

Sofia's look was full of sympathy but at that moment she said nothing, just squeezed my hand very tight. It was, I thought later, as though we made a silent decision to find a private place in which to tell our secrets, and we were soon heading east along Via San Donato. The street had once been the city's glittering jewel where the ruling Bentivoglios had built an ostentatious palazzo and adopted the church opposite as their own. San Giacomo Maggiore still welcomed worshippers but the palazzo was long gone, torn down by the bare hands of Bologna's citizens, so it was said. In its place was a rough grassy area, known as the Guasto, with brambles and nettles choking the boundary walls. We went through a gap which passed for an entrance and began a circuit of the makeshift park. In the centre a group of ragtag boys were kicking around a pig's bladder, yelling words of support or scorn at their fellow players, but otherwise we were alone; the entertainments of Piazza Maggiore were more attractive to most of Bologna that day.

Sofia's memories of her homeland were a tapestry of heat and colour ripped apart when a slave ship moored in the river's mouth near her village. Her father was working in the fields and did not see his wife and daughter snatched from the hut in which they cowered. She remembered little of the voyage and later found out that she had spent it lingering between sleep and wakefulness thanks to some herbs her mother had hidden inside the folds of her clothing. I found it hard to picture this part of Sofia's story; I had never seen the sea, and my only idea of a ship came from a fresco in San Petronio which shows the three Magi standing bolt upright in a little tub with a sail. The bullying rants of the man who bought mother and daughter were only too easy to imagine, though, and I could feel the pain of the terrified little girl who was called 'monkey' rather than by any name and ordered to dance and sing for visitors until she was dropping from exhaustion.

By the time she reached the end of her story, Sofia was struggling to keep her voice steady. I touched her on the arm but was stopped before I could say anything by the pig's bladder, which flew through the air to land at our feet.

'Sorry, Signoras.'

The young boy flashed us a cheeky grin and grabbed the ball before running back to his friends. I could not hide my surprise.

'He did not even notice your . . .' The sentence tailed away.

'My colour? No, children usually not. It is parents who teach them to.'

We were now on our second circuit of the park and I began to tell my own story – how my parents' love had been replaced with the grinding routine of the Baraccano and its daily cruelties: the meals taken standing up; sewing considered of poor standard slung over shoulders and carried around all day. I described how the grey world of the orphanage was lightened only by my friendship with Laura and the rich fabrics which filled my senses. Finally, I told Sofia of the confraternity's leader and his regular defilement of the girls; and how he had caused Laura's death.

Sofia stopped walking all of a sudden and turned to face me, anger set in every feature.

'That man should be – what is the word? – punished.'

'I agree – but we might as well ask for worldly fame. Even if anyone were to believe us, they would protect their own.'

'What about church people?'

'The Church is very good at blinking when required.'

Chapter Nine

Antonio della Fontana was not the only man in the city who wanted to welcome summer with a swagger, and as the red bricks of Bologna warmed in the May sunshine the workshop was never without at least one customer being measured or fitted. My undershirt for Signor Malatesta earned his grin of delight (even the Maestro dubbed it 'good work') and my reward was to be put in charge of alterations for those clients who wanted their wardrobe updated but without too much expense. The Maestro privately called them 'cheese-parers' but even he would not turn away such work; for the cheese-paring now might well be the prelude to later outlay on a daughter's wedding or an anticipated honour. I became skilled at remaking a pair of breeches by unpicking the original and rejoining the less worn pieces with wide strips of a contrasting colour: black on ochre looked well, or crimson on dark blue. The worn cuffs of a doublet could also be made stylish again with a ribbon strip which looked as though it had always been there.

When the day arrived for Fontana's final fitting, I was determined to keep myself out of the way and my repugnance hidden. A customer whose doublet had detachable sleeves, worn at elbow and cuff, had chosen to replace them with a new pair. This was real tailoring at last and I had already cut out the pieces, marked by the Maestro, in a deep-green damask figured with a pine-cone design. The construction would keep me busy all day and tucked away on my cushion in the far corner of the workshop. Customers came and went but I scarcely noticed them until a loud rapping on the counter was followed, as always, by Fontana's strident voice. In a moment his body was filling the doorway.

'Good afternoon, Rondinelli, lads. And you too – Elena wasn't it?'

The others responded with smiles and greetings, but I just nodded before turning my cushion away so that it faced the back wall. It was a movement which would be seen as one of respect rather than revulsion. As I pushed my needle through the thick damask using my thimble ring, I imagined myself far from the workshop on a country walk with Sofia, until Fontana's constant chatter was no more than a background murmur. Apart from our excursion up to San Michele on Calendimaggio, we had never ventured through any of the city gates, content to wander along lanes between smallholdings which clustered together just inside the walls. But there was one place which I longed to visit. Beyond the Saragozza Gate, a mule track wound up a high wooded hill to the sanctuary of San Luca, where Our Lady, in the form of a gilded icon, kept watch over Bologna.

Every July a solemn procession of priests brought the Madonna's image down to the city for a short stay to remind her of her duty to keep its people from harm. I had sometimes been among those who thronged the streets to welcome her, but I found no joy in the event. The prayers of those who jostled against each other under the porticoes seemed to carry a desperate edge – asking that the mulberry trees did not contract blight or rains destroy the crops again. Though held in high summer it was not a celebration so much as an entreaty. Even so, I yearned to follow the route of the procession, away from the pounding of the mills and the stench of the alleys, up through the woods until I reached the summit and a silence I could only imagine. But I knew the risks of such an outing, even if Sofia were to agree to come with me. Two young women alone outside the city would be considered good quarry for those who cared little for God or law.

It was the word 'Baraccano' which interrupted my thoughts, dragging me back into the workshop, and I heard Fontana boasting about his charitable works.

'I do what I can to keep the place going. It's shocking how many girls find themselves orphaned, with nowhere to go.'

Noises of approval from the journeymen.

'Not that it's all hard work, boys. There are some very pretty girls, know what I mean?'

I tried not to imagine his slow wink.

'I must admit I take advantage of that from time to time. A little grope. But I always own up to it in the confessional, and I've not yet met a priest who denies me absolution. They agree with me – God will forgive the odd peccadillo in return for all my charity. The scales are balanced in my favour, don't you agree, boys?'

The tailors were silent now and some of the air seemed to

have been squeezed from the room. I heard Fontana's steps as he strode up and down.

'Perfect, Rondinelli. The quilting works very well.'

Once again, the rustle of fabric.

'But I have to tell you, boys, there was one girl there – a real honey – hair like a raven's wing, ruby lips. And the body! Oh lads, she was a glorious couple of handfuls.'

I twisted my head and caught sight of the lewd gesture Fontana was making with both hands, as though he were testing fruit for ripeness.

'Took my pleasure there, I admit. Don't get me wrong. I left her a virgin, just as I found her.'

Ulisse guffawed and I heard the Maestro clear his throat in warning. I crushed my thimble ring into my palm, willing Fontana to be quiet, but he had not finished.

'Can't remember her name now. Doesn't matter. Silly girl committed self-murder.'

I heard nothing more, all sound muffled by the blood pounding in my ears. I pulled myself to my feet and strode over to Fontana until we were face to face in front of the Maestro's table.

'Laura! Her name was Laura!'

Fontana raised a derisive eyebrow at the journeymen before replying.

'Yes, I think you are correct. Did you know her?'

'She was my friend and she killed herself because of what you did to her.'

Fontana sniggered.

'I don't think I can be held accountable for the sacrilegious act of some orphan.'

The bile rose in my throat and I felt light-headed. I staggered a little and put out a hand to steady myself against the table. There I touched the cold metal of the Maestro's shears, which were lying close to the edge. I reached back and closed my hand around them. I wanted to cause Fontana pain. I raised the shears above my head, ready to plunge them into whatever part of his body they found first. But before I could, the Maestro stepped forward and twisted them from my grasp.

'Enough, Elena. Go outside to calm yourself. I am certain the Signore will put your outburst down to grief. Is that not right, Signor Fontana?'

'I am not certain about that, Rondinelli, but the girl is fortunate that you stopped her doing something very foolish. An assault on me would most certainly result in her hanging.'

I could no longer breathe in the room and staggered out of the workshop, legs trembling beneath me. The alleys were clogged with afternoon shoppers and I elbowed through them until I reached an archway which opened out onto Piazza Maggiore. There I leant against a pillar and took deep breaths, my heart beating as though I had run the length of the city. The market had long since ended and the piazza stretched out in front of me, its vast space dotted with knots of people, but I was back at the Baraccano again.

I had woken in the middle of the night to find that our hands were no longer clasped and Laura's bed was empty. Where could she be? Leaving the dormitory before the bell was forbidden and there was no excuse which would serve for absence – a chamber pot under every pallet saw to that. If Laura was found elsewhere in the building, she would pay with her beautiful black hair, cut to a stubble by the rough hands of one of the lower mistresses. I had to find her and bring her back before anyone noticed that she had gone. Still in my nightshift, I slipped out of the dormitory and into the corridor. All the sleeping quarters were arranged on an upper floor which ran around the four sides of an inner courtyard. My first thought was to run round it calling my friend's name but I was afraid that I might wake the other girls, or worse, one of the mistresses. Instead, I forced myself to stand still and think: Laura would not have left one dormitory just to hide in another. She must be somewhere else.

I turned right down the passageway which led to the work corridor. The row of workrooms had been built at the front of the *conservatorio*, over the arched portico and across the entrance, facing the wide street so as to welcome in all the light Bologna's skies could offer. I pushed open the door to the first workroom, my bare feet already numb with cold. This was the sewing-room where Laura and I spent most of our time, and I hoped it would be her choice of sanctuary. The shutters had been fastened for the night and only a dim light filtered through the gaps. It took a few moments before I could even make out the shapes of the sewing-tables but once I could see the large obstacles, I felt my way around the room, hoping to find Laura crouched in a corner. But she was not there.

Further along the corridor was the throwing-room, where girls used spinning-wheels to twist fine silk filaments together to make thread – work which the throwing-mills had made pointless, though the *guardiana* would never admit it. But I could not find Laura there, and nor was she hiding in the weaving-room next door amongst the piles of silk veils for which the city was famous.

At the end of the corridor were steps leading down to the ground floor and another square of rooms around the courtyard, each with a particular purpose and intended to keep the Baraccano functioning. I first approached the door of the dispensary and my spirits lifted. Though I had only been allowed entry on a few occasions, because of painful menses or a headache which would not leave, it would have been my choice of refuge. It was a small room, warmer than anywhere else in the orphanage, and the air was always heavy with the scent of herbs and spices. The walls were lined with shelves full of little jars, labelled as to their contents, together with leather-bound volumes of recipes for poultices and draughts. The dispensary mistress liked her comforts, and blankets and cushions were piled on a wooden settle. Laura should have been curled up amongst them but she was not.

Next door was the infirmary, its four cots empty. They were intended for those who suffered serious malady, but it was rare that any girl was considered sufficiently ill to warrant a bed. I did not even try the door to the kitchens for they were always kept locked, to prevent any of us stealing food. Next to the kitchens and right at the back of the Baraccano a gate led out into a second courtyard, on the far side was a separate building from, day and night, came the roaring of caterpillars munching on trays of mulberry leaves. The reelers also worked there, boiling the cocoons until they released the precious end of their filaments, creating a stink which never left the girls. I dismissed the thought that Laura would choose that as her hiding-place.

I passed the gate and reached the refectory, banging open its double doors, heedless now of the noise I was making, desperate to find Laura safe. I walked past the rows of long tables and benches, ducking my head underneath every so often in case Laura crouched there. I even ventured up onto the dais where the mistresses sat, an offence which would carry a serious punishment indeed if I was seen. Beyond refectory tables and benches, the room contained just two other items of furniture: a pair of deep chests, one in each alcove. My fear growing, I heaved up the lid of each in turn and peered inside, but they contained only tarnished silver chalices and trays. There was only one place left to search and it was a room I had no wish to visit.

I wiped my sweating palms down my nightshift and began to climb the winding staircase leading to the boardroom of the confraternity. The treads creaked and I sent up a prayer to San Francesco that the door would be locked. But when I reached the top, I knew that my plea to the saint had been in vain – the door was ajar. The shutters were closed as always but this time there were no flickering candles and it was a few moments before I saw her; silhouetted against the thin light coming through the window, Laura's dangling body was hanging from a beam by a long silk veil. My hand went to my mouth and I tottered backwards into the arms of Mistress Serafina.

I spent my last few months at the Baraccano as though from behind a grille, catching glimpses of life and snatches of conversation but unable to take part. Some of the other girls tried to be kind but the mistresses kept their distance; to them I might as well have been a carrier of plague. It mattered not. I wanted nothing but to be away from that place, and the only person I wished to see was Laura. And when I finally arrived at Signora Ruffo's, she asked only that I learn. That I could do.

When I turned back into Via Clavature, the shutters were already coming down on the apothecary shops which huddled around the hospital of Santa Maria della Vita. At one of them a matron was fussing over the ingredients for a poultice while the apothecary, no doubt eager to close up, shifted from foot to foot. At the far end of the counter was a bowl of dried lavender heads.

I checked that the apothecary was looking the other way and then rubbed some between my fingers before hurrying off, my hand held up to my face. I could no longer picture my mother, but the smell of lavender always took me back to afternoons we spent filling little bags with the dried flowers to place among our clothes. At the corner of Clavature, I concealed myself behind a pillar with a good view of the workshop, and it was not long before Fontana came out and strode off in the opposite direction. But I remained hidden, waiting to catch the journeymen away from their master; I had disrupted their afternoon's work and for that I must show contrition.

The bells across the city had just begun to clamour out Nones when the three men appeared at the entrance to the workshop and turned in my direction. They seemed more subdued than usual, their talk low-voiced and serious. When I stepped into their path, all three came to a halt and fell silent. I dipped my head in greeting.

'I must beg your forgiveness, sirs. You worked hard to please Signor Fontana and I spoilt the satisfaction which was your due.'

Filippo and Stefano nodded their acceptance of my apology but Ulisse snorted.

'You are right there, girl. I wager his tip would have been a lot larger if it hadn't been for you making an elephant out of a fly. Have you no restraint?'

My fingernails bit into my palms as I fought to keep in a retort, but it was gentle Filippo who delivered it for me.

'Perhaps it is Fontana who needs to learn some restraint, Ulisse. Had you thought of that?'

Ulisse shrugged.

'I still think she needs a man to take her in hand.' He glared at me. 'And don't go thinking that's an offer.'

Stefano, silent until then, burst out laughing and clapped him on the back.

'I think she could do a lot better than you, Ulisse. Come, boys. I need a cup of wine after today.'

Stefano and Ulisse moved off down the alley, but Filippo hung back and touched me on the arm.

'Good night, my dear. I am certain the Maestro will show understanding.'

I smiled, wanting to believe it was true, and hurried towards the half-lowered shutters.

Inside the Maestro was standing by his cutting-table, staring out of the window. Though he must have heard me come in, he did not move. Nevertheless, I bobbed a curtsey towards his turned back.

'Maestro, I beg pardon for my intemperate behaviour and I thank you for saving me from worse.' I twisted my thimble ring, only now realising that I had failed to take it off before I left. 'I should like to tell you what happened at the Baraccano, sir, but I cannot. It was too . . .' My voice faltered.

Rondinelli turned a weary face towards me.

'You do not need to tell me – I can divine that from Fontana's account. And he calls himself a man of honour . . .' His lip curled. 'I presume that it was all of you?'

'Yes, Maestro, as soon as we were more woman than child. But Laura was his particular . . .'

'Favourite?'

I nodded and Rondinelli met my eyes.

'I am sorry for her suffering. And yours. I would that there were some way of unravelling his reputation, but men like him own justice in this city.' He paused and looked away. 'It is I who must ask your forgiveness – Fontana has my back against the wall.'

'Maestro?'

'After you left, he made it clear that unless I dismiss you immediately, he will withdraw his custom. *That* I might be able to weather, but he also threatened to blacken the workshop's name throughout the city. He will say that it is too dangerous to frequent and that the workmanship is inferior.' He shrugged. 'I would lose all my customers, Elena. And my livelihood. So would three other men.'

For a moment, I was unable to speak but then I pulled myself up straight.

'I understand, Maestro. I would not wish your workshop to come to ruination because of me.' I swallowed. 'Send word to him that you have done what he asked. Before he begins spreading rumours.'

'Elena . . .'

But I was out on the street before he could say any more.

I cannot remember the walk home; only that my feet led me there while my thoughts remained at the workshop going over and over what had happened. Once back in my room, I sat on the floor hugging my knees and begging San Francesco for the impossible: the day to run its course again. If only I had not listened to Fontana's boasting, or not turned in time to see that lascivious gesture. If I had just blocked out his voice and concentrated on my stitching. But I had not, and his failure to remember Laura's name had filled me with rage. While she lay in unconsecrated ground somewhere near the Baraccano, and without even a marker, her abuser postured and preened his way round Bologna. Beneath my desire to become a tailor had always lurked an even more impossible dream: to avenge Laura. And now I had allowed both ambitions to slip from my fingers like thread through the eye of a needle.

At first, my thoughts shuttled back and forth. One moment I was certain that Rondinelli would not be able to manage without me and I would be welcomed back within a week; the next all I could see ahead were the grim doorways of Via Santa Croce where young women who lacked the protection of one man gave themselves to hundreds.

It was not until the first stripes of grey light broke through the shutters that I was calm enough to think more clearly. I felt no anger towards the Maestro; he had offered me the chance to sew a new life for myself. It was I who had slashed its seams. As for the other workshops in Drapperie, if they were wary of taking me on before, they certainly would not risk it now. And even Signor Martelli would baulk at taking to wife a woman who had affronted Antonio della Fontana. But I had to earn money to live and there was but one respectable place I could try.

Chapter Ten

As soon as the mills along the canal cranked into life, I dressed and splashed my face with water before tucking my hair into a clean cap. My route took me through a tangle of streets and alleys, always heading south until I came to the high wall which curved around the Collegio di Spagna. As I approached its massive doorway a group of students glided out, easily recognisable by their long robes and flat caps. They turned in my direction, chattering amongst themselves in words I did not understand, but I must have been invisible to them since I found myself forced into the gutter. Not many paces beyond the *collegio* I could tell that I was close to my destination. The stink from Via Altaseta hung over the surrounding streets even on a still day and, when the wind blew from the south, the whole city held its nose. In factories along both sides of the street huge vats of water bubbled over furnaces, boiling the worms in their sticky cocoons and releasing the first thread of silk. There would always be work for a young woman inside those forbidding buildings, but I could not bring myself to wear the perpetual stench of a silk-reeler. At least, not yet.

I turned into a street parallel to Altaseta and arrived at a house about halfway along. Signora Ruffo had sent me there a few times, when there was no other choice, but I had not called on Nonna Agnese for many months past. Everyone knew her as Nonna, as though she were grandmother to the whole of Bologna, but it was not a title of affection. I knocked on the door and prepared to wait. Though Nonna's fingers were still nimble and her eyesight sharp as a needle, her legs were thick and swollen and a caller could recite two Paternosters in the time it took her to lurch from the sewing-table to the door. Finally, it creaked open a little and a sharp nose poked through the gap.

'Who are you and what do you want?'

'It's Elena, Nonna. I used to work for Signora Ruffo. May I come in?'

'Why?'

I took a breath.

'I need work, Nonna.'

A long pause followed and then the door was dragged open. I stepped straight into a small, square room which smelt of a mixture of old clothes and boiled cabbage. There was but one window, facing into the side alley, and Nonna Agnese was already hobbling towards the chair and table placed directly in front of it. The room contained no other furniture.

'Shut the door behind you.'

The old woman sank down with a sigh and looked up at me with a gleeful expression.

'How are the mighty fallen! So what brings you so low that you need Nonna Agnese?'

I tucked my hands under my apron and lifted my chin. I had already decided that the truth, told baldly, was the best tactic.

'I tried to become a tailor, but I did something wrong and now I just need some work.'

'A tailor? Ha! And who would take on a silly young girl as 'prentice?'

'Signor Rondinelli.'

'Oh him. I might have known. You know what they say about Francesco Rondinelli.'

I felt my anger rising.

'He is an excellent tailor, I know that much. It is not his fault he cannot keep me on. Do you have any spare work, or not?'

Nonna Agnese waved at her sewing-table, which was piled high with torn garments and fabric remnants.

'I have plenty, but Borso will not be happy if I waste money paying a slip of a girl.'

I had never met Nonna Agnese's thuggish son but I knew that he ran the grid of streets around Altaseta as if it were his own Papal State, deferring only to the sisters at Corpus Domini.

'But he will not want you to fall behind with your mending, either. Just think what that would do to his reputation.'

In fact, Borso would probably take a club to anyone who complained about late work, but Agnese refused to think ill of her darling boy and believed everyone loved him as much as she. She pummelled her thighs, wincing.

'Piecework only, mind. There will be no wage paid.'

'I understand. Shall I sort out some bits and you can tell me what needs to be done?'

'Not so fast. You will choose all the quick and easy tasks.'

I would actually have chosen those which offered some difficulty, but I need not have worried; they were exactly the ones Nonna gathered together, commenting all the while.

'This doublet is split along the seam. Some lazy fool has probably been stuffing his face. Let out both sides with some ribbon.' She held up another garment. 'Someone's torn his breeches. Wonder what he's been up to? Invisible mend should do it.' More shuffling through the bits of fabric. 'This pair of sleeves are worn at the elbow. Nice bit of brocade, that was. You will need to find a remnant somewhere amongst this lot to blend in.'

'Or a strong contrast,' I suggested.

'Suppose so. Suit yourself. If the customer doesn't like it, I'll blame you.'

Once we had collected together a bundle of work and the haberdashery I would need, Nonna Agnese tied it all up in a piece of shabby linen.

'No later than this Lord's Day, understand? I won't have people thinking badly of my Borso.'

I was not convinced that people could think any worse of Agnese's son than they already did, but I nodded my agreement before getting out of the house as fast as I could.

If my landlady wondered why I was always at home now, she did not say anything; as long as she got her rent, she did not seem to care how I came by it. I found that if I worked every day, I could earn enough from Nonna Agnese to pay for my room, even if that sometimes meant that my stomach griped with hunger. I had moved my table and chair under the window to squeeze every moment of light from the day, and if the moon was full, I carried on into the night until my eyes were dry and sore. To stop my back from aching I would sometimes move from my chair to sit tailor-style on the floor or on my pallet. Nonna Agnese paid me the same amount to mend a split in a work tunic as to reshape a damask sleeve for a nobleman who had fallen on hard times. I ought to have demanded more for jobs which took twice as long and required real skill, but I did not dare risk losing the work altogether and, anyway, I much preferred the difficult tasks. I always delivered the work early and sometimes received a grudging word of praise from Nonna Agnese. The old woman had made it clear that I should never approach the house if Borso was around, and I was certain that she was passing the work off as her own. It mattered not. I did not intend to remain a mender for long.

Bologna's red roofs were sucking in the summer heat now, and every day sweat trickled down my neck as I worked, despite the wide-open shutters. I had not been into the centre of the city for weeks, and relied on a food vendor at the corner of the street for meals which I eked out to last several days. I had no time for walks with Sofia but I did not want her to think I had abandoned her once again, so, very early one morning I slid a scrap of paper under Signora Ruffo's door, saying only that I was too busy to meet and would explain everything when I could. I missed Sofia more than anyone, Laura excepted, but there were days when I felt so lonely that even Ulisse's snide remarks would be welcome.

It was one Lord's Day morning at the beginning of July, the sun already creeping across the neat piles of fabric on the table, when I was startled by the widow banging on my door.

'There is a . . . person to see you.'

I had no chance to reply before she went on.

'Immediately, miss. I do not want someone like that outside my house.'

I put down my needle wondering who could have made her so uneasy. Perhaps Borso or one of his henchmen had come to warn me off doing Nonna Agnese's work for her. When I arrived downstairs the widow had disappeared into her own quarters and the front door was firmly shut. I opened it to find Sofia pacing up and down the street outside, wringing her hands. She came straight up to me, held me by the shoulders and gave me a little shake.

'Where have you been? I keep hoping to bump into you but it never happen. I even wait outside tailor's but you are not there. I only know you live in this street and I am knocking on every door to find you.' Sofia paused for breath. 'I am so worried.'

I took her hands in mine.

'I am sorry. I did something very rash and had to leave Signor Rondinelli's. And I have been working so hard.' My voice broke a little and I realised for the first time how completely worn out I was.

Sofia slipped an arm through mine.

'But you have time for short walk now. You do not say "no".'

I managed a faint smile.

'I do not say "no".'

We strolled arm in arm alongside a narrow canal, its

sluggish waters flanked not by silk mills but by vegetable plots and some straggly vines. We glimpsed through a gate an old woman scattering food for her chickens and she raised her hand in greeting. Bees hummed in makeshift hives and the scent of honeysuckle drifted over walls. As we walked, I told Sofia everything but swore her to silence.

'I don't want anyone knowing what I am doing now. Especially not Signor Rondinelli. Being a mender is such lowly work and he would despise it.'

'I think you are wrong. You are still sewing – yes?'

'If you can call it that. It is little more than tacking one bit of fabric to another so that someone can wear a garment for a few more months.'

A magpie bounced along the stone wall beside the path and Sofia turned her head to look at it.

'I find out if Signora Ruffo needs some extra work. New girl is not so good.'

'No! I could not bear to go begging to the Signora after the way I left. I am a mender for now and I must bear it, but I have not given up. I will be a tailor yet.' I patched a smile onto my face. 'Now tell me what you have been doing.'

'I have news. Do you remember young artist – Carracci – we met on Calendimaggio?' Sofia rushed on without waiting for a reply. 'He want to paint me.'

'Silly boy. You refused, of course.'

Sofia looked down, shaking her head.

'I said I think about it.'

'Why would you do that?'

'He will give me a few *soldi*. And I like to.'

I stopped walking and pulled her around to face me.

'It is a trick, Sof. He will get you alone in his studio and say he needs to see you without your apron, your partlet, then your overdress. Before you know it, you will be half-naked and he will be molesting you.'

'I do not think so. He is nice boy, not strong man. If he does anything, I will fight him away.'

'And if he brings a friend? I do not think you should do this.'

Sofia drew herself up tall and the changed set of her face was a warning.

'But I do, Elena. Carracci wants to paint the colour of my skin – my face and hands, not my body – and to show me as a working woman. I wish him to do that.'

She was not to be dissuaded. I shrugged.

'Then please agree to one thing – tell him that I must come to the sittings as well.'

'You will be my chaperone?'

I laughed.

'Yes, and if necessary, we can fight him off together.'

Chapter Eleven

I had never seen Sofia look so handsome as when she arrived outside the widow's house on the following Lord's Day. She was wearing a dress of brown woollen *garbo* with a little velvet trim across the bodice. A fine cream partlet covered her shoulders and a caul of the same fabric was wrapped over her tightly braided hair. The only flash of colour was provided by a loosely knotted coral necklace which Sofia's fingers played with as she posed before me.

'What do you think, Elena? Is this suitable? Oh, why I ask? It is only good clothes I have.'

I took her by the shoulders and held her at arm's length.

'You look very fine. I see a proud and respectable seamstress. And that is what our young painter friend will see too.'

The Carracci workshop was in Via Augusto Righi, not far from the Reno but hard to find in the warp and weft of alleyways surrounding the place where the canal finally slipped underground. To get there, I was following the plan of Bologna which anyone brought up in the city holds in their head. Even my years of seclusion in the Baraccano had not erased it, and I was able to walk to any destination within the walls with very little thought. Sofia considered the ability mystifying and, as usual, clung to me tightly for fear of becoming completely lost. The description Annibale gave led us to a pinched little house squeezed in among similar buildings in a street too narrow to be reached by the sun at any time of day. It was an odd choice for an artists' workshop, I thought, but perhaps the Carraccis could afford nothing better.

As we approached the front door it crashed open and Annibale came rushing out, almost colliding with Sofia. I briefly wondered why he would be leaving when our arrival was expected but, after I looked a little more closely, I saw that the person in such a hurry was not Annibale at all. This young man was taller, the face a little more mature, but otherwise he could be the artist's twin.

'Greetings, ladies. My brother awaits you – go straight up. Agostino Carracci at your service – and I am in a tearing hurry!'

He gave the briefest of bows and then ran off down the street in the direction of the Two Towers. After we had stepped inside and closed the door, I called up the wooden staircase.

'Master Carracci!'

I thought I heard a distant response so we began to climb, pausing at the closed door on each dingy landing to catch our breath. It was not until we were ascending the final flight that the Carracci family's choice of workshop was suddenly revealed as a wise one. Sunlight spread down the stairwell and, instead of a landing, we stepped straight out into a long room, both ends of which were almost entirely open to the sky, the shutters thrown wide. It was impossible to see it from the street, but here was an extra floor which sat like a fine, feathered hat on top of the house. Standing in the middle of the room and twisting his hands together was Annibale Carracci. He executed one of his awkward, low bows.

'P-please, come in. If you would sit here, Signora Sofia.' He gestured to a straight-backed chair near the side wall, in front of which stood an easel and blank canvas. 'And, Signora Elena, there is a seat over there for you.'

I settled on a padded divan under the front window and looked around. Every wall was covered in completed paintings either hanging from hooks or propped up on the floor, while half-finished ones stood on easels, making the room feel as busy as any Bologna street. The floorboards were splattered with paint of every colour and in a slight alcove at the far end of the room a large table, similarly splashed, was covered with little bottles of coloured pigments together with pestles, mortars, palettes and brushes. A workmanlike smell of linseed oil mixed with varnish filled the room. I took from my bag the mending I had brought but left it lying in my lap while I watched Annibale give Sofia careful directions about how to sit. I was relieved to see that he did not touch her with so much as a finger. Once he was happy with the pose, he turned to me.

'Would you have a couple of spare pins and a needle, Signora?'

'Of course – for what purpose?'

'I would like to attach them to Signora Sofia's bodice.' He flushed. 'Or rather, for you to attach them. Your work gave me the thought. They are marks of the profession you share.' He paused. 'Umm, if you both agree?'

Sofia smiled her assent and I attached two pins and a needle onto her overdress in the exact place Annibale indicated. Meanwhile, he shuffled his easel this way and that until he was satisfied with its position. Once seated again on the divan, my view of Sofia was blocked by the canvas, and by the young artist who appeared almost to dance in front of it. Though I had intended to spend the time attaching ribbon to a pair of frayed cuffs, I found myself transfixed by his sweeping strokes of charcoal, his head constantly bobbing as he looked first at the sitter, then his drawing. Only when the broad outlines of her shape were complete did he settle into a calmer rhythm, and gradually the smudged features of Sofia's face appeared. I was used to seeing a length of silk fabric transformed into a flowing gown, or a closely fitted doublet formed from a few *braccia* of brocade, but I had never seen something apparently created from nothing. My own hands fell still and I felt an unusual calm as I admired the boy's astonishing skill. I would be facing a long night of sewing to catch up but at that moment, it did not seem to matter.

The sound of feet bounding up the stairs made me start and I watched the doorway. Perhaps Annibale's apparent innocence was the perfect lure, after all. My body tensed, though I knew not what I could do if we were in danger. So much for being a chaperone! There was only one way out of the workshop, and nobody down in the street would hear the cries of two women up so high. I felt a little reassured when the figure which appeared at the top of the stairs turned out to be Agostino. He was grinning broadly and already speaking before he was fully inside the room.

'I would wager that my little brother has not even offered

you ladies some refreshment.' He went over to the easel and ruffled Annibale's hair before taking a step back to appraise the canvas. 'Wonderful work, as always, Anni.' He turned to me. 'This boy is a better artist than me and our cousin put together. Do not mistake me, we are not at all bad, but this lad – Saint Luke has touched him with genius. We intend to spend our careers riding pickaback on his.'

Annibale's blush was the deepest yet.

'It is not true. You and Ludovico are fine artists and when we work together it is because it pleases us.'

'It does, little brother. Now, your sitter must be tired with holding her pose and I think we all require some refreshment. I know that I do.'

Agostino went to the top of the stairs and yelled a request for watered wine and bread to someone called Maria, who must have been behind one of those closed doors the whole time. Annibale took the hint from his brother and put down his charcoal.

'Of c-course, you must be tired, Signora Sofia.'

Sofia stood up, stretching her neck and shoulders, before coming round to Annibale's side of the easel to admire his work. I was about to join them but thought better of it – the artist and his sitter had their heads bent together in quiet conversation and they did not need another opinion. Instead, I walked over to a completed painting which hung near to where I had been sitting. It was of the Madonna and Child with Saint John but rather than her usual blue, the Madonna was wearing a pink dress – a fine silk, if I was not mistaken – with a partlet which looked as though it had been woven from golden thread. The fabrics were so finely painted that I felt as though I could reach out and touch them, almost as though I were in the scene with Our Lady.

Agostino's voice, directly behind me, brought me back into the studio.

'That's one of my better ones. The fabrics have come out well, do you not think? The house was piled high with cloth when we were young, so I ought to be able to paint the stuff.' Before I could reply he had bounded away across the room again.

'Let us clear some space on the table, Anni, we don't want to be eating ground lapis.'

I began to make a circuit of the studio, stepping round easels and peering at the canvases which hung on the wall. Many showed scenes I knew from the frescoes at the Baraccano – the crucified Christ, saints with their familiar symbols – but others were so very strange. I could understand the reason for painting portraits of fine ladies and gentlemen with grim expressions; such people would no doubt hand over many *soldi* to have their importance made visible. But they sat next to scenes of ugly butchers surrounded by hunks of meat, or street urchins glugging wine. Who would pay to own such a thing? As I approached the far corner of the room, Agostino ran over and threw a paint-spattered cloth over a set of what looked like framed drawings piled up together. I caught a glimpse of naked limbs, apparently entwined.

'My apologies, madam. Annibale should have turned those to the wall. He gets so lost in his work that he forgets everything.'

At that moment a well-rounded serving-woman stepped into the room carrying a tray with a jug, cups and a bowl of bread pieces. She dipped a curtsey in the direction of Agostino.

'I have told you to stop doing that, Maria. It makes me uncomfortable. You are as important as any one of us. How would we eat otherwise? And no eating, no art!'

Maria dimpled a smile and placed the tray in a space between two large pestles, before scurrying back down the stairs. Annibale immediately grabbed a hunk of bread and returned to his easel, where he continued to sketch with one hand whilst eating with the other.

Agostino slapped a hand to his own forehead.

'Forgive the boy. Once he is working, he will stop for nothing.'

Sofia looked anxious.

'Should I go back to my place?'

'No, madam. He will be perfectly happy adding some details. Please, both of you, have something to eat and drink.'

Agostino poured cups of watered wine for us both and held out the bowl of bread. It was freshly baked and smelt delicious. I had never eaten in such an informal manner before and I was uncertain how to manage it. I watched as Agostino dipped his bread in his cup of wine before lifting it to his lips, and after a sideways look at Sofia, we both did likewise. It tasted exquisite and I only realised when all the bread was gone that I had not even muttered a grace. Annibale was beginning to shuffle with impatience, so Sofia took up her pose once again and I pretended to do my mending, though I found it much more interesting to watch Annibale and Agostino go about their work. Agostino had pushed plates and cups to one side of the table before taking a few small pieces of bright blue stone from one of the glass jars. He put them in a mortar and began to crush them with the pestle, making a soft crunch which was the only sound in the room. I was surprised to see him doing the preparation work himself. Did they not have an apprentice? A young boy whom they were training up as an artist? I could not imagine Signor Rondinelli tidying his own haberdashery drawers. Then I remembered what Agostino had said about the Carracci studio. Annibale would, in any normal family workshop, have been that apprentice, preparing pigments and cleaning brushes, but perhaps Agostino had been telling the truth when he said that Annibale was their most talented member. It must, I thought, take great humility of spirit to recognise that your little brother was already a greater artist than you could ever be. And yet Agostino continued to paint, to produce the best work of which he was capable. The thought brought warmth to my cheeks and I looked down at the threadbare sleeve I was trying to repair. Mending old clothes was far from the best work of which I was capable, and yet I was allowing one day to unravel into the next without making any effort to get closer to becoming a tailor. I gave a sigh of exasperation, which caused Agostino to look in my direction.

'Are you in need of something, Signora Elena?'

'No, nothing.' I gave him a faint smile. 'I was simply wondering how much satisfaction there is to be gained from taking the easy path.'

Agostino flashed me a grin.

'Very little, in my experience. I would rather be the worst artist in Bologna than not be an artist at all.'

Chapter Twelve

It took me several days to gather enough courage to visit the Maestro again. In the meantime, I said nothing of my plans to Sofia and continued to patch together worn and faded bits of fabric to satisfy Nonna Agnese's bodkin gaze. Finally, I set off for the tailor's workshop late one afternoon, knowing that the journeymen would already have left. I could not bear to make my petition in front of them, particularly if they were already taunting a new apprentice. The city carried a permanent stink now in the relentless summer sun – the smells of silk-making overlaid with those of excrement and sweat. The Accursio clock was striking Vespers when I turned into Via Drapperie but it was still light and the *sbirri* were not yet doing their rounds, clearing the streets of unaccompanied women. During my walk I had tried to construct clever arguments with which to persuade the Maestro that he should defy Fontana; but I could think of none. My reason for entering his workshop again was what it had always been: my eagerness to be a tailor.

Most of the shops in the labyrinth of streets behind Piazza Maggiore were already shut up for the night and I wondered if I had arrived too late, but as I approached Rondinelli's workshop, I could see the flickering of candlelight behind its half-open shutters. For a few moments I stood outside, tucking damp strands of hair back into my cap and then wiping my hands on my apron. Finally, I tapped on the shutter and waited. No one came but there was a shout from within.

'Who is it at this hour?'

'It is Elena.'

'Who? I cannot hear you.'

I cleared my throat.

'Elena, Maestro.'

There were footsteps from inside and the shutter rattled open.

'Thanks be to the Good Lord that you are here. Come in, girl. I need your help.'

It was not the reception I was expecting, but I hurried in behind the Maestro to find the workshop looking as though a brawl had recently taken place. Bolts of fabric, half-unrolled, were spread across both cutting-tables, and scattered amongst them were spools of thread, pins and needles, bodkins and slashing tools. The Maestro was now ferreting among the items on his table, muttering to himself.

'My shears. Where are my shears?'

They were balanced precariously on the edge of his table, half-concealed by a piece of linen, and I pulled them out and offered them to him, handles first.

'Thank you. Now, please, could you sort all this,' he waved a vague arm around, 'before I am driven to madness?'

I did not reply but immediately began by collecting up the small items and placing them on the top of the set of drawers. I could put them away later but what the Maestro needed now was space to work, so I re-rolled each bolt of fabric before heaving it up onto a shelf or stacking it in the corner of the room.

'Not that one!' The Maestro grabbed a roll of brocade – maroon but with subtle loops of golden wire which glimmered in the candlelight. 'That's what I am working on.'

In the time it would take to say a couple of Paternosters, the Maestro was standing at his table, chalking up the brocade against a linen toile, oblivious to my presence. I opened the haberdashery drawers to find a worse muddle than when I had first started at the workshop. Clearly, the Maestro did not have a boy apprentice yet. There was nothing for it but to empty out each drawer in turn and start all over again. For at least an hour of the clock neither of us spoke, and the only sounds were the slicing of shears through fabric and the shuffling of sewing items in the wooden drawers. Then, without turning around, the Maestro held out a pair of newly cut sleeves.

'Neat as you can – and take notice of the button marking. The client likes his doublets tight around the wrist.'

The light was too faint to sew in my accustomed place on the floor so, once I had found matching thread and needle, I hoisted up my skirts and settled cross-legged on the table. Lulled by the silence and the familiar smells of fabric and thread-wax, my shoulders loosened for the first time in many weeks. The workshop was more of a home than anywhere I had lived and given the choice, I would have stayed in that little fabric cocoon for ever. I had completed one sleeve when the Maestro sank onto a stool and yawned. He looked around the room.

'I see you have bestowed your customary orderliness on my workshop. How go the sleeves?'

I handed him the one I had finished, and he stood up and held it close to the nearest candle sconce. He performed his usual checks, pulling and examining the seam.

'Excellent work, despite this dim light.'

It was then I looked up at the window and saw that there was complete darkness beyond. I slipped down from the table, twisting the thimble ring I still wore and pacing in a circle.

'Oh, by the saints. I shall be arrested if I go out alone now. Even this' – I tugged at my work-dress – 'won't stop them claiming that I am a whore.'

Rondinelli put down his shears.

'Be calm, Elena. I shall walk you back to your lodgings. They will not bother an accompanied woman.'

'But Maestro . . .'

'Do not argue. You have saved me from a terrible fate. Now I will not have to work all night to avoid a client's complaint of lateness. Come, let us make haste.'

He extinguished all the candles and locked the shutters, and we walked into the still, warm air. The city was unusually quiet, dulled into silence by the July heat. Though the Maestro walked alongside me down the backstreets, he kept a respectful distance.

'By the Reno, is it?'

'How did you know?'

He gave a short laugh.

'It is where I lived when I first came to the city from Firenze. The rooms are – how shall we say? – modestly priced.'

'They are – and modestly appointed too.'

I no longer knew how to speak of the reason I had turned up at the workshop that evening, and we had walked almost the length of Via Galliera in silence before the Maestro cleared his throat.

'How do you manage now, Elena?'

I hesitated but found that I could not lie.

'I am a mender, sir.'

Rondinelli sighed.

'That is a waste of your skills.'

The anger rose in me without warning and I turned to face him, eyes wide.

'That I know, sir, but it is the only work available to me. You were the one tailor on Via Drapperie who even allowed me to show my work.' My voice was rising now. 'Though I do not know why you did so, since you had no intention of taking me on until you were forced to by Prospero's retirement. Perhaps it gave you amusement to praise my work and then toss it away. And perhaps this evening has given you similar amusement – get the girl to do some tidying up with a piece of sewing to keep her happy, and then send her home again. Is that it?'

I stopped, my body shaking. It was the longest speech I had ever made to Francesco Rondinelli and I saw him recoil.

'That is not true. I mean, neither is true. Your test was

real. I knew that Prospero could not work much longer and I was looking for a replacement. But I wanted to find out how serious you were about our profession. When you kept propping up that portico pillar day after day, I knew that it was not just a passing fancy. And as for this evening – no!' He was shouting now. 'I was all heels-over-head when you arrived. It was as though God had answered a prayer.'

A shutter banged open above us and a woman's voice cut through the heavy air.

'Hey, you two! Take your lovers' *battibecco* elsewhere.'

To hide my embarrassment, I scurried off down the street, the Maestro close behind.

'Wait! I said I would escort you home and I will.'

I slowed and he caught up when we reached the road that ran alongside the canal, its water glinting in the moonlight. Rondinelli gave me an enquiring look.

'Why did you come to the workshop tonight?'

I could not reply.

'Elena?'

'I came to ask you to allow me to work again. But I know not how I thought that could be managed. Please consider the request unmade.'

We walked on in silence for a few steps before he spoke again.

'Where do you do your mending?'

'At home. In my room. Why do you ask?'

'Then it could be managed. How would it be if you worked at home for me? You could take away a pair of sleeves, a doublet even, and then deliver them back to me – outside my opening hours, of course. No one need know.'

He paused. 'Especially not Fontana.'

I did not perfectly understand but I knew that the Maestro was offering me something more than Nonna Agnese's mending, and my tone softened.

'Altering for the cheese-parers?'

'I think we are agreed on one thing, Elena – that your skills are wasted on simply mending and altering. I propose that I give you ready-cut garments and you sew them – just not at the workshop.'

It was more than I could ever have wished for; but there was a flaw in his plan.

'What about the journeymen? They will notice the arrival of completed work and wonder at where it came from.'

'I will simply tell them that I have trouble sleeping and am working at night. They will not suspect. And even if they do, they cannot prove my story wrong.' He paused for a moment. 'You could arrive only after they have left, and we will need a system of signals with the shutters so that you know it is safe to enter. Only come in if they are half-shut – never if they are closed or fully raised. Does that put an end to your concerns?'

And he gave me one of his rare smiles. I almost laughed with delight.

'Yes, Maestro. Thank you, Maestro.'

We had arrived at my lodgings and I gestured towards them.

'It is here.'

Rondinelli turned to leave, calling over his shoulder.

'I will expect you tomorrow evening to pick up your first piece. You have the other sleeve to finish and there is no time to waste.'

I bobbed a curtsey to his retreating back before hurrying inside, with a smile which would last the rest of the evening.

The next few weeks were the happiest I had known since the day I left Rondinelli's in disgrace. Each day I sewed at my window, following the instructions given me the night before. Then I would set off for the workshop, the work in a cloth bag, timing my walk so that the journeymen had already left. Only once in the first days did I come close to bumping into them. It was a Saturday evening and I was so excited to show Rondinelli my first pair of breeches that I arrived a little early. I was weaving in and out of the alleys towards Drapperie when I saw the three men trudging towards me in an entirely different direction from their usual route home. I stepped behind a large matron carrying a basket on each arm, hoping not to be seen, but my anxiety was baseless because they immediately turned into The Sun, no doubt intending to sink a few cups of wine to end their week's work. I waited until the workshop shutters signalled it was safe before hurrying in to warn the Maestro, but he had been unconcerned.

'By Vespers they will not be able to recognise their own mothers, never mind you. They won't be back.'

He was right, of course, and I began to relax into the rhythm of my working days, which always ended with a visit to the workshop. I had expected that the Maestro would simply check my sewing and then either require some improvement or give me a new task. Indeed, Rondinelli always submitted my work to the closest scrutiny but it was never rejected, and once I had the next garment tucked into my bag with necessary thread and trimmings, he would spend time teaching me. I learnt the neatest way to bind a buttonhole when the fabric was rich and heavy, how to cut fabric with as little as possible ending up in the *cavolo*, and he even allowed me to mark up a linen toile from a client's measuring strip. I noted, with gratitude, that the dimensions provided could not possibly be those of Fontana. The light evenings allowed me to attend my lessons for a couple of hours and still walk home safely alone, but I did not want to think about how things could be managed in the dark days of autumn and winter. In fact, I did not want to think about the future at all. It was enough that I could see my skills improving every day and that the Maestro considered it worth the candle to spend time on me.

My days of rest had also taken on a regular pattern. Each Lord's Day afternoon Sofia called up to my window and we strolled east alongside the Reno to Via Righi. The streets were deserted because most Bolognesi were gathered in the city's piazzas – gossiping, eating, playing *pallone*. Once, as we approached the Carracci house, I thought I saw Signora Ruffo coming out of their door and hurrying off in the opposite direction, but Sofia convinced me that I must have been mistaken. Each week we climbed up the flights of stairs, greeting Maria as we passed her door, knowing that for a few hours we would bask in the sunlight in congenial company.

Annibale had reached the point where he was brushing thin layers of paint onto Sofia's image, building up the shapes and colours, while Agostino and Ludovico buzzed around him like bees around their king, or sat at the table dashing off red-chalk sketches at astonishing speed. I glimpsed pages of cherubs, praying hands and haloed heads – which were explained when I learnt from their conversation that Ludovico was deep in negotiation for a joint commission for the three of them to paint a church altarpiece. I dared not bring my own work to the studio, for fear a tiny splatter of paint might bring ruin to a whole garment, but I did arrive with scraps of fabric and spent my time practising skills such as slashing and buttonholing. Every so often Agostino would pause in his tasks and stroll over to offer wine or ask after my welfare and I marvelled at the novelty of having my needs attended to. One day he lingered a little and watched my hands at work – which had the result of turning each of my fingers into a thumb. I lay aside my practice piece and gave him a questioning look.

'My apologies, Signora Elena. I was simply remembering the hours I spent as a boy watching my father in his workshop.'

'Did you not consider the profession yourself, sir?'

'Never. I did not have the patience – no more did Annibale. Our father was disappointed at first that neither of us wished to follow his craft, but he finally acceded – once our youngest brother showed signs of taking up the needle.'

'My father was a tailor too, sir, but he had gone to God long before I was fully grown – and there were no sons.'

'Yet you are heir to his skills.'

I dipped my head.

'I aspire to be.'

'And you are apprenticed?'

I could not hide a smile.

'If I were, I would be the only woman in the city to have

achieved such a thing, but I work for a fine Maestro and I have not yet given up hope.'

'That you must never do.'

And he rushed away to continue grinding the umber pigment required for Sofia's skin colour.

Chapter Thirteen

The city was sweating now under a dome of relentless August heat, and as the month progressed, I was forced to step round piles of horse dung on my way to and from the workshop. During the day I sometimes heard the clopping of horses, roped together in twos and threes, below my window. They had been brought inside the city walls to be stabled in outhouses and sheds – wherever there were a few *braccia* of space for the beasts. The frenzy which marked La Porchetta had begun. On the day itself, the narrowest of streets would resound with galloping hooves as riders competed in perilous races, forcing their mounts round tight corners, often colliding with each other or crashing into buildings. Every year, so it was said, two or three competitors were mangled, and horses often had to be put to death with a blow from the hammer after breaking a leg. Even spectators risked being crushed against a wall or pillar; it seemed like poor pleasure to me.

Entertainment in the squares was safer, and when I heard

that Sofia had never been allowed out for the *festa*, we agreed to meet in the precinct under San Francesco's campanile where jugglers and magicians, actors and musicians were trying to persuade crowds of Bolognesi to open their purses. We spent a couple of hours of the clock strolling from one amusement to the next, and for a while Sofia was standing transfixed by a mime while I browsed among the bric-a-brac stalls. I was admiring a set of six Venetian glasses, chipped and cracked but still threaded with shimmering white filaments, when I sensed a man close behind me. Expecting a groping hand, I whipped my head round only to see Filippo's fatherly smile accompanied by a slight tip of the head.

'Elena! What a delight it is to see you. And how do you fare?'

'Well, sir, I thank you. And are you all in good health – Stefano, Ulisse, yourself, of course?'

'We are, we are. But I note you do not enquire after the Maestro. Could that be because you already know?'

I felt my cheeks colour but made no reply.

'Do not be perturbed, my dear. I have told no one – not even my fellow journeymen. But I knew it was your work all along. Every tailor has a particular way with the needle and I recognised those garments at once as yours, not his.'

'I beg you, sir, to keep the confidence. I would not have Signor Fontana learning what the Maestro is doing for me – not for all the world.'

'Be easy. He will not hear it from me. I pray that one day you will join us once again in the workshop. Until then, do not forget – your work is most accomplished. You will soon put us all to shame.' He glanced behind him. 'But I am wanted. Farewell, my dear.'

He slipped away into the crowd where a young man, accompanied by a pinched-looking woman, was tapping his foot. *The son and daughter-in-law*, I thought. *Poor Filippo.* At that moment, Sofia swayed towards me, causing the usual ripple of disquiet. She looked puzzled.

'I hear people say it is time for the pig. What that mean?'

'Ah, this you must see.'

Sofia's forehead grew even more furrowed and I took her arm.

'Follow the crowd, Sof. You cannot call yourself a citizen of Bologna unless you are in Piazza Maggiore for the pig-throwing on La Porchetta. But we will keep to the outer edge of the square – it is safer.'

The centre of the city was already crammed with bodies and we had to push our way past Neptune's fountain to enter the main square. Some young bravoes had clambered onto the fountain; two clung to the god's sinewy legs, while others splashed about in the pool below, flicking water at passers-by and lounging over the statues of mermaids. On seeing the two of us, one young man began caressing a mermaid's breasts, his leering expression fixed on my body as he did so. I lowered my eyes and propelled Sofia round the corner, where we found a space to stand under the portico of the Palazzo Pubblico, surrounded by groups of women, most with child or accompanied by infants. At that moment Agostino Carracci walked past, accompanied by his brother and cousin. He smiled and raised his hat in greeting before heading towards the centre of the crowd. Sofia looked disappointed.

'Why cannot *we* be in the middle?'

'Wait and see.'

The sound of marching feet preceded the arrival of the Legate's *sbirri*, who filed in from Via Mercato di Mezzo and formed a cordon around the edge of the piazza. Neptune was straightaway left alone with his mermaids. The *sbirri* wore no uniform and their weapons were wooden clubs, but there was no mistaking why they were there; any justice to be delivered would come from them. As if by a pre-arranged sign, all faces turned towards the Palazzo d'Accursio which sprawled along the western side of the square; there our leaders, the Quaranta, attended by their wives, had appeared like living portraits at every window and were now throwing objects down to the people below. Sofia turned an excited face towards me.

'What are they doing?'

'Showing us how generous they are with things they can easily afford – small coins, sweets, cakes.'

I scanned the façade, wondering at Fontana's absence from such a public display of largesse – but the puzzle was soon solved. Above the central door was a stone balcony, pillars on either side, and at that moment the curtain behind it was pulled back and the Papal Legate, recognisable by his scarlet cape and hat, stepped out. He was accompanied by a gaggle of important citizens who were busy shoving each other aside to reach the front. Among them was the unmistakeable bulk of Antonio della Fontana, and at his side a tiny woman, presumably his wife. Convinced that the best gifts would descend from the balcony, the crowd at the front surged towards it and people were soon scrabbling on the pavement. The Legate intoned some words, impossible to hear over the clamour, and then the bell in the Accursio Tower was tolled – a mournful sound for a day of celebration, it always seemed to me. There was a moment of silence and then a loud roar reverberated around the piazza as a man dressed all in white came out onto the balcony.

'Who he?'

'The Legate's chef. Watch – you will see what he has been cooking.'

He was followed by four heavyweights holding aloft a roasted pig, garlanded with flowers and laurel. There was a steady, rhythmic baying from the crowd as the men lowered the animal to waist height and swung it to and fro until, on some unheard command, they jettisoned it over the balcony rail, down onto the crowd below.

Sofia gasped.

'Now I understand why we stay here.'

The piazza became a heaving mass of bodies, all shoving each other aside with the aim of grabbing some of the cooked meat. When the first screams went up, the *sbirri* took them as an invitation and strode into the crush, wielding their cudgels without discrimination. Sofia's hand was at her mouth now and she squeezed her eyes shut. Tears trickled from under her closed lids. I was confused. One moment she had been enjoying watching the antics of the Bolognesi, but now I felt my friend's weight against my shoulder and realised that she was about to swoon. I looked around in appeal but the attention of those around her was most determinedly fixed in the other direction. No one, it seemed, was willing to give aid to a girl with brown skin. I scanned the crowd for Agostino and the other Carraccis, but either they had left or they were far away across the other side of the piazza. Sofia was a dead weight now but I was afraid to lower her to the ground, in case the crowd suddenly swept in our direction. Just then, a figure loped towards us inside the line of pillars and lifted Sofia into his arms. He gave me his broadest smile.

'Do not distress yourself. We will get her to safety without delay. Stay close.'

It was then I saw that Giorgio Malatesta was not alone and that the Maestro was already clearing a path for us through the crowd, weaving in and out but aiming always for the arch which led to Via Clavature. Once there my employer sprinted ahead down the empty alleys so that by the time Malatesta reached the tailor's shop with me trotting behind, the shutters were already up and the Maestro had brought down a padded chair from his quarters. Sofia was beginning to regain her senses when Malatesta lowered her into the chair, but Rondinelli still waved a vial of salts of hartshorn under her nose. Sofia spluttered and coughed before looking around in confusion. I knelt at her side.

'You swooned, Sof, but these gentlemen have brought you to safety.'

The Maestro and his friend had already removed themselves to the far side of the workshop and were making a good show of being deep in conversation. I glanced in their direction before whispering close to Sofia's ear.

'What happened? Is it your menses?'

Sofia shook her head.

'I remember something. Our village square full of people. Men with clubs. Then we are dragged away – me, Mother. I had forgot but suddenly I am there again.'

The tears were falling freely now and I stroked Sofia's arm, wondering how I was to get her back home. As if he had read my thoughts, the Maestro approached, his brow furrowed in concern.

'We need to get her home before the streets are full of drunken revellers. Where does your friend live?'

'At the far end of Mercato di Mezzo – Signora Ruffo's palazzo.'

'I know it well. And the Signora.' He paused. 'Is she able to walk?'

Sofia stood up and wiped her eyes on her sleeves.

'I am, sir. But I give you too much trouble. Elena will take me.'

'Nonsense!' Signor Malatesta strode across the room and offered his arm to Sofia. 'We will all walk together – is that not right, Francesco?'

'Indeed we will.'

Once the Maestro had locked the shutters, he and I led the way, with Sofia and Signor Malatesta following a little more slowly, she still clasping his arm for support. To avoid Piazza Maggiore, we went straight across Via Mercato di Mezzo and threaded in and out of side streets, always keeping a direction parallel to the main road. All the time we walked, the Cathedral of San Pietro loomed above us as though it owned the city, but when we reached its precinct it was deserted, rejected once again by the Bolognesi in favour of their favourite saint and his basilica in Piazza Maggiore. Little was said on the journey: from time to time, Signor Malatesta confirmed Sofia's ability to continue but the Maestro and I walked side by side in silence. Finally, our little group turned left and approached

Signora Ruffo's palazzo from the road where I had waited so long to give my apology to Sofia all those weeks ago. Now Sofia released her arm from Signor Malatesta's and made an attempt at a wobbling curtsey, from which I immediately had to steady her. But she was determined to recognise her benefactors.

'I thank you, sirs. It was most kind.'

I went with her to knock on the entrance door and waited until a young woman – my own replacement, I assumed – opened it. After a squeeze of Sofia's arm and a promise to see her again soon, I turned to give my own thanks to Malatesta and Rondinelli. But they had already strode off along Mercato di Mezzo, and were disappearing out of sight. I was disappointed; I had wanted to let them know that their actions had saved a difficult circumstance from becoming so much worse. Instead, I made my own slow way back to my lodgings where I fell onto my pallet and slept a full hour of the clock, only waking when the night-time revelry spilt out of the city's centre, following the lines of the canals.

Chapter Fourteen

About a week later I was doing a little tidying for the Maestro before leaving for home while he stood cutting a pair of sleeves from a lustrous damask. He had fallen into silence, as he always did once our work was complete, but nevertheless the warm workshop with its smells of wools, silks and linens was a far more comfortable place than my damp room down by the canal. I had just finished ordering the drawer of thimbles and threads and was about to begin rewinding the abandoned bolts of cloth, but I needed to make haste; outside the light was already fading and I did not want to risk walking home in the dark. It was then that I heard sounds in the distance and by straining to listen, I could just pick out shouts and running footsteps echoing through the city's porticoes. My first thought was that some drunken lads were rattling home, their bellies sloshing wine, but there was something more organised, more disciplined, about the progress of those noises through the narrow streets. It sounded like the Legate's *sbirri* were out and about and, if so, I was glad to be indoors.

I closed the drawers and was smoothing the wrinkles from a thick brocade when I noticed that the Maestro's shears had fallen silent. He was standing with his back to me, utterly still, head cocked towards the half-closed shutters, listening to the approaching officers. It was possible now to make out their chant: 'Come out, you filthy sodomites!'

So that was their quarry. One night it was prostitutes they were after, the next cutpurses. Tonight was obviously the turn of the sodomites. I cared not whom they sought, as long as it was not me.

The shouting was getting closer now and the footsteps had become a sort of march. They were at the far end of Via Drapperie now and heading in the direction of the workshop. This was certainly no time to be setting off for home; I would ask permission to wait inside until they had gone.

'Maestro . . .'

The face he turned towards me was twisted as though in pain and, without a word, he lunged across the room, steering me backwards until I was pressed against the wall. Though he thrust his face into my neck, he neither kissed nor bit, and while one hand kneaded my left breast the other grappled with my skirts, failing to find its way inside them. I gasped and my body became rigid, my palms sweating with fear. In that moment, I was back at the Baraccano, forced to give Fontana what he wanted. But there was a difference: I did not have to succumb to this assault. I was already biting and scratching when, over the Maestro's shoulder, I saw the first of the *sbirri*, a wiry man with unkempt red hair and beard, duck under the shutters, wielding a cudgel. Others, similarly armed, were crowding in behind their leader who, as soon as he saw what was happening, held up a hand to halt them.

'It's all right, lads. Looks as though we've been misinformed. He's giving the girl one – even if she isn't very willing. Go to, mate.'

And they were gone, racketing off down the main street, their cries bleeding away into the distance, like dye from a fabric. The Maestro stepped away and lowered his head.

'Forgive me, Elena.'

'*Forgive you?*' I was struggling to keep my voice from trembling. 'For what you have just done?'

'I could think of no other remedy.'

I was fighting back tears now and could not follow what he was saying.

'Remedy? For what? Whatever I might have done, I do not deserve such a *remedy*.'

'I express myself badly.' He was pacing around the workshop now. 'I needed to persuade them that I am no . . . sodomite.'

'Strong remedy indeed for a false accusation of sodomy.' My whole body was shaking now. 'No, do not raise your pleading eyes to me . . . Maestro.'

I spat the last word, before striding off to the other side of the workshop to slam bolts of cloth onto shelves. I flinched when he approached, and he came no closer.

'Elena . . .' His tone was pleading. 'You know what they would have done. Smashed and befouled my workshop just as they did to my Jewish neighbours before they fled the city. And I would now be a mass of broken bones and bleeding flesh.' I heard him swallow. 'If I survived at all. I had to convince them they were mistaken.'

I knew that he spoke the truth but I could still feel his groping hands – and the ones that came before. I shuddered and remained with my back to him, addressing the empty space in front of me.

'I put my trust in you, Maestro. I told you what we suffered at the Baraccano to give Antonio della Fontana his pleasure. You were full of solicitude then but now I see you are just as bad.'

'No, Elena, no! Do not compare me to that vile man.'

I twisted round to face him.

'The only difference between the two of you is that your actions were driven not by lust but by fear.' My voice was rising. 'You have used me just as he did. All you had to do was speak to them.'

'And you believe they would have held off the cudgels long enough to listen?'

'If I spoke up too. I would have vouched for your not being a sodomite.'

There was a long silence before the Maestro gave out a strangled sob and buried his face in his hands. I had never seen a man weep before and I found his tears contemptible. What possible excuse could he give for them? A thought flashed into my mind. No. It could not be. But it was the only explanation: the *sbirri* had made no error and his inept fumblings were due to inexperience. How foolish I had been! I should have realised that kind Signor Malatesta with his constant grin was more than the Maestro's friend.

'Oh.'

The Maestro lifted his head and looked into my eyes.

'I was so afraid, Elena.'

Rondinelli was still standing on the other side of the room, twisting his hands in anguish, but I could offer no comfort. Francesco Rondinelli was a sodomite and deserved all the insults that are flung at his kind. I grabbed my cloth bag and ran out, preferring to take my chance on the streets rather than be escorted by such a man.

I counted every hour by the Accursio bell that night, yet when the shutters were finally edged with ribbons of sunlight, my thoughts were no less tangled than they had been when I first lay down on my pallet. Rondinelli could be as abject and full of remorse as he was able, but I could find no forgiveness within me for his assault. His abuse of my body, though feigned, had stirred the silt of memory – something he must have known when he pressed his weight against me, trapping me beneath him. And yet to save his own skin he had molested me – even if it was a pretence. I shivered away the memory. He had given no thought to me. I was not God's creation to him – rather an object of which he could avail himself, if there was need. Just as Fontana had availed himself of all us Baraccano girls, whenever the urge came upon him and he was unable to moderate his desires. I had always known Rondinelli to be morose, even wordless at times, but I had come to respect him, to call him Maestro with no hint of mockery; but that was a title he no longer deserved. How could I look up to a man who treated me with such disdain?

And if his treatment of me were not enough, he had admitted to sodomy – an evil, a mortal sin. The Church said it was so and thundering priests reminded us from the pulpit time without number. I had thought all who practised it to be ugly, dirty and without any virtue. I could make no sense of it. Sodomy was condemned by God and yet that same God had given Rondinelli such skills with shears and needle – skills that he had freely shared with me. And then there was Signor Malatesta. Kind, benevolent Giorgio Malatesta who treated everyone with solicitude and seemed such a good friend to Rondinelli. Except now it was clear that what bound them together was not friendship but something abhorrent. Behind all my muddled thoughts, there was another question about the events of that evening that snagged like a tiny knot in a piece of thread, but I could not work it loose.

Since there was little to be gained from lying sleepless, I rose and dressed and ate a little dry bread washed down with tepid water from my covered jug. My bag was on the chair where I had flung it the previous night, and contained a doublet in need of no less than a dozen buttons and buttonholes. Though I was uncertain whether I ever wished to duck under the shutters of the workshop again, I could think of nothing else to do, so I took up my needle and thread and settled at the table in the morning sunlight. The sewing task was not a difficult one but my needle was often stilled, either by languor or by thoughts I was too tired to unravel. Finally, I must have drifted into a doze, because I was startled by a banging on the front door of the house. My landlady received few visitors but there was one elderly matron who came from time to time, and I predicted an afternoon of chattering voices and raucous laughter coming up through the floorboards. I picked up my needle to resume work but a few moments later there was a light tap on my own door and I rushed to answer it, grateful for any distraction.

'Your landlady feels the heat too much to be rude today.'

'Sofia! I believe my thoughts must have conjured you up. Come in, come in. But why are you not working?'

'Signora Ruffo say that she will not work in the fires of hell and we are all to rest until the weather stops boiling.'

I smiled.

'I think she probably said until the boiling heat passes – but I like your description better.'

'Oh, your language is too hard!'

I moved my sewing to one side and settled Sofia in the chair with a cup of water before sitting cross-legged on the floor nearby. She sipped her water and made a grimace before looking at me with a raised eyebrow.

'What has happened?'

A priest could have delivered a whole Mass before Sofia had the chance to speak again, because I did not stop until I had gabbled my way through all the events and feelings of the previous night. When I finally came to a halt, there was a long pause before Sofia finally spoke.

'He was frightened, Elena. You tell me yourself, it was not real assault – he was pretending and he say sorry straightaway. Yes, he did bad thing but he is not Fontana. Do not punish your Maestro for what that man did.'

I got to my feet and began pacing the room.

'That is not the heart of the matter, Sof. It *felt* real and for a moment I was back in that gloomy boardroom at Fontana's mercy.'

'I know.' Her voice was gentle. 'Memories can – how do I say it? Come back like a fire from embers.'

'How would you know?' I snapped back. 'He never abused you. You were the fortunate one.'

Sofia moved her hands to her lap and sat up tall.

'Not so fortunate when the slavers came.'

'Sorry, sorry.' I walked over to the table and touched her on the shoulder, but she was stiff and unyielding. I should have stopped there – changed the subject of our discourse entirely. But, of course, I did not.

'That apart, Sof, what of the sodomy? I do not know if I can look upon him again, knowing the sort of man he is. Or Signor Malatesta. They are common criminals.'

Sofia shrugged and it was at that moment that my anger finally reached the surface, like a silk cocoon in a boiling vat.

'Why are you always so calm and serene, Sofia? Will nothing stir you? Rondinelli and Malatesta are in the wrong. What they are doing is not only against the law, it is a mortal sin. Everyone knows that.'

'Not everyone, Elena.' She took another sip of water. 'Men beating women and children with clubs – I would call that a sin. Or a bully like Fontana using bodies of young girls. That is a sin also. But two men who love. What is so wrong? In my village there are – were – two men like Rondinelli and Malatesta. They share hut. No one care.'

I still do not know why I said what I did.

'Well, who knows what sort of thing *your* people get up to?'

The look Sofia gave me was enough to curdle milk. She did not reply but rose from her chair and hurried out of the room, her footsteps pattering down the wooden stairs. The front door slammed shut and I ran to the window.

'Sof! Sofia! Let us not wrangle. Please come back!'

But she did not even acknowledge my shouts and continued down the road until the porticoes hid her from sight. I turned back into the room and slumped onto my pallet, tears slipping down my cheeks for the first time since Rondinelli had pounced upon me.

Chapter Fifteen

I awoke shivering, though my room still held the late afternoon heat, and got up to wrap a shawl around my shoulders. While I knew that I should eat, my stomach was closed and I could not face the cheerful enquiries of my local food vendor. Instead, I pushed my chair close to the window to catch the last light of the day and began work on the ninth buttonhole, taking care to centre it exactly over the button on the opposite front of the doublet. As I worked, I was also embroidering excuses for giving such offence to Sofia: I was tired, I told myself, and still reeling from Rondinelli's assault. If only she had shown some disgust at the sodomy, I would never have said what I did. But the truth was that I saw her serenity as a reprimand for my own intemperance. I wanted her to display her anger as I did, but that was not in Sofia's nature. And, though I was loath to admit it, there was some truth in what she said; Fontana and Rondinelli were not two copies of the same book. One was a bully, using the bodies of young girls who had no power to resist, and the other held an equal in affection. Which was truly the sinner?

A loud rap on the front door startled me and I stretched out of the window until I wobbled, hoping to look down on Sofia's dark curls. We could start our conversation again and this time I would take more care not to offend. But the visitor was wearing a feathered cap and the feet which took the stairs two at a time certainly did not belong to Sofia. I opened the door to Francesco Rondinelli, the widow behind him, wringing her hands. Before he could speak, she thrust herself forward.

'I do not approve of male callers but this gentleman' – here she simpered up at Rondinelli – 'tells me that he is your employer. His dress marks him out as a man of good standing, so I am making an exception. It will *not* become common practice.'

I curtseyed my assent and she bustled off down the stairs. When I turned into the room, Rondinelli followed but left the door wide open, which at least showed some sensibility. I did not invite him to sit and he stood in silence, tugging at his lace cuffs, before glancing over at my sewing.

'I see you are busy with the doublet.'

'I committed to complete it and I will.'

'My thanks.' He tugged at his cuffs again. 'There is no urgency. The customer is out of the city at present.'

'I will deliver it tomorrow evening.'

He looked up, trying to fix my gaze.

'That is not the reason I have come, Elena. I am here to ask you to continue our arrangement. To work at home as you have been doing. I know that you cannot forgive me for what happened – for what I did – but the workshop needs you.'

I walked across to the window and stared, unseeing, across the street. How hard it was for him to accept fault. Once again, it seemed, I was required to be Rondinelli's saviour: to be his apprentice but only on his terms. I glanced down at the doublet with its three missing buttonholes. I could make this piece of work my last and never have to look on Rondinelli or Fontana again. For a moment such a prospect seemed to offer comfort and safety, but when my thoughts wandered down the path of how I would earn a living, there came unbidden a picture of Nonna Agnese bent over her table poking at bits of old clothing. And it would not take much for me to sink even lower – to end up wearing the constant stench of a silk-reeler until my very body gave off the odour. Or for my body to be all I had to sell. The thoughts were enough to scare me. I turned to face him.

'I will continue, but I ask one thing: please keep distance between us in the workshop.'

His head drooped, whether in shame or agreement it was hard to tell.

'You have nothing to fear from me, Elena. You know now where my inclinations lie.'

All at once, I understood what had been nagging away at the back of my thoughts the previous night.

'I do. But who else did? How did the *sbirri* know to come for you?'

'That I cannot answer. Giorgio – Signor Malatesta – and I have always taken great care. Men like us learn to live two lives. One in public and one in private. We have told no one else. So Elena, please . . .'

I blurted it out before he could finish.

'I have told Sofia. She found me distressed. But she is no gossip – and neither am I.

The ruse to deceive Fontana continued as though nothing had changed: Rondinelli gave me work which might take one day or a few, and left the shutters half-open for me once the journeymen had left. He praised my skills, as before. He gave me suggestions to help me improve and I followed his advice. He ensured that I left while it was still light and the streets were safe. But, in truth, everything was different. There was little in the way of greeting or farewell, and certainly no curtsey from me. Nor could I bring myself to call him Maestro, and I contrived to avoid any other form of address. We had no conversation beyond the work in hand. He kept at a distance, as he had promised, and even when he was trying to show me a method, I stood a pace away. Though I could see the anguish in his twisting hands, I had no intention of relieving it.

Things were no better with Sofia. I accompanied her to two awkward sittings at the Carracci studio, but we met and parted outside their house and spoke little beyond what was necessary. I knew that my words had caused her offence, but I would have preferred that she shout her anger rather than give me that cold stare. Annibale glanced at us both with a raised eyebrow and Agostino attempted to lighten the gloom with his bantering remarks, but they asked no questions. For a couple of weeks, I scarcely exchanged words with another Christian soul but simply sewed, or trudged in searing heat to Via Drapperie or the Carracci studio and back to my lodgings.

It was near the middle of September when, without notice, summer left Bologna, like a besieging army whose departure had long been craved. Outside my window, millworkers lingered and chatted on their way home, no longer silenced by the shroud of heat which had been wrapped tight around the city. Rain showers washed away the smells of drying vomit and urine in the alleys around San Petronio, and the workshop was finally free of the odour of warming fish – a stink which had drifted over from Via Pescherie for weeks without number. I checked my cloak for holes and loose seams; though I did not need it yet, it would only be a matter of days before the citizens of Bologna, as one, donned their winter clothes.

On that evening the walk to Drapperie had been cool and I was glad of the glowing brazier that had been kept going to warm 'the goose'. Rondinelli asked me to shape the shoulders of two sleeves I had completed, before tying them onto the body of the doublet. When I had finished, he put the whole on a mannequin and stood back to appraise it.

'Excellent, Elena. Signor Baciani will be most pleased, I have no doubt. As am I.'

I almost dipped a curtsey out of habit but held back and nodded my thanks instead. The streets outside were silent, the only sound some drunken shouting way across Piazza Maggiore, far from my route home.

'I should go now. It's fast growing dark.'

I placed the cut pieces of an undershirt in my bag and left the room without any farewell, but just as I was passing through the gap in the counter, something crashed against the shutters outside and I drew back, terrified that the *sbirri* might have returned. Rondinelli was beside me now and we both watched in horror as a body crawled under the shutters, unable to raise itself from the ground.

'Cecco . . .' The voice was little more than a harsh whisper.

Rondinelli gasped, then threw up the shutters and lifted the injured man into his arms before carrying him into the workshop and lowering him onto the cutting-table. The *sbirri* may have been fooled by his little performance but Malatesta, it would seem, had failed their test. Taking the shears, Rondinelli cut him free from his clothes.

'Fabric, Elena, quickly! Anything soft and warm.'

I ran to the shelves and dragged down bolts of fine wool, then used them to support Signor Malatesta's head and to wrap around his broken body. His nose was mangled and misshapen and his hands covered in gashes, where he had tried to ward off his attackers. Far more concerning were the bruises already ripening on his limbs and torso, and the deep gash on the crown of his head. He was drifting in and out of his senses and it was impossible to know what invisible damage had been done to his body. I moved a covered jug of water from the journeymen's table to the top of the still-warm stove and began tearing strips of soft linen from the end of a roll. Meanwhile Rondinelli was bent over the cutting-table, holding Malatesta's hand and murmuring words of comfort as though to a much-loved wife. He even winced each time Giorgio let out a stifled moan. Though the sight made my lip curl, I fetched the jug and dipped each piece of cloth in the water before squeezing it out and handing it to Rondinelli. He lay some over the bruises and began to mop up the blood that trickled down Malatesta's face – but he was unable to staunch it.

'It is no good! The head wound is too serious and I have

nothing to treat it with. Where are the barber surgeons when you need them? All tucked up on their pallets, no doubt.'

I took a handful of bloodstained linen from him.

'I think we need more than a barber surgeon. Let me go to the *ospedale*. Perhaps they can take him in.'

Before Rondinelli could answer, Signor Malatesta grabbed my sleeve and croaked a reply.

'I must not go there. Would draw attention to Francesco. Bring someone.'

The hospital surgeon began by parting Malatesta's hair in several places until he revealed the worst wound – a long gash already surrounded by dark red bruising. Rondinelli had let Malatesta's hand drop at the arrival of the doctor but stood close by, eyes fixed on the patient's face. I withdrew to the corner of the workshop and leant against the artisan's table, waiting for my breathing to steady. After Signor Malatesta had given his instruction, I had picked up my skirts and raced down Drapperie before swerving into Via Clavature, my feet finding their own way in the gloom. Halfway down the street a flaming torch in a sconce on the wall marked the entrance to the hospital of Santa Maria della Vita, and I had to bang on the door repeatedly before a sleepy porter opened up and I could gabble out my request. I had feared a blank refusal but at the mention of Rondinelli's name the surgeon-in-charge was summoned and, in a few moments, he had thrown on a cloak and grabbed his bag before running behind me, his boots not even properly fastened.

Now, after razoring around the wound, the doctor used tweezers to remove the splinters in the cut and then dripped some wine fortified with opium into Signor Malatesta's mouth before sewing the two edges of the wound together with as much care as if he were repairing a tear in an expensive silk robe. Malatesta cried out with every piercing of the needle but I kept telling myself that this at least meant that he was still alive. Finally, the surgeon dabbed the wound with the leftover wine to prevent infection. He would give no further prediction, saying that the patient's recovery was in the balance and only passage of the night would tell.

'He is most fortunate. There do not appear to be any broken bones and the skull has not been stove in.'

Rondinelli's voice rose.

'But what of his organs? Are they intact?'

'That I cannot tell – but a bed in the hospital would be the wise choice. We can transport him there now and I could keep watch on him each hour of the clock.'

Rondinelli shook his head.

'I thank you but no. My friend does not wish his whereabouts to be known.'

'Then you must summon me if he appears to worsen. In any case, I will visit again in the morning.' He clicked his tongue. 'You young men and your brawls. Let us hope he lives to learn his lesson.'

I saw Rondinelli's fists clench and, in that moment, I understood his anger. Signor Malatesta, it seemed, was to blame for what had happened to him, just as Laura had been; the lessons to be learnt were theirs, and did not belong to those who made them suffer. But the surgeon was speaking again.

'He cannot remain lying here. Is there a bed or couch he may use?'

'Upstairs. If you would be so kind as to help carry him.'

The two men formed a sort of litter from a length of sturdy damask and carried Malatesta to the back of the workshop before starting up the stairs. They were narrow and twisted and each movement drew a groan from Malatesta but, at last, I heard them lower him onto the bed and he fell quiet.

Once I had dragged the shutters down behind the surgeon, I crept to the top of the stairs where one door was ajar, a flickering light within. I was about to knock when I heard a whisper.

'Come in, Elena. He is sleeping now.'

Rondinelli's bedroom was as neat as I would have expected: a bed, on which Signor Malatesta lay, his breath laboured even in sleep; a small side table and wardrobe; and an armchair on which Rondinelli perched, still alert even though his eyes were dark with exhaustion.

'How does he look to you?'

The truthful answer was that Signor Malatesta looked as if he were disappearing, his body becoming one with the pillow and coverlet, but I did not wish to load Rondinelli's shoulders with greater burden.

'He is peaceful. That is a good sign, is it not?'

'I think so.' He looked up. 'Oh, Elena, you must forgive me, but I cannot leave him to escort you home.'

I nodded.

'May I remain downstairs until dawn? I do not trust the *sbirri* tonight.'

'You are right not to.'

In the workshop, I wrapped myself in the blanket Rondinelli had given me and curled up on the floor, on the very cushion I had used when I underwent his sewing test. It seemed such a long time ago. I was certain that I would not sleep and when I heard loud banging on the shutters, I was at first convinced it was still the middle of the night and the *sbirri* had returned for a second attempt. But warm sunshine had already crept across the floor and the voices outside were those of the journeymen arriving for work.

'Hush.' I put my fingers to my lips as I lifted the shutters and let the three of them in, their brows furrowed in puzzlement. Filippo spoke first.

'Is the Maestro unwell? Is he still abed?'

Ulisse sniggered.

'Well, the two of them have not been lying together, of that we can be certain. Ow!'

He rubbed the arm where Stefano had slapped him. I could feel a flush rise to my face.

'It is Signor Malatesta. He was attacked last night and your Maestro is tending to him. The surgeon has been but . . .' I could not give voice to my fears. 'He will be visiting again soon.'

The faces of all three artisans showed their shock at the news, and Stefano even turned pale and had to hold onto the table for support. At that moment, Rondinelli came down the stairs, doublet undone, running his hands through his hair.

'I need you to work with as little noise as is possible today, boys, and not a word to anyone about Signor Malatesta's presence.' He looked hard at Ulisse. 'No one must know that he is here.'

They all mumbled their assent and then spread through the workshop, assembling their tools for the morning's work. Rondinelli approached me, though his eyes kept darting towards the staircase and his thoughts were clearly elsewhere.

'Do you feel safe to walk home alone now, Elena? Or would you like Filippo to take you?'

'No need. There is little to fear now it is light.'

Chapter Sixteen

I spent the next days stitching tedious seams on the undershirt. Though I longed to know how Signor Malatesta fared, I could not be sure that my presence at the workshop would be welcome. I certainly had no wish to bring Fontana's wrath down upon Rondinelli by being seen there, so any visit I made would have to be at my usual time. The undershirt required no embroidery – just lace trim at neck and cuffs – and by the end of the week it was complete and I could delay my visit no longer. Doubtless some customer was in need of it.

When I arrived in Via Drapperie around Vespers, the alley was in shadow and all the tailors' workshops were locked for the night – including Rondinelli's. Upstairs, I could just discern a dim light round the edge of the window in the bedroom. I hesitated in front of the shop. The light could mean that it was still a sickroom where Malatesta was being tended by his friend. Or perhaps it was all over and had become the place where Rondinelli nursed his grief. At one moment I was all for returning home, and even took a few steps back down the street, but whatever had happened, undelivered work would be of little help to my employer. I took a breath and tapped on the shutters, hoping that the sound would not carry too far in the still evening. No answer came and I was just about to try once more when I heard shuffling steps from within, and a cracked voice called out.

'Who is it? What do you want?'

'It is Elena. I bring the shirt. I can just pass it under the shutters, if you will raise them a little.'

'Elena! No – I mean, please – come in.'

The shutters clanked open a couple of *braccia* and I slipped underneath. The man I faced was scarcely recognisable. Rondinelli had clearly not shaved for days and his eyes were red-rimmed, the skin around them dark and stretched. He was wrapped in a grubby nightgown and the odour that clung to him suggested that he had not washed for a considerable amount of time. That evening the usually elegant tailor resembled one of the beggars who crouched by the doors of San Petronio importuning those who came and went. Yet a glance around the workshop told me that work was continuing, and it was that which gave me some hope. Rondinelli saw my expression and shrugged.

'As you see, I can look after him and supervise the workshop, but anything else is beyond my abilities. The boys are doing their best but they have slowed down and we are behind with commissions.'

'How does Signor Malatesta fare?'

'The surgeon seems surprised that his spirit clings on. The

injuries we could not see were worse than those we could.' He cleared his throat. 'Giorgio is between life and death, Elena.'

If Rondinelli had been a woman, I would have offered a touch of the hand, even an embrace, but it was strange to see such grief in a man, and my employer at that. There was a short silence while I thought of what I could offer him.

'I will sit with him. You tend to yourself for an hour of the clock. After that you will give me as much work as I can take from you.'

Rondinelli nodded and I followed him up the stairs to the room where Giorgio Malatesta lay just as I had last seen him. Except that he was not as I saw him then. His cheeks were sunken as though his sinews could no longer support them, and his breath came short and sharp. A fine sweat covered his forehead and as I sat down by the pallet a groan escaped his mouth. On the bedside table stood a cup of water and I dipped my fingers in it to wet his lips. Meanwhile, Rondinelli stood unmoving, arms hanging limp by his sides. I turned.

'Go! Wash and eat. I will not move from this spot.'

In fact, more than an hour of the clock passed and it was already getting dark outside before Rondinelli came back into the room, clean and dressed at least.

'Elena – my apologies. Once I had eaten, I sat for a few moments and I must have fallen asleep. Is there any change?'

'None – but he is no worse. Fix your prayers on that. I must leave now or I will be out after dark. Give me all the sewing you need to be done.'

Down in the workshop Rondinelli filled two large bags with cut fabric for doublets, breeches, undershirts – garments for which customers were already banging on the counter.

There was no time for detailed guidance and I swept away his attempts to give it.

'I will work it out. Are you able to leave the shutters open each evening as before?'

'I will try to remember – if not, you must knock.'

I struggled under the shutters with the bags and hurried off down the street, eager to get home before the last light left the sky.

I spent the rest of the month of September working every moment for which God gave sufficient light. When it was too dark to see my stitches, I curled up in a blanket on the floor, my sleep sliced through by visions of an endless winding staircase or a ghostly, dangling figure. My pallet had another use; on it were laid out in piles the pieces of silk, linen, brocade – each pile the promise of a finished garment. The fabrics could not remain stuffed into bags all day, gaining creases and lint, and there was nowhere else to put them; my table was only large enough for the current work. I had begun with a doublet and breeches, the measurements and colours of which suggested they were intended for the same customer. The suit took me just two days but I scarcely stopped in that time, even to eat, and I made decisions on buttons, trim and thread which were accompanied by prayers to San Francesco. When I delivered it on the second evening, Rondinelli nodded his approval at my choices, too tired even to speak. Once again, he took a short pause while I sat with Signor Malatesta, but I wondered how long it would be before his own health was lost. As for

Malatesta, there was no change and not even the surgeon, it seemed, could tell whether his body was mending inside or not.

After that I completed a garment every day, my fingers now sore and bleeding from the constant stitching. One afternoon, as I worked, my thoughts flitted as usual between hope and fear for Signor Malatesta, and I even found myself pitying Rondinelli – his affection, though sinful, was clear as day. Hitherto I had not dared ask him the question which had been itching away at me: who had ordained the attacks against himself and Malatesta? For they surely had the same source. The *sbirri* are so stupid that they would lose their way from their nose to their mouth – they must have been carrying out someone's bidding. In name they are the Papal Legate's men, but the whole city knows that he employs a loose halter and they can be bought by anyone of stature for a few *soldi*. And what wrangle could the Legate have had with two men who lived quiet lives, even if they were sodomites? As I picked away at the question, I could summon up only one answer: Antonio della Fontana. There was no other man of influence who both knew Rondinelli and delighted in exercising his control over others. He had done so at the Baraccano and in his own home, as Sofia knew only too well.

The thought of my friend reminded me of the pain my remarks must have caused her. I had been so much concerned about my own hurt that I had spoken without thinking, as guilty of poor judgement as Signora Ruffo's shunning clients. I wanted to close the rift between us, make an invisible mend as in a torn sleeve, but there was no time in the day to visit her and I had even stopped going to her sittings at the Carracci studio. The three men had shown themselves to be honourable and I had no fear for her safety or reputation. There would be no Lord's Day leisure for me until something changed at the workshop, for good or ill. Each evening I returned to Drapperie to deliver my work and give Rondinelli some respite, hoping for good news. But there was none, except that all the garments I sewed had been received with approval by his clients. That gave me some comfort, at least.

It was a fortnight after I delivered the first undershirt that I arrived at the workshop as usual, carrying a pair of slashed breeches which I had barely completed in time: two layers of fabric had more than doubled the work. Once again quiet shadow filled Drapperie and only at the far end was light spreading under half-raised shutters onto the cobbles outside. I stepped through the gap in the counter and into the workshop, intending to call up the stairs as was my custom, when fear snatched my breath. The room was in complete disorder: half-unwound bolts of cloth trailed onto the floor; pins, needles and buttons were scattered over the cutting-tables; jugs and cups had been abandoned on any surface; even Rondinelli's stool had been knocked over and still lay where it had fallen. I was certain that the worst had already happened, for surely only the death of Signor Malatesta could explain such disarray. I stood in the middle of the room, unsure what to do, when I heard the floor above my head creak, followed by the sound of footsteps clattering down the narrow staircase. I braced for my encounter with Rondinelli and the news he would bring. The man who rushed into the room still looked ghastly: his hair and beard had clearly not seen a comb since the previous night; he wore no doublet and his crumpled undershirt sagged out of his breeches; his eyes were still sunk into their sockets with dark arcs below them. And yet all these clues to tragedy were belied by the wide grin, one worthy of Giorgio Malatesta himself, that lit up Rondinelli's features.

'He is recovered! Not yet completely well, of course, but the surgeon says that he is out of danger and all he now requires is rest. Come! Come upstairs! He will be glad to see you.'

The room was dark and stuffy with the scent of lavender heavy in the air, coming from the large bowl of dried flowerheads placed on the bedside table near the patient's head. It took a few moments for my eyes to become accustomed to the gloom so that I could make out Signor Malatesta, pale and propped up on pillows but awake and smiling, and the sight lifted my spirits more than I would have thought possible. He beckoned me to come closer, his voice low and hoarse.

'I must thank you, my dear. This one,' he patted Rondinelli's hand, 'tells me that you ran for the surgeon. Your quick thinking – and running! – made all the difference.' He paused for breath. 'And you have been taking care of him and his work for me.' He smiled up at Rondinelli. 'We both owe you much.'

'I was glad to be of help, Signore. And I rejoice at your recovery.'

Rondinelli swallowed and moments passed before he spoke.

'I also told him of my loathsome assault upon your person – which makes your actions even more praiseworthy. I used you to save my own skin and I beg your forgiveness, Elena.'

His hopeful expression told me that he was waiting to be absolved but I said nothing, shaking my head in refusal: still he did not grasp the import of what he had done and would need it chalked out. After a long pause, and stammering at first, I looked Rondinelli in the eye.

'You did use me, Signore, and that gives me pain, but there is something you have not yet understood. The worst part was that you made me remember things I wished to forget. You may not think your assault was real or lasted very long, but for those moments I was once again a young girl, forced to carry out Fontana's vile bidding and in fear that my virtue might be taken at any moment. Always knowing that this would not be the last time and that worse might come.' I was shaking now and my voice broke as I lowered my head. 'For Laura, much, much worse.'

There was a quiet 'oh' from Rondinelli before he stepped forward and took my right hand in both his own.

'Elena, I have been cruel and thoughtless and no man, nor woman neither, could reproach you if you left now and never returned. But I beg you to forgive me – and to remain at the workshop.'

There was no doubting the sincerity in his eyes, and I managed a smile as I released my hand.

'I know you did not intend to cause me harm . . . Maestro. And I have had my fill of mending for Nonna Agnese.' I cleared my throat. 'Do you require some help downstairs? When I saw the state of the workshop, I feared the worst.'

I glanced over at Giorgio Malatesta, who was beaming at us both.

'Blame Cecco. When the surgeon pronounced his verdict that I would make a full recovery, he immediately told the boys to leave off early and drink to my health. Sounds like they took him at his word.'

The Maestro laughed.

'I have never seen them move quicker!'

I headed towards the stairs but turned, knowing that there was a question I must ask.

'Do you know who attacked you, Signor Malatesta?'

'Only that they were *sbirri*. Oh, and I heard them call the leader Volpe – a nickname on account of his red hair and beard, I would hazard.'

'That sounds like the same man who came to the workshop. But who might have directed them? Told them their target?'

The Maestro shrugged.

'We are at a loss. We were considering the matter before you arrived.'

I bit my lip.

'Could it possibly be . . . Fontana?' Their eyebrows rose but I rushed on. 'He has the necessary power, not to mention the affection of men like them.'

The Maestro immediately shook his head.

'But what could be his motive? He is a loyal customer who likes our work. What benefit would it be to him if the workshop failed? I know you hate the man, and with good reason, but I do not think he is behind these attacks.'

Signor Malatesta sighed.

'I cannot fathom who it might be.' He gave a weak smile, nothing like his usual grin. 'But that is no surprise, as I cannot think in a straight line at present.'

I could see that he was beginning to tire.

'Do not brood on it, sir. You must rest. I will restore order below.'

Chapter Seventeen

Within a few days Giorgio Malatesta was well enough to return home and the workshop relaxed into its customary rhythm – as did I. Each waking hour was no longer filled with toil. The Maestro still entrusted me with sewing tasks which required all my skills but sometimes as I sat at home sewing my neat stitches, I longed for more – to fit and cut so that I could take credit for a whole garment. But even San Francesco could not bring about that miracle. The Lord's Day was once again a day of leisure for me and, as the leaves on the trees took on the hues of safflower dye, I wanted so much to walk along the lanes inside the city walls with Sofia. Her portrait must be close to finished now, I thought, and I wondered whether young Annibale had been able to catch my serene friend with his paints. My apology to her was overdue and so on the last Lord's Day in October I once again followed the course of the canal towards Via Righi. I made sure that I arrived outside the house before the usual time; I did not want an audience of the

Carraccis, however well intentioned, for my confession. I was certain that Sofia would forgive me when I told her how sorry I was, and how busy I had been because of the attack on Signor Malatesta. She might need to visit a few trees or some such but I had no doubt that we would soon be reconciled.

I had been pacing up and down in front of the house when I heard footsteps behind me, and turned to find that Sofia had rounded the corner and we were face to face. I had never seen her features so stern. She said nothing but stood and glared at me, waiting for me to begin.

'Sof, Sofia, I have come to apologise to you – again!'

I gave her a rueful smile but received none in return. I pressed on.

'I would have come sooner but I have been so very busy doing extra work for the Maestro.'

There was no flicker of understanding on Sofia's face, so I changed direction.

'I was very wrong to suggest that your sufferings were less than mine. Fontana has injured us both—'

'Stop!'

I had never heard Sofia raise her voice and I was left mouth agape while she berated me.

'I am weary of hearing about how hard you work and how much you want to be tailor. This I know. I work hard too – but I am just seamstress, not so important. And I am weary of hearing that name – Fontana. On and on you go about him and your friend Laura. I suffer because of him too. My mother and father die too. I am dragged from homeland – where people are good people – do you hear? – not savages. All you think about is Elena and what Elena want.'

Tears were trickling down my cheeks now.

'But I thought . . . I thought you were my friend too.'

'I wish to be, but always there is Laura. She is – how you say it? – in my way. I cannot be in her place. And you do not even know my name.'

'What do you mean? It is Sofia.'

'It is not. My name is Suhailah but that is too difficult for you, for all of you people of Bologna. So you change my name as if it not important.'

'Oh.'

I wanted to defend myself but at that moment I knew her words were just. My friend had kept her pain hidden, like a wound under a bandage, and I had never even noticed it, because I was too busy thinking of myself. She lifted her chin, as though already rejecting anything I might say.

'I am needed for my sitting. Are you coming?'

I nodded and trailed behind her up the stairs, knowing that I was there on sufferance, but when we reached the top, we both stopped in surprise. The studio looked completely different, as was the mood within it, and instead of the usual friendly greeting, our presence at first went unnoticed. Agostino was sitting on the floor tailor-style, a sketch-pad resting on his crossed legs, his silverpoint darting across the page. All the canvases had been removed from the walls and were propped up in a pile in one corner, allowing Ludovico to rough out huge shapes in charcoal on the bare plaster. Annibale was stationed in the middle of the room at his easel, scribbling notes on a large sheet of paper and calling out ideas and instructions to his brother and cousin. I was uncertain what to do – perhaps we were not welcome that day – but finally Agostino noticed our arrival and leapt to his feet, putting his work aside.

'Time for a pause, boys. The young ladies are here.'

The other two stopped their work, though Ludovico did so with a deep sigh, and Annibale set up the chair and his easel, now bearing Sofia's image once again. She took up her usual pose on the high-backed chair and I slunk over to the divan, trying to be as inconspicuous as I could. Agostino appraised the portrait for the length of a Paternoster, before walking over to me.

'I – we – are pleased to see you again, Signora Elena. We thought we had perhaps offended you in some way.'

'No, not at all. I would not wish you to think so. I have had much work to do for Maestro Rondinelli.'

'But you have more leisure now?'

'Yes – things are as they were.'

Not exactly true, but I could not even begin to tell Agostino Carracci what had happened since we last met.

'I am glad of it. May I sit here?'

I smiled my assent, and immediately became conscious of how close his body was to mine on the narrow seat. Like most men, he carried the smell of his craft and I found that linseed oil had a most appealing scent. He put on a mock-formal expression.

'We Carraccis would like to invite you and Signora Sofia to join us in celebration in fourteen nights' time. I will ensure the portrait is framed by then and we can share some bread and wine again as we did all those months ago. Would the two of you find that acceptable?'

'Certainly, sir. I am sure that I can speak for Sofia also. We would be delighted.'

Agostino clapped his hands together.

'Then it is fixed. As fortune has fallen, we have two things to celebrate. Ludovico has managed to secure us that commission I mentioned for an altarpiece. It is but a little church – and outside the walls . . .'

'But a great achievement all the same, is it not, sir?'

Agostino turned to me with a grateful smile.

'It is a beginning at least. The church itself could not afford to have it done, but a benefactor has stepped in and now we can begin work.'

'That is indeed cause to celebrate, and the benefactor deserves praise for his good taste!'

'He does. Antonio della Fontana does so much for our city.'

The man was everywhere but, heedful of Sofia's words, I tried to push him into the dark recesses of my thoughts, at least for now.

Agostino glanced over at Annibale, who was gazing around as though lost.

'Excuse me, Elena . . . Signora Elena. It looks like my brother has run out of pigment.'

The rest of the afternoon passed quicker than I wished, for the walk home promised to be an awkward one. As soon as we reached the bottom of the stairs, I started my prepared apology to Sofia – it would be a struggle to think of my friend by her new, to me, name. 'Suhailah . . .'

But she waved my words away.

'I know that you are sorry – you do not need to say. But please remember that I am your alive friend.'

It was an odd way of speaking but the meaning was clear; she did not want to be pushed aside by Laura any more. And she was right. Whatever I did, I could not bring Laura back.

I slipped a tentative hand in hers and she squeezed it tight. By the time we reached my lodgings, we were giggling over grumpy Ludovico and wondering whether a smile had ever crossed his lips.

It was a few evenings later when the Maestro and I were alone in the workshop and he had just pronounced a doublet I had completed as 'of excellent workmanship'. It was in a damask which flickered between ruby-red and cherry depending on the light, and I knew that my finely stitched details, including invisible buttonholes and bound cuffs, had only enhanced the garment. He was just about to explain my next task – a richly decorated velvet cape – when there was a loud banging on the shutters.

'You in there, Rondinelli? Need to talk to you.'

The Maestro became completely still, the cut-out pieces of velvet draped over his arms.

'It's Fontana.'

I did not need to be told: his was a voice which still broke into my dreams at night. I looked around, wondering where I could hide, but there was nowhere in the workshop. The Maestro pointed up the stairs.

'My room and stay completely still. The floorboards creak.'

I scuttled up the stairs and crouched down on the top tread, unwilling to step inside the Maestro's chamber now it was no longer a sickroom. I would have chosen not to hear the conversation which was had in the workshop below, but every word reached me.

'Good evening, Signor Fontana. How may I be of service?'

'Now I do not have much time. There's a cargo of silk bound for Genova tomorrow morning and the warehouse is all downside-upside – but I've got a very particular commission for you: the best set of clothing you can make.'

'A special occasion, Signore?'

I could hear Fontana pacing around the room, stopping from time to time, and could imagine him picking up and dropping items with his customary arrogance.

'My eldest daughter's wedding. She is but fifteen years old and I have made her a fine match. Not that she seems very pleased . . . ungrateful miss. Says she wants to be a nun and compose music or some such nonsense, spends fully half her time at Mass. The convent dowry would be cheaper, there's no doubt of that, but it would be a pity for her to become a dried-up husk. She is a pretty girl, fine figure already. In fact, she would tempt me if she were not of my own flesh.'

A shiver ran through me. There was a brief silence. What was he doing?

'This is a fine doublet, Rondinelli. A good shape – your fitting, I presume – and the stitching is excellent. Your work or one of your journeymen?'

'Um, an apprentice actually, Signore. Very skilled.'

I felt my face flush.

'I can see that. Better even than any of those three craftsmen, I wager. I am impressed, Rondinelli. Your choice of apprentices must be improving. By the by, what became of that young girl you got rid of?'

There was a short silence before the Maestro replied.

'I know not, Signore.'

'On the streets, I would wager, and spreading the pox to those unwise enough to use her.' There was a pause. 'So this is what I want. You as fitter and cutter – no one better – but we'll give this new young man of yours a chance with some of the sewing. Of course, if it's not good enough I will expect you to do it all again with no cost to me. Are we agreed?'

'Signore.' I could imagine the Maestro's nod. 'One question – the date of the marriage?'

'The thirtieth day of November. Yes, I know, I know. It is an unusual time, and I would have preferred Lent so that I could avoid spending out twice for wedding *and* Carnevale. But if we don't grab this man fast he may be snatched by some other family. And I need the connection. Should be plenty of time for you to make the outfit if you hold the boys' noses to the grindstone. I will be back the day after tomorrow to choose the fabric and to meet this young apprentice of yours.'

I heard Fontana stride out of the workshop, shouting a farewell as he left. I waited a few moments until the Maestro called up.

'The coast is clear. You can come down.'

I found him slumped on his stool, head in his hands.

'Did you hear any of that?'

'All of it. Why, by all the saints, did you agree?'

'I thought you could work in your usual way from home. It was not until he said he must meet you that I understood the mistake I had made.'

I paced the room between the two sewing-tables.

'You must tell him that your new apprentice has left.'

The Maestro gave a mirthless laugh.

'What, between now and Friday? He would see that as a

deliberate refusal to give him what he wants. What am I to do?'

I continued my pacing as I tried to line up my thoughts like a neat row of stitching. Rondinelli was right; the absence of 'the new apprentice' would only arouse Fontana's suspicions, but equally if he found out that I was still employed, then the Maestro could wave farewell to his commissions – and probably to the workshop altogether. What we needed was a way for me to do the work without Fontana realising who was behind it. I slumped onto the wooden chest under the window and traced its grain with my finger while I tried to think. Could we somehow pass off Ulisse as the new apprentice? But Fontana had met him several times and he would have to be heavily disguised. Then Fontana would wonder where Ulisse had gone. It would never work. The Maestro was as silent as I, his gaze directed at the floor. I idly flicked the catch on the chest up and down, earning a glance of irritation from him. The chest, it seemed, was always an object of anger. I had only ever seen it opened when a customer's failure to pay had resulted in an unsold garment being thrust into it, usually accompanied by a curse. It was full of clothes of all sizes which lacked owners. A thought – not an entirely welcome one – began to form.

'Maestro,' I started slowly, fearing his derision. 'How would it be if I became your young male apprentice?'

'This is no time for nonsense, Elena.'

'It is not nonsense. I could find a suitable outfit in this chest and pass myself off as a youth. Fontana shows no interest in a face unless it is attached to a female body, and my shape could be hidden under breeches and doublet. If he was told I am a boy, I think he would believe it.'

'But your hair, your lack of beard. No! He would never be fooled.'

'The hair is easily solved, I will tuck it inside a cap, and I know of someone who can help make my complexion a little less soft. I think the ruse could work, Maestro, as long as the whole workshop sings to the tune.'

Antonio della Fontana was true to his word and the Accursio clock had just struck ten on Friday morning when we all heard him arrive at the counter. Ulisse had been given the role of receiving customers that day – the Maestro deemed it to be the place where he could do least damage – and he was suitably obsequious as he ushered Fontana into the workshop accompanied by the cloying scent of hair oil. The Maestro flashed one wide-eyed glance at me before I made myself busy laying out shears and needles for the journeymen. Fontana clapped the Maestro on the shoulder.

'Morning, Rondinelli.' He looked around. 'Morning boys,' then came up to me. 'And you must be the new apprentice.'

I almost found myself making a curtsey but managed at the last moment to turn it into a small bow – respectful but without sweeping too low.

'Signore.'

The Maestro stepped forward.

'Signore, this is Cristoforo, whose sewing skills you admired. He will be pleased to work on your wedding suit. Is that not so, Cristoforo?'

I nodded and, pitching my voice as low as I could, gave the

answer we had decided upon.

'I will be most honoured, Signore, and hope to be of good service.'

'I hope so too, boy. As everyone knows, I believe in helping all the young people of our city, whatever their station. It is my small gift to Our Lord as thanks for my good fortune. Generally, I must own that I favour the girls. They give me so much in return.' And he gave a large wink.

I felt the bile rise in my throat. *The man has no shame*, I thought. *He tells the world what he is doing and no one hears.* I forced myself to make another small bow before walking away to the back of the workshop.

I had felt strange and uncomfortable the previous evening when I first put on the dark brown breeches and doublet we had found in the chest, completing the outfit with a cream undershirt and hose. Brand new, the clothing looked too fine for a mere apprentice and the Maestro had to rub the garments in dust and lint to make them appear well worn. My breasts were squashed by the binding I had tied around my chest and there was an unfamiliar bunch of fabric between my legs. I could not imagine how long it would take to use the privy! My calves felt naked with only hose for covering and I found myself skulking behind the cutting-table to hide them until the Maestro summoned me into the centre of the room. It had been harder than I imagined to pin my hair inside a flat cap of the kind favoured by aspiring apprentices, and tendrils kept escaping. An early morning visit to Annibale, who was sworn to secrecy, had provided a stick of charcoal, but it took several attempts before I was able – with the Maestro's help – to sketch an emergent beard on my face. I then spent an hour practising how to move around the workshop as a boy, with the Maestro shouting orders at me until I was close to giving up. But the lack of skirts flapping around my ankles gave me a freedom I had never known and in time I was taking longer strides, bending and squatting in a way that was impossible in women's clothes. When all was done, the Maestro declared me ready to take on the role. The greatest concern remained the three journeymen; the Maestro and I knew we could rely on Filippo to play his part, but of Stefano and Ulisse we were less certain.

On that Friday morning I was once again in hiding on the stairs when the journeymen arrived at work. The Maestro asked them to sit on their table because there was something important he needed to tell them, and I could feel the unease fill the room as they waited to hear what he was going to say. Such a serious announcement, they would assume, must be bad news.

'I want to introduce you to our new apprentice, boys.' It had been agreed that this was the point when I would step into the room, and as I did so, the Maestro gestured in my direction. 'He is called Cristoforo, and Signor della Fontana has requested his work most particularly for a set of garments for his daughter's wedding.'

Three heads twisted in my direction and I sketched a bow towards them. Stefano and Ulisse were stony-faced, clearly livid with anger that some upstart boy would be chosen over them for such a prestigious task. It was Filippo who cocked his head on one side with an appraising look before bursting out in laughter. Ulisse now looked confused as well as angry.

'What is there to laugh at, Filippo? Do you want your

livelihood taken away by some pretty boy who doesn't know a needle from a bodkin?'

Stefano nodded in agreement.

'The boy scarcely has fluff on his face. Maestro, we do not deserve this insult.'

Filippo wiped his eyes.

'Look more closely, lads. Is that face not a little familiar? "Cristoforo" indeed!'

Stefano and Ulisse slipped off their table and approached me. I met their looks with a steady gaze.

'Holy Madonna!' Stefano was moving his cupped hands in a gesture of disbelief. Ulisse pushed him aside.

'Let me see.' He peered at me. 'Elena? Maestro, what is this about?'

Then the Maestro explained how I had continued to work since my dismissal and how Fontana had come to choose my stitching.

'That is why we must keep up the pretence that Cristoforo here is a new apprentice who – for some reason we will avoid mentioning – is very skilled.' I flushed at that. 'It is of the greatest importance that you call her Cristoforo and treat her as you would a boy apprentice. Understood?'

Filippo and Stefano had chorused their 'Yes, Maestro' and Ulisse gave a sullen nod.

Now the three journeymen were sliding the brightest bolts of cloth from the shelves onto the Maestro's table and he in turn draped a length of each roll, one after another, against Fontana.

I had to admire their knowledge of the customer's taste: the colours ranged through greens, blues, yellows, reds – including a scarlet so vibrant that bucketloads of scale insect must have died to produce it.

'Oh, I don't know, Rondinelli,' Fontana snapped.

He was becoming exasperated, never a good omen for those around him, as I knew only too well. Once at the Baraccano he had been unable, for some reason, to reach the peak of his pleasure on the body of one poor girl called Domenica. She had certainly paid the price, returning to the refectory bruised and battered, and with a bloody nose. Mistress Serafina ensured that the punishment did not end there and for a week afterwards Domenica ate only bread whilst standing with a sign around her neck stating 'For presumption'. The lesson all we girls had learnt that day was that Fontana's frustration was something to be avoided. I stepped forward, gave a small bow and in my new low voice addressed our client.

'May I ask what colour the bride is wearing, Signore?'

Fontana turned a puzzled face towards me, and the Maestro gave an almost imperceptible shake of his head.

'What, boy?' Fontana's voice was louder now. 'What has that to do with anything?'

'It is just that I am certain you wish to wear a colour which will look well against her gown.' I chose my words carefully. 'You would not want her garments to detract from your own.'

Fontana scratched his beard.

'Hmm. A good thought, young man. Her gown for the *nozze* procession is a burgundy. All the fashion, I am told. The other stages of the contract are of no concern; we will scarcely be in the same room. Let the suit be as handsome and as showy as you like, eh Rondinelli?'

I reached out for a brocade of vibrant blue shot through with gold thread that glittered like fireflies on a dark night.

'This would look very well against burgundy, Signore.'

And put the poor girl in the shade, I thought. *But that cannot be my concern.*

The Maestro took the bolt of fabric from me and held it up against Fontana.

'It is a fine cloth, Signore. You will not find its like in Bologna.'

'Do you give me your word on that, Rondinelli? I do not want to come face to face with the groom's second cousin wearing the same.'

'I swear the cloth is unique, Signore. I should also warn you that the price reflects that.'

Fontana waved his hand in the air.

'The cost is of no matter.' He turned to me. 'An excellent choice, young man. I expect your stitching to do it justice.'

I nodded and helped the journeymen clear the table of fabric bolts, ready for the Maestro to begin his sketches.

For the rest of the morning, tailor and client sat at the cutting-table, heads bent together in conference, while the Maestro drew and annotated sheet after sheet. I joined the others, who were finishing items for customers, and I could not help but smile as I settled tailor-style beside them without having to hide my legs under my skirts. From time to time, the Maestro threw a command over his shoulder for samples of shirt linen or matching threads and one of the tailors would slip down to find what he wanted. At one point, Ulisse was ordered to fetch some decent wine and he scuttled off to The

Sun, jug in hand, but not before hissing at me that a proper apprentice would carry out the errand for him.

There was only one moment when I feared that our ruse would be found out. Filippo was rummaging through the drawers, searching for some thread to hold the stuffing in place in a codpiece he was making. He called across to our backs.

'El— I mean Cristoforo, where did you put the strong black thread?'

I slipped off the table and hurried across to him, deliberately lengthening my stride.

'Here, sir.'

My voice came out comically deep and was followed by a snort from Stefano's direction. The Maestro turned and glared at us all.

'Keep the noise down, boys. Signor Fontana does not need to hear your nonsense.'

There were mutters of apology and Filippo grimaced at me before we all settled to work once again.

By the time Fontana left the workshop the designs for his wedding suit were complete, including undershirt, hose and a full-length cape. As the Maestro ushered him through the entrance, the journeymen put down their needles and Filippo blew out his cheeks in relief.

'My apologies, Elena. I did not mean to put your disguise in jeopardy.'

'It mattered not, sir. I am certain the Maestro and Fontana did not notice. They were too preoccupied with the designs.'

At that, Rondinelli came back into the room.

'Well done, boys.' He looked towards me. 'And an excellent

fabric choice . . . Cristoforo. I think that to avoid further mistakes,' he flashed a disapproving glance at Filippo, 'we should call you Cristoforo at all times. If that is acceptable?'

I nodded: swapping back and forth between the two names would be bound to end in more errors. Moreover, I found that I rather relished the idea.

Chapter Eighteen

Now that Cristoforo was Rondinelli's official apprentice, I no longer had to skulk into the workshop after business had finished for the day. How much I had missed the warm fug with its odours of fabric and waxed thread. Even the stink of male sweat (and worse!) could not detract from the feeling that this was where I belonged. I had taken to putting on my boy's outfit before I left my lodgings in the morning and wore it back home too, always making sure that my landlady was not peering out of her front window when I came and went. It was much simpler than trying to change at the workshop with the tailors milling around, but I also found that wearing the clothes all through the day helped me to play the part. There was another advantage which filled me with astonishment. I had not realised what a different place the city was for a boy and how much easier my life became when I was Cristoforo. Never did a man tell me to get back indoors. No longer did I have to endure catcalls and obscene suggestions as I walked down the street. No one grabbed at my skirts or tried to slide a hand across my breast in a crowded alley. I could even leave the workshop after dusk had fallen, if necessary, without fear of molestation or the tender attentions of the *sbirri*. It was true that an ageing sodomite often leered at young Cristoforo from his post propping up a pillar of the *ospedale* in Via Clavature, but he never spoke or approached and his expression was an offer rather than a demand. I knew that the Church would view the Maestro and that importuning wretch as equal in sin – but to me they seemed as different as white is to black.

On the day of the celebration Sofia arrived at my lodgings wearing, as usual, her formal dress – the one which had been painted in such careful detail for her portrait. I, on the other hand, had spent the last three evenings making something new for the occasion out of a length of dark blue *garbo* which the Maestro had allowed me to take from the chest because it had a slight fault running through its length. I was able to avoid the fault with my cutting and the wool was not as heavy or thickly woven as some, so the garment looked well enough. The weather was soft and mild for the time of year and across my shoulders was the shawl I reserved for best wear – it was of a fairly rough silk but in a beautiful dark rose. It had been a gift from Signora Ruffo for my saint's day and, much as I loved it, a flicker of guilt now seemed to be permanently attached to it like a sample of poor embroidery. I slipped my arm through Sofia's and we strolled beside the canal, dodging the rats which slithered along the bank and into the reeds. When I had told Sofia of the Carraccis' indebtedness to Fontana, she had laughed.

'If you threw a stone in Bologna, it would hit someone who owe Fontana for something. Do not judge a man on that.'

But now I had a new reason for anxiety.

'What if he is there? He might want to join in the celebrations . . .' My voice died away.

'I do not think that likely. The studio of some poor artists is not the sort of place Fontana would spend time, however pleasant the young men are.' She looked sideways at me. 'I think you like Agostino, yes?'

'I like his good humour – and his modesty. It must be hard to know that your skills are likely soon to be eclipsed by your little brother.'

Sofia giggled.

'And his good looks are of no importance, of course.'

I smiled.

'Not in the slightest.'

We had arrived at the Carracci house and began climbing the stairs. Halfway up, Maria popped her head round a door.

'Good afternoon, ladies. Signor Agostino said to go straight up. I will bring refreshments shortly.'

The studio had been swept and tidied, and in the middle stood Annibale's easel bearing the framed portrait of Sofia. The artist himself shuffled from foot to foot beside it, his head lowered. We both stepped up close and I marvelled at the skill which could make fabrics appear from paint: the metallic thread of Sofia's partlet glittered in the sunlight and the painted caul which kept her bound hair in place was as transparent as its true-life counterpart. On her breast, scarcely visible, were the pins and needle – subtle reminders of her craft. Though the background of the painting was dark, her skin glowed against it and the colour of her lips was reflected in the simple coral necklace knotted at her throat. But it was, I thought, the eyes above all which refused to allow the viewer to look away. Her bold stare told of suffering endured and overcome, of pride and determination, as though the artist had lived every moment alongside her. And yet I knew that Annibale, all nervous stammering, had scarcely exchanged a word with his sitter. How was this young man, no more than a boy in fact, able to see all that and then describe it in paint? No wonder Agostino poured praise upon his little brother. Sofia gave my arm a squeeze before turning to Annibale with her broadest smile.

Behind them, the whitewashed wall was now covered with disconnected charcoal sketches: there were angels hovering high and low; legs which lacked torsos twisted into positions I doubted any human could hold; hands with index fingers pointed every which way; there was a dove and the face of an elderly man; and part of a river even washed across one corner. I approached the wall and was trying to disentangle the themes when Agostino came alongside me.

'Is the altarpiece to be of Christ's baptism?' I asked.

'That is a relief,' Agostino laughed. 'At least there is some hope that people will recognise the completed scene if you can spot the elements already.'

'And who will paint which part?'

I could not imagine how three young men with such different temperaments could work together on one painting.

'We will decide nearer the time – perhaps not until we begin. Though I can tell you now that Ludovico will insist on taking the head of God.' He pointed at the elderly face. 'He loves to surround a head with light. Is that not right, Ludo?'

'That's right.' The voice came from the alcove at the far end of the room. 'I do light better than either of you.'

In Agostino's voice the words would have been softened with a chuckle, but Ludovico appeared to be stating a fact. Agostino bent his head towards me to whisper in my ear.

'That is why Annibale and I leave the negotiating to him. Once he thinks he is right, there is no budging him.'

Annibale was now hovering in front of the portrait, bending his head this way and that before darting forward to make the smallest of touches with a fine paintbrush. Agostino glanced over at him and shook his head.

'Stop it now, Anni. You cannot gild refined gold.'

Annibale put down his brush and we all gathered around the table, where Maria filled the cups and handed them around. Agostino raised his in a toast.

'To Annibale's fine portrait – only possible because of his fine sitter!'

I sipped my wine and almost spluttered. Whether at Agostino's behest or by her own choice, Maria had watered the wine a great deal less this time. A flicker of alarm went through me – was this when the three men would try to breach our defences? I glanced from Annibale, who was blushing with pride, to smiling Agostino thumping his younger brother on the back and then Ludovico, mouth downturned as always, and the thought flew out of the open window. I felt as safe here as in the Maestro's workshop. I sipped the wine, feeling it loosen my limbs and tongue, and when the conversation turned to the most suitable colours for the robes in a baptism altarpiece I found myself arguing most forcefully for the inclusion of splashes of vermilion. The late afternoon sun was now slanting through the rear window upon our group, and its warmth made me regret the choice of fabric for my new dress. At least I could remove my shawl, and no sooner had I done so than Agostino asked if he may lay it aside for me. He placed it on the divan and all at once I was filled with melancholy. I had spent so many hours sitting there – sewing, watching, listening to the conversation amble back and forth between the three brothers – and now there was no reason to return.

The farewells were prolonged and much repeated, and it was not until Sofia and I had left and we were nearing my lodgings that I noticed I had left my shawl behind. When I told her, she giggled.

'That is very good excuse, is it not? You have to return now to see handsome Signor Agostino.'

'But he will think that I left it by intention. That it was a ploy to visit again.'

Sofia gave me a sideways look.

'Which of course it was not.'

'No! I swear that I left it by mistake. What am I going to do?'

I stopped walking and held my wrist to my forehead: the afternoon had been long, my dress too hot, and now a throbbing had begun between my eyes. Sofia held me by the shoulders.

'It is quite simple. You will go inside, drink water, lie down for short time. Then in a few days you will return for your shawl. Just make sure you do not arrive as young Cristoforo!'

Antonio della Fontana's wedding apparel was of an extravagant design, far removed from the Maestro's personal taste, as the whole workshop knew. Yet Rondinelli left us in no doubt that we would carry out the man's wishes to the highest standard of craftsmanship. The ruff was of enormous proportions and kept Ulisse sweating over the poking-stick for hours while he moulded in the tubular sets. The breeches were of a heavy linen in two colours – the underlayer in cream, which was then paned with strips of a dark burgundy. Nestled within them was a massive codpiece, a clear sign that Fontana disavowed fashion in favour of show. Stefano joked that he and Filippo would need the wool of a whole sheep to stuff it. I (or rather Cristoforo) had been charged with the doublet in the blue cloth of gold and I was mindful of the honour. The Maestro himself would add a sweeping velvet cape when all the other items were complete. For now, when not checking on everyone's work, he busied himself taking new orders at the counter, with a warning that there would be a slight delay before requests could be met. The mention of an important commission for Antonio della Fontana always seemed to sweeten the bad news. Since there remained more than two weeks before the wedding, the Maestro urged us to take our time and as soon as the light dimmed, the day was over. This was not the sort of work to be done by candlelight.

On the fourth day since my last visit to the Carraccis' studio,

I determined that I must retrieve my shawl straightaway or I would never find the courage to do so. To that end I took my women's clothes to work and, at the end of the day, asked the Maestro if I might change on the stairs.

'You may use my room, if you wish. No one will disturb you there. Are you visiting someone this evening?'

Ulisse sniggered and I felt a flush rise to my cheeks.

'No, rather yes. Just a friend – I left something behind.'

Ulisse bent close to hiss in my ear.

'As long as it wasn't your virtue.'

I flashed him a glare before grabbing my bag from the corner.

'Thank you, Maestro.'

As I changed out of my apprentice clothes and wiped off my beard, I could hear the three journeymen gathering up their belongings and chattering their way out of the door. For a few moments all was silence and then there was a new voice, murmuring low.

'It is such delight to see you, Cecco. I have been tallying the hours until we could be alone.'

'I too. Come here.'

Silence followed. I bundled Cristoforo's clothes into my bag and stood perfectly still, wondering what to do. The Maestro had clearly forgotten I was there, but if I did not make myself known I risked being locked in – or worse, being a witness to something I did not even want to imagine. There was only one remedy: I clattered down the stairs, gabbling all the while.

'My thanks, Maestro. I do not know what my friend would have thought had I turned up to collect my shawl dressed as

a boy. Only Sofia knows of Cristoforo's existence, of course.'
I arrived at the foot of the stairs. 'Signor Malatesta! Good evening.'

Giorgio Malatesta was on the opposite side of the workshop from the Maestro and showing immense interest in a bright purple damask which I knew he would never wear. He turned towards me with a wide grin.

'Elena! It is a pleasure to see my saviour again.'

'And how goes your recovery, sir?'

'Very well, I thank you. I am told that I will soon be chivvying my printworkers as though nothing had happened.'

'Is that your occupation, sir?'

'Yes, I am a *cartolaio*. We create some books for the wealthy men of the city – and some women too.'

'You are too modest, Giorgio.' The Maestro turned to me. 'His is the best *cartoleria* in the city.'

Their obvious affection confounded me.

I had been so put out by the awkward interaction that I turned into Via Calzolerie not fully noticing my whereabouts. And so I was heedless of a well-dressed couple walking towards me, her arm linked through his, until we were almost upon each other. I glanced up. The gentleman's startled look must have been reflected in my own. He gave the briefest of nods.

'Signora Morandi. Elena. Good evening.'

It was Signor Martelli. I could have wished myself on the other side of the city.

'Good evening, sir.'

I had hoped that was the end of the encounter, but he made no attempt to step aside.

'May I introduce my *wife?*'

The emphasis on the last word was marked.

'Madam.'

I made a curtsey, longing to escape, but they made no move. Martelli cleared his throat.

'I hope that you are well, Elena, and that your . . . choices have not brought you to grief.'

'N . . . no, sir. That is, I am well and . . . practising my craft.'

He would get no further detail from me.

'My own prospects are, as you see, most favourable.' He gazed down at his wife, who simpered back with lowered eyes. 'Your decision was, I think, for the best.' He attempted a chuckle. '"Man proposes and God disposes", as the Holy Mother Church tells us.'

'Indeed, sir.'

'Well, we will wish you good evening.'

And they were gone. It was my day, it seemed, for discomfiting meetings and I had scarce cooled my face from that one before I reached the Carraccis' studio. It was impossible to know which of the Carraccis would be there at that time of day but I hoped it would not be all three. Or, even worse, Ludovico alone: he would, no doubt, be most displeased to be disturbed from his work on account of a forgotten shawl. Perhaps the best to be wished for was that they were all out save Maria, who would bustle about in her sensible way and without recrimination. But there was another circumstance for which I dared to hope: to find Agostino alone – even if an unchaperoned conversation should, for my reputation's sake, be very brief.

There was neither sight nor sound of Maria on the stairs and as I neared the top I could hear male voices, just two as far as I could tell, speaking low. Perhaps Agostino and Ludovico were discussing plans for the altarpiece. I crept up the last few steps to the open doorway but there I came to a stop. Agostino was indeed in the room, standing with his back to me in front of two easels, but the man alongside him was not Ludovico.

'Fine work, Carracci, very fine indeed. And so true to life that I find my breeches rising. That minx on the right is enjoying herself, is she not?'

Agostino cleared his throat.

'Each will depict one of the ancient gods and his love, Signore. Here we have Mars and Venus, and Bacchus and Ariadne. These are but the preliminary drawings, but the engravings will be of the highest quality and the twelve prints will be bound in leather. It will be a book worthy of the most discerning customer.'

'Yes, yes. There's no need for all that nonsense with me, Carracci. You know that I can't wait to get my hands on them. Would that I could get my hands on the girls too, eh? I can think of several fellow-merchants who will writhe with envy – or something else – when they see these. So all I ask is to be first on your waiting list – fair exchange for the altarpiece, do you not think?'

At that moment, Fontana stood to one side and in the gap between the two men I could see the two works on display. Each showed a man and woman – both naked – and on the verge of sexual congress, but there was no modesty or shame depicted, only sheer lust. It did not take great intellect to understand the purpose to which they would be put. I must have gasped because Agostino twisted round.

'Signora Elena. Did you want to speak to me or . . .'

But I did not hear the rest of what he said; I was already running down the stairs.

Chapter Nineteen

The street was thronged with millworkers plodding home and I fell in step with them, brushing away the tears that threatened. Was there no place in this city where Fontana's disgusting fingers did not reach? Until now, I had felt respect for the Carraccis – especially Agostino – but now that respect was unravelling like a clew of dropped yarn. Little wonder he had been so keen that those works were covered up in a corner of the studio. He was no better than Fontana, fanning that man's wickedness with lewd and lascivious drawings. He might as well have helped tie the noose around Laura's neck. And he would have needed more than his imagination to draw those sinuous bodies; all that wine and hospitality looked very different now. I stopped in my tracks, causing someone to curse behind me. Though the portrait was finished, there was nothing to stop young Annibale from luring Sofia back with some excuse about needing to add final touches or with the promise of a further portrait. A few blushes and stammers were all the weaponry the boy needed to persuade my kind-hearted friend to help him. I must warn her.

I hurried on, past the turn to my lodgings, towards the bridge over the Reno. The workers had now sloped off to narrow houses which hung over the canal, and I was alone on the street lined with smallholdings leading to Signora Ruffo's palazzo. Dusk was softening the edges of the trees and an owl swept past me, hunting for the small creatures that scuttled through the undergrowth. Dry leaves swished under my feet and a runnel of water trickled beside the stone wall. Had I been dressed as Cristoforo, the sights and sounds would have pleased me, but as Elena, I was far too aware of the perils my surroundings could be hiding. I pulled my cloak tight and rounded the corner into Mercato. When I arrived at the Signora's front door, I stared at the fierce sea-creature on the knocker for the length of an Ave Maria but I was no closer to deciding what to say. I only hoped that the new girl, whoever she was, fetched Sofia without too much fuss. Finally, I banged hard on the door and waited for what seemed like a lifetime in Purgatory before I heard footsteps inside and the latch lifted. Then my hand went to my mouth: it was Signora Ruffo.

'Elena!' The tone was not one of welcome. 'I did not expect to see you here again.'

I made my deepest curtsey.

'Signora Ruffo. I am sorry to disturb you . . .'

'If it is Sofia you want, she and Agnella are very busy with a client. Is there a message?'

'Pl — please.' I stumbled over the words. 'Please tell her to avoid the Carraccis' studio. They are not as they appear. Their motives are not well intentioned.'

'What? The Carracci boys? What are you talking about, girl?' The Signora laughed. 'I am yet to meet a finer set of young men. I would not allow Sofia to go there otherwise. Who has told you such nonsense?'

My fists clenched in anger but I kept my voice low.

'No one has told me anything. I have seen with my own eyes the sort of . . . pictures they draw. It is not all altarpieces and respectable portraits, you know. Sofia is in danger.'

'Ah.' Signora Ruffo nodded her head slowly. 'So you have seen Agostino's engravings.' She opened the door wider. 'I will not discuss these matters on the doorstep, Elena. Come inside.'

The workroom looked no different from when I had left it months before. There was even a regular client near the screen, fussing about the fit of the sleeves on a voluminous pink silk dress which Agnella was adjusting while Sofia stood at arm's length passing the pins. Sofia looked startled to see me and raised her eyebrows in question, but I had no chance to explain because Signora Ruffo escorted me to her embroidery table at the far end of the room.

'Wait there.'

While I sat twisting my hands, Signora Ruffo checked the girls' work and then bade farewell to her customer. When she returned, she sat down opposite me with a deep sigh.

'I need to set you straight about the Carraccis – and Agostino, in particular.'

I bowed my head and deemed it best to say nothing.

'The drawings he makes with – what shall I say? – themes of love, are made into engravings and then books. He sells them to respectable customers, married men only, you understand, to be appreciated in the privacy of their homes.'

I opened my mouth to speak but the Signora carried on.

'There is nothing amiss in what he does, and the money he makes allows all three artists to produce those fine altarpieces and portraits you speak of. They could not survive otherwise.'

I looked up with a glare.

'And the models? Where does he find those? How can you be sure he does not debauch young girls like Sofia for his . . . art?' I spat the last word.

'I know because I help him to find his models. They are not unwilling dupes. They are courtesans – streetwalkers – who are glad of work which is safe and clean. And I chaperone them. They are treated well, I give you my word.'

My eyes must have widened. I would never have believed that the Signora kept company with such women. Now she had punctured one of my complaints like a pig's bladder but I still could not forgive the Carraccis.

'I am glad of that, at least, but Signor Agostino needs to take more care who his customers are.'

'What is your meaning?'

'I have just left Signor Antonio della Fontana leering over two examples of those drawings and putting in an order for a book full of them.'

The Signora sighed.

'Ah. There is a man I have never liked. To tell truth, he causes me to shiver. Let us hope he admires them while alone or . . . in the company of his wife.'

I was out of my chair now and shouting.

'Or perhaps he uses them before a visit to the Baraccano, to prepare himself for molesting any girl there he takes a fancy to. Will no one stop the man?'

A startled look crossed the mistress's face but she had no chance to reply, because a whimper came from the other side of the room and we both turned to see Agnella slumped to the floor in a swoon. In moments the three of us had lifted her onto one of the soft chairs and Sofia was holding some remedy under her nose which worked faster than any salts of hartshorn. I knelt at the girl's feet and rubbed her hands, which were cold as marble.

'What is it, Agnella? Are you unwell?'

Agnella's reply was a whisper but she cleared her throat and tried again.

'Fontana. He is not here, is he?' She was shaking now and looking around the room, eyes wide.

'No, my dear. He is nowhere near.' I squeezed her hand. 'He cannot do it again.'

Sofia brought a blanket, which we tucked around the girl while the Signora stood silent and brooding. Finally, she spoke.

'Tell me everything.'

I did not want to speak in front of Agnella so I took Signora Ruffo aside and we paced back and forth in front of the open windows while, in an undertone, I described Fontana's abuses at the Baraccano and Laura's self-murder; how Mistress Serafina had made it possible and how even the *guardiana* had chosen not to see; and how Sofia had suffered a different kind of abuse in Fontana's house. When I had finished the Signora sat down at her table with a deep sigh.

'There have been rumours, Elena.' My eyebrows rose. 'No, not about the Baraccano in particular, but about his inclination towards young girls. And the city's courtesans talk of him favouring the very youngest among them. But to be capable of *that*. And I thought I was doing good by allying myself to an orphanage . . .'

My anger had dissipated.

'You *were* doing good, Signora. You gave me and Agnella a home and an occupation – and others too, I warrant.'

'But I asked no questions. I saw the Baraccano girls arrive here in wordless pain and I did not ask the reason.'

'Pain which you helped to ease. To feel safe in this house is a balm – one which is already soothing Agnella.'

We both looked across at the girl who was now conversing with Sofia, her complexion no longer as pale as milk. I sat down opposite the mistress and waited for her to speak again.

'And yet you left me in the lurch. I hear from Sofia that you have found a position in a workshop.' She smiled. 'I should have known you would succeed.'

'I must beg forgiveness for my ingratitude, Signora. I could not bear to marry Signor Martelli and live above a tailor's workshop without ever being allowed to thread a needle.'

'It matters not now. Who is the tailor?'

'Francesco Rondinelli. He is most skilful, and I put my trust in him and his . . . friend Giorgio Malatesta.'

'He is indeed and there is no need for the coyness, madam. Affection takes many forms. They are good men both and you do well to trust them.'

'I thought the same was true of the Carraccis but now I am not certain.'

'I would swear by all the saints, Elena, that Agostino does not know the nature of the man he is dealing with. He would be the first to condemn him, if so.'

'Even though Fontana is paying for their first altarpiece?'

'Even so.'

'Signora, as you know them well . . .'

'No, Elena. He needs to hear from someone who has suffered at Fontana's hands. From you.'

I gazed unseeing out of the window and listed in my mind all those I had told of Fontana's sin: Sofia, the Maestro, Signora Ruffo – and now I was about to add Agostino Carracci. It felt as though I was hawking Laura's suffering around like a common pedlar. And to what end? Half the city owed some debt to Fontana, while the other looked to him as a second father. And the Church had given him absolution as though he had bathed in holy water. It was then I decided that Antonio della Fontana should pay the price for his wrongdoing, not at the hands of a foolish young woman with a pair of tailor's shears, but in a way which would hurt him much more – though I had no inkling of what that might be.

I turned back to the mistress.

'I will speak to Signor Carracci, Signora. But not now. I must get home before the *sbirri* are abroad.'

The following day Fontana arrived at the workshop for a final fitting on his ruff – too loose and he would cut a poor figure, but too tight and his discomfort would be visited on the whole wedding party. He swept in, filling the room with his presence as usual, and it was a few moments before I noticed that trailing behind him was a girl, small in stature, comely and fine-featured – but for the anxious furrows on her brow. Fontana addressed us all.

'This is my daughter Madalena. Her mother insisted that I bring her to see my wedding suit. Not that her opinion counts for anything, of course. Madalena, this is Maestro Rondinelli.'

The Maestro made a respectful bow.

'You are most welcome, madam.'

She gave him a deep curtsey in return.

'Signore.'

Fontana waved vaguely towards the back of the workshop where the tailors and I stood in a deferential line.

'The journeymen and an apprentice.'

I expected a daughter of Antonio della Fontana to acknowledge us with no more than a curt nod but she crossed the room, clearly expecting to be introduced. The Maestro rushed over and hovered in front of each tailor in turn.

'This is Filippo, my longest-serving journeyman, and Stefano and Ulisse. And this young man is Cristoforo – the apprentice.'

Madalena dipped her head and we all bowed from the waist. It was only when I straightened up that I saw her quizzical look.

'Cristoforo,' she repeated, in a tone which was neither question nor statement. She walked over to the mannequin that wore Fontana's doublet and put out a hand to stroke the pile, only pulling back at the last moment.

At a nod from the Maestro, Ulisse took down the ruff from the beam, its tasselled band-strings dangling from the two ends. Fontana lowered himself onto a stool and Ulisse settled the ruff around his thick neck before tying it at the back. Fontana ran a finger round the inside of the collar.

'Not bad. A little tighter, boy, and I will be pleased.'

The remark sounded harmless enough but anyone who knew Fontana could hear a threat lurking beneath those words. Just the thought of our client's displeasure caused Ulisse's hands to tremble, but he untied the band and was able to find enough slack in the strings to make the collar a little more snug on the second attempt. Once again, Fontana tested the fit with his finger.

'Excellent. And the sets are well formed. Your work, boy?'

'Yes, Signore. The whole piece, Signore.'

'No dithering then – untie it for me.'

Ulisse removed the ruff and hung it up again before peacocking his way back to us, a triumphant smile on his face. Fontana immediately rose and headed towards the door, addressing us over his shoulder.

'I am in much haste this morning – a confraternity meeting, followed by a visit to the Baraccano. Charity, boys, is what the Lord asks of us and is what we must give, if we are able. Farewell.'

The man had clearly forgotten that he had brought his daughter with him at all, and was out the door before she had gathered her wits. The Maestro came to her aid.

'Cristoforo! Escort the young lady and ensure that she is reunited with her father. We cannot have her walking the streets unchaperoned.'

'Maestro. This way, madam.'

Madalena dipped a brief curtsey to all the assembled tailors and followed me through the gap in the counter onto Drapperie. I twisted my head in each direction and saw her father striding off down Via degli Orefici, no doubt on his way to one of the civic buildings in Piazza Maggiore. I pointed and we followed him, she lifting her skirts and trotting alongside me as fast as she was able. I knew that it was not my place to address her, even had Fontana's mention of the Baraccano not made me speechless with rage, so we progressed in silence until we entered the piazza. Fontana was still ahead of us but had been waylaid by a well-dressed citizen, giving us time to catch up. Madalena slowed down a little and looked at me sideways.

'You are no more a boy than I am.'

She took me so much by surprise that nothing came from my mouth. We stopped and she gave me a sweet smile.

'Do not concern yourself. I will not be telling anyone – especially not my father.'

We were now facing each other in the middle of the piazza, while citizens swirled around us on all sides. I could still see Fontana out of the side of my eye, head bent in whispered conversation with his companion.

'Thank you. But why would you keep my secret from him?'

'Because when it comes to my father it is much safer to be a young man than a young woman.' My face must have registered my shock. 'Did you think that I do not know what sort of man he is? The signs are there for all to see – yet no one does.'

'But he does not – I mean – with you he is . . .'

'He manages to control himself with me, but I can see the force of will it requires. He will be glad to have me married to take away the temptation.'

'And you? Are you glad to be marrying?'

Her short laugh was mirthless.

'I can think of little worse. I long to be a nun and fill a convent chapel with music of my own composition, but my father will have none of it. He needs the connections, you see, and the holy sisters offer little of that.'

I dared not touch her arm in sympathy – a fine lady being manhandled by a tailor's apprentice would draw the attention of the whole piazza. Instead, I performed an awkward bow, my head passing near hers, so that I could express myself in a whisper.

'I am sorry for your afflictions, madam.'

At that moment, I noticed Fontana taking leave of his companion and could do no other than escort Madalena towards him.

'Your daughter, Signore. I fear she did not know your next destination.'

He looked startled.

'Yes, yes. Thank you, Cristoforo.' He turned to Madalena. 'Silly girl.'

And he grasped her wrist so as to drag her away towards the huge portal of a nearby palazzo.

Chapter Twenty

I must own that I dawdled back to the workshop the long way round, all the while unpicking my short meeting with Madalena. There was a time, and not so long ago, when I would have envied the young woman all the advantages of her birth. The walls of Fontana's palazzo were solid and thick, fortified against chill draughts and miasmas in winter as well as the relentless August sun. Madalena would never have shivered under a blanket while the room rattled, nor been baked in her bed like a fish in the oven. She would dine on dainty slices of meat and candied fruits, whilst wearing clothes made of the finest brocades and damasks. Her days, I thought, must be full of repose with servants bowing and curtseying to her every wish. All this because she had been born of illustrious parents – and, what is more, parents who had contrived to stay alive. And yet I found myself full of pity for her. My life was harder to the touch than hers, of that there was no doubt, yet I had never been a piece of property to be bought and sold, nor were my eyes filled with shame at the mention of my father.

I had reached the workshop and went in, though my mind was still with Madalena and my expression likely vacant. Signor Rondinelli looked up from his cutting.

'Well?'

'Maestro?'

He sighed.

'Did you deliver her safely?'

'I did. He had forgotten all about her. Poor girl. Her life must be a torment.'

A snort came from the direction of the journeymen's table. Ulisse, of course.

'I wish I suffered that kind of torment. Living in luxury, no work.'

The Maestro did not even turn his head.

'You will have no work soon, if you do not finish that sleeve by the end of the day.'

Ulisse bent back to his sewing, but not before he had shuffled along to make room for me beside him on the table. The black breeches I was slashing matched the doublet he was working on and I could see that neither would disgrace the other. The workshop fell silent and, as I stabbed the slashing-tool time after time into the thick brocade, I once again felt the satisfaction of doing what I loved in the place where I felt at ease. It was strange to think that I enjoyed a privilege which Madalena's high birth could never bring her. My next thought was so unexpected that it caused me to cease slashing and gaze unseeing across the room. I would not now describe that first idea as a plan; it was too shapeless and ill formed, lacking design or embellishments, but even then I felt certain there was a way that both Madalena and I could get the better of Antonio della Fontana. A nudge from Ulisse brought me back into the room – and not a moment too soon. The Maestro was stretching his back and rolling his shoulders, always a prelude to a detailed appraisal of each garment being worked on. I flashed Ulisse a grateful smile and returned to poking at the brocade.

Ulisse had resented my presence in the workshop from the very beginning: ever since the day of that first test when the Maestro compared his work unfavourably to mine. Not a wise remark, as it turned out, for Ulisse had borne his grudge like a burden and I had thought that he would never let it fall. At one time, I had even considered that he must have been the informer against the Maestro and Signor Malatesta – but it made no sense. Anyone who named a sodomite to the *sbirri* would know to expect violent consequences – consequences which risked the workshop, and thus Ulisse's own living. What is more, the arrow of his malice always had me alone as its mark, no one else. The Maestro and Signor Malatesta no longer seemed interested in who was behind the attacks, as though they had paid one fee and there would be no further demand for money. I still blamed Ulisse for the violence but now believed it to be the result of a loose tongue rather than malevolence. Ulisse was a gossip, and who knew what he might have let slip in The Sun once he had downed a few cupfuls of wine; it only needed the right ear to be listening. As the Maestro passed along the line checking our work, it came to me that it had, in fact, been some time since Ulisse had released one of his barbs in my direction. Perhaps he found Cristoforo a more acceptable workmate than Elena.

For only the second time, I changed back into Elena's clothes at the workshop and hurried off towards the Carracci studio. The day was hovering on the edge of dusk and, though the *sbirri* showed little interest in that part of the city, I did not want to linger in its darkening streets. There had seemed little purpose in planning what I would say to Agostino. I did not even know if I would be able to speak to him alone, never mind how to find the words to tell him about Fontana. The stairway of the Carracci household was silent and Maria's door did not open to allow a friendly greeting as I passed by. On the top step, I sent up a quick prayer to San Francesco and then paused to hear any conversation which might be taking place within. I had no wish to interrupt another of Agostino's negotiations. There was nothing, not even footsteps crossing the floor of the studio, so I stepped across the threshold. He was sitting cross-legged on the divan, the soles of his bare feet facing upwards in a position I did not even know the human body could assume. His hands rested on his knees, and his eyes were closed, as though he were asleep, yet the upright pose of his body denied that was so. I spotted my shawl hanging from a hook in the corner of the room and was much tempted to grasp it and run back down the stairs. But Agostino must have sensed my presence, because he slowly opened his eyes and then leapt to his feet.

'Good day, Signora Elena. You have returned. I am so glad.'

My nod was curt and I did not return his greeting, but he was not to be diverted from his course.

'I caused you distress last time you visited. I would not, for all God's kingdom, have wished you to witness what you did. I beseech you to accept my apology and allow me to explain.'

He looked sorry enough and his eyes resembled those of the

most abject beggars on the steps of San Petronio – but I did not want to hear his excuses.

'There is no need for explanation. Signora Ruffo has told me of the reason why you produce those . . . works of art.' I did not even attempt to remove the sneer from my words. 'She said that they bring in money to allow your other work. She also assured me that your models are willing and well looked after.'

'They are. They are. And I sell only to respectable men.'

'Respectable men?' My voice was rising now. 'You call Antonio della Fontana a respectable man?'

Agostino recoiled, his brow furrowing in puzzlement.

'Is he not? He is married. He performs charitable works all over the city. Were you yourself not a beneficiary?'

Poor Agostino. How he must have regretted that choice of word, for it unleashed all the anger I had kept in check for so many months. I paced up and down in front of him, words tumbling from my mouth – words for which my mother would have given me a slap. This was not the simple cutting-line of facts I had given the Maestro. I wanted Agostino to know exactly what sort of man his prints inflamed and what they led to: every slobber and grope, every bruise and bite, every demand to suck and rub. I even disclosed the secret I had kept from everyone – Sofia, the Maestro, Signora Ruffo: that Fontana loaded *us* with his guilt, muttering 'whore', 'cunt', 'slut' in our trapped ears and, favourite of all, claiming that we privately longed for every moment of our ordeal. And, of course, I told him of Laura – of her shame and the only means she could imagine to make Fontana stop.

When the words were finally spent and I had stopped my pacing, I dared to look again at Agostino. He was motionless, open-mouthed, his face pale. Were he anyone else, I would have assumed that my intemperate language had outraged him, but that seemed unlikely for the artist of 'The Gods and Their Loves'. He shook his head slowly from side to side.

'I can scarce believe it, Elena. He parades around this city like a jovial saint, all smiles and ridiculous yellow breeches. Makes us believe that he is full of beneficence and all the time . . .' Agostino's hand shot to his mouth. 'And I have colluded with him. Given him fodder for his vile appetites in return for a commission. It is a pact worthy of Judas!' He sank back onto the divan, head in his hands. 'I beg your forgiveness. I had no conception . . .'

I sat down beside him.

'You are not alone in that, Agostino. My Maestro has clothed Fontana for years and knew little of the real man.'

'He has duped the whole city, it seems. But for how long?'

'There have been rumours, Signora Ruffo tells me, but the whole truth remains hidden. As for how long – I only know that there are decent married women in their fourth decade who shudder at the mention of his name.'

Agostino raised his head, his expression grim.

'We must give up the commission. I cannot bear for our work to be connected to that man. It would be like daubing the altarpiece with blood. And if he thinks that I will let his filthy hands near my print-book . . .'

He was shaking with anger now and, as if by its own will, my hand moved across the gap between us and touched him on the arm. The fabric of his sleeve was soft and worn, so unlike the stiff damasks and brocades of the workshop.

'By all means find an excuse not to sell him the print-book, but the church deserves its Carracci altarpiece. All he did was provide money – your work stands on its own merits.'

'And Fontana meanwhile just trots along to the Baraccano whenever the urge is upon him and is granted access to the bodies of those poor girls.'

He was on his feet once again, raking his hand through his hair and striding from one end of the room to the other. All at once he stopped.

'I have it! You must make a denunciation – you and others who have suffered – the *auditore* would have to hold a trial if you made an official complaint.'

I gave a hollow laugh.

'And you think he would value the testimony of some cloakless orphans above that of the city's greatest philanthropist? The case would be thrown out before it even reached the halls of the Palazzo Pubblico.'

'So what is to be done?'

And it was then that for the first time I clothed my half-made plan in words, starting with the news of Madalena's forthcoming *nozze*. Agostino straightaway drew two stools up to the paint-splattered table, pushing aside the mortars and jars of pigment. While I gabbled through my imaginings of what should happen on the day of the *nozze*, jumping from point to point as things occurred to me, he scribbled notes on a torn sheet of paper. Every so often, he would interrupt with a suggestion, but there was no sneering or disbelieving laughter. He even committed his brother and cousin to the plan, without consulting them. And therein lay one of the weaknesses of our strategy; it required so many people to commit with full heart to the actions of that day – and one person in particular. Finally, Agostino asked the question I had been trying to dodge.

'Do we know that Madalena will agree?'

I shrugged.

'I do not *know* it. In our short discourse I learnt of her strong desire to be a holy sister and of how much she despises her father.'

'That may be so, but this plan brings public humiliation upon her – and upon the groom – on the day of her *nozze*. It is a lot to ask of any woman, Elena, never mind a young girl who has been brought up in Fontana's household.'

'Do you think I do not know that?' I rubbed my temples. 'Sorry – you are just giving voice to my own fears. If Madalena refuses, we can proceed no further. Worse yet, if she gives her consent then succumbs to shame at the last moment, all will be lost and there will be consequences for many.'

'Then we must determine her feelings. Are you able to meet her?'

'Surprisingly, we do not move in the same circles!'

Agostino laughed. 'But did she not say anything – about how she spends her time, perhaps?'

'"Composing music" is all I can remember . . .'

'. . . and any music teacher would visit her at home.'

'Exactly so.'

I tried to think back to any mention of a place she might be found but could remember none. She did not even say which community of nuns she aspired to join. Then a comment made by Fontana came back to me.

'I have it! Fontana said that she spends a great deal of time attending Mass.'

'But did he say which church? There are so many close to Fontana's palazzo.'

'That is not where she would choose to go. If Madalena's interest is music, there is only one church worth her time.'

'Of course. San Petronio!'

There was no hope that Madalena would be permitted to attend Mass alone or to have a conversation with a rough apprentice like Cristoforo: especially not a conversation which called for time and freedom from interruption. My first step must be to arrange a meeting in a secluded place. I was trying to think of somewhere suitable when I noticed that stars were visible through the wide window at the front of the workshop. I jumped up.

'I must go. It is already dark.'

Agostino walked to the hooks on the wall and took down my shawl and a woollen cloak.

'It is a cold night. You will need both.'

I thanked him and was at the top of the stairs before I realised that he intended to accompany me.

There was, of course, no certainty that Madalena would be at Mass the following morning. It was neither the Lord's Day nor a feast day, so only those whose faith was like breath to them would be shivering through Prime in the vast cavern of San Petronio. My short conversation with the girl led me to believe she was one of that number, but who knew what strictures there were on her daily life? Though my errand might turn out to be pointless, I crept out of my lodgings while it was still dark, wearing Cristoforo's doublet and breeches with my own cloak wrapped tight against the cold. As I hurried alongside the Reno, I remembered the warmth of Agostino's cloak, against which my own now seemed as useless as a silk veil. Sunrise lacked an hour but heavy cloud smothered the city and dawn, when it finally came, would likely be no more than a slight lifting of the darkness.

There were few abroad at that hour, and when I reached the steps of San Petronio, there was no queue of worshippers waiting to enter the huge portal. Once I stepped inside, I found that I had to remain still for many moments for fear of bumping into pew or pillar. The darkness at first seemed absolute but gradually the windows of coloured glass began to take form as grey slabs, and the pools of candlelight in each side chapel allowed shapes to appear. Though I could yet see little of God's glory in the basilica, I could hear it. To the right of the far-distant altar the voices of a small choir soared and plunged their way through the Mass, their cadences like threads twisting in and out of each other to form a fine fabric. I knew nothing of how such beauty was created but I understood only too well that if Madalena were to compose music such as that, she needed the freedom of a convent, not the fetters of a marriage. The Kyrie sank to its close and I shuffled forward, feeling my way into a pew halfway down alongside the Bolognini chapel.

When I was a small child, of perhaps six years, my father brought me to look at its frescoes, which fill the walls of the side chapel from floor to ceiling. Its pictures of the Inferno were, no doubt, used by many a parent to frighten their children into obedience. In them the damned, all naked, suffer every torture of the artist's nightmares, and the cavorting devils are brought to life by the flickering candles placed beneath. But my father had no wish to scare me with demons. The object of our visit was the opposite wall of the chapel where the artist had painted the story of the Magi's journey to worship Our Lord. And my father's interest was most particular; he was there to admire the clothing of the participants.

I can still see him, peering up at the highest scenes, sighing with frustration that he could not see them clearly.

'Is that a brocade they have used for his sleeve, do you think, Elena?'

No reply was required, as he went on to answer himself.

'I think so. The pattern is so marked that it must be raised.'

'See the ermine edging on Herod's cloak!'

'The shepherds are wearing *garbo*, I have no doubt of it. And those are *perpignano* hose – otherwise they would not fit so well.'

It was, to him, as though the witnesses at the Christ Child's birth were citizens of Bologna who had just recently been dressed by one of its tailors; it was a commission he would have relished. I followed his pointing finger, as it moved from male figure to male figure, and repeated the names of the fabrics after him. There was but one woman depicted in the frescoes – the Virgin herself – and my father made no mention of her clothing. No wonder. It was of plain dark blue with no embellishment. Perhaps it was then I learnt that a tailor would always outshine a seamstress.

Now the gloom was slowly giving up the morning's scattering of worshippers: an elderly man two rows before me wheezed and coughed his way to salvation; to my right, a prim matron mouthed prayers, her lips never still; and close by her, propped against a pillar, sat the legless beggar who habitually filled a corner of the doorway at the top of the steps, his hand outstretched for alms. I peered the length of the basilica and there she was: Madalena, seated at the end of the first row of pews, as close to the choir as she could be, her head bowed in worship. I had expected her to be flanked by armed bodyguards but there was just a lady's maid, hands tight in lap, sitting close beside her. I waited until the singers reached their final crescendo and the priest raised his hands in benediction, before I stood up and headed round the back of the church and down the far aisle, to intercept Madalena. I bowed low and tried to draw her aside, hoping that her maid would hang back. But it was not to be, and the woman hovered behind her mistress, seemingly determined to hear every word which passed between us. There was nothing for it but to pretend a chance encounter.

'Greetings, madam. I did not expect to find you here today but you have saved me a journey. I have a message from my Maestro for your father.'

Her fine-plucked eyebrows rose in surprise but she nodded her permission.

'He requests that Signor Fontana returns, at his convenience, for the final fitting of the ruff.'

I could only hope that Madalena realised the request made no sense at all and that I needed to speak to her alone. The puzzled frown lasted but a moment before she grasped my meaning.

'Yes, of course. I will let him know.' She turned to the maid.

'Maria, please could you take my thanks to the priest and tell him that the sung Mass lifted my soul. The boy will remain with me until you return.'

217

Maria bobbed and scuttled away, and I took the opportunity to gabble out my purpose.

'I need to speak with you, madam – in private. It concerns your future.'

'As you can see, I am like a prisoner under guard. Do you have a suggestion?'

'Who is making your wedding outfits, madam? Could we meet there?'

'Signora Properzia Ruffo. Do you know of her?'

I grinned.

'I know her very well. She used to be my mistress. When do you visit her next?'

'Tomorrow afternoon. Meet me there.'

The lady's maid was hurrying back, clearly anxious that her mistress should not be late home lest it was she who paid the price. I gave another low bow before striding off down the aisle, hoping that the maid was not given to spying for her master.

Chapter Twenty-One

It was as Elena that I arrived at Signora Ruffo's the following day and it took Madalena a few moments to recognise me, now I was no longer Cristoforo. She had already told the Signora of our meeting and we held our whispered discussion between pinnings, tucked away in the corner among the shelves of fabric. The ever-present lady's maid was easily distracted by chatter with Sofia and Agnella, and only glanced over every so often to check that I had not spirited her mistress away. Madalena needed none of the persuasive reasons I had rehearsed on my walk along Mercato; her determination to become a nun ranked alongside my own to be a tailor and even when I made vivid the shame that was like to descend on her father – and hence herself – she did not flinch from the plan. Nor did she seem in any way deterred by the physical exertion it would require from her. My concerns about the convent were also put at rest. Madalena visited Corpus Domini each week for a Mass and the abbess, she assured me, had no doubts about the depth of her faith.

Signora Ruffo took a little more persuasion. The sewing task alone would upend her commerce for weeks and I knew that she would have difficulty in attending to her worthy clients while the workroom was festooned with lengths of rough sky-blue wool. I was also asking something much more of the Signora, for she would be the last player left in our little scene and there was no way of knowing whether the audience would like what they had been shown. It was Agnella who won the argument for me – terrified little Agnella who agreed to her part before I had finished asking and even took on herself the extra task of finding the girls. With that example, the Signora could not rightly refuse. Sofia needed no asking at all and I knew that she would be my steadfast companion on the day. But I also feared that she would baulk at what the Carraccis were about to create; suffering may have made her as durable as hemp yet she was pure of spirit. I decided that she should be kept away from their work until the final moment.

As it turned out, Sofia was not the only one banished from the Carraccis' studio. Maria darted out of her own rooms that afternoon to bar my way.

'I wouldn't go up there now, dearie.'

I immediately conjured up the very worst imaginings: either Agostino was enjoying a woman or courting the likes of Fontana. Perhaps even Fontana himself. Clearly, it did not take much for my good opinion of Agostino to unravel as fast as a picked seam. I tried to push past Maria but she was a sturdy woman and showed no sign of budging.

'Why not? Is someone with him?'

She twisted her hands.

'It is not that. They are all three working on something . . . particular. Very odd, I call it. Never seen them paint anything quite like it before. But I know that Signor Agostino would not wish to cause you any disquiet.'

The knots in my shoulders released.

'Do not concern yourself, Maria. I know what it is – he is making it for me.'

Her eyebrows rose.

'All the same, dear, he said not to let you up.'

At that moment, a voice travelled down from the upper floor.

'Who is it, Maria?'

She opened her mouth to reply but I preceded her.

'It is me, Elena. May I come up, please? I need to speak to you.'

The only reply was a clattering of footsteps down the stairs and then there were three of us crushed onto the tiny landing.

'Thank you, Maria. You can get back to that magnificent stew you are preparing.'

She withdrew but not before throwing me a quizzical look. I said nothing. If Agostino was not going to invite me upstairs, I wanted to hear his explanation. He gave an awkward shrug, though at least he was not avoiding my eyes.

'I don't want you to see it here, Elena. The boys and I agree that it is an ugly piece of work. Well executed, of course.' He hazarded a smile. 'But not something I want you to associate with us, with me, for ever. Please wait until the day, then you will see its purpose. Here it looks too . . . coarse.'

I nodded.

'I will not argue with you. I only wished to tell you that Madalena welcomes our plan and that the female company is aboard. Now I need to persuade the Maestro and his workshop.'

'That is good news indeed. How many men are necessary?'

'The task requires four. But I have some unease about Ulisse – I fear he may not be wholly trustworthy.'

'Can we not help?'

'Thank you, but the canvas must be your prime concern. Signor Malatesta may be persuaded . . .'

But it was the Maestro's nod of agreement I had to win first – something which I dared not attempt until Fontana had given his approval of the wedding suit. He was due for his final fitting on the next afternoon and ever since early morning the whole workshop had vibrated with tension; when Ulisse dropped a handful of pins, I feared that the Maestro might slap him. As it was, a bawling-out was all he delivered. Even before Fontana swept in, the journeymen and I were lined up in front of our sewing-table like a row of Baraccano girls awaiting inspection, and the Maestro was pacing back and forth rubbing his palms together. Fontana's complete outfit was displayed on the mannequin, artfully placed so that the gold thread of the brocade shimmered in the thin winter light.

Once again, Fontana had brought someone with him, but this time it was a well-dressed servant who trailed in behind his master and then tried to make himself inconspicuous under the hanging beam. His task would be to carry the finished garments home without them getting soiled or creased and, to that end, he had a length of linen draped over one arm; it resembled nothing quite so much as a winding-sheet. Fontana made extravagant bows in all directions accompanied by loud greetings and laughter, as always. We all bowed in return. Then he approached the mannequin and made a circuit of it, peering at every feature from the stiff ruff to the soft linen undershirt, which the Maestro had deliberately left visible through the unbuttoned doublet. Finally, he stood back and applauded, for all the world as if he were in the audience of a Passion Play. The servant shifted from foot to foot, seemingly unsure whether he should join in, but decided against it. Perhaps he thought there was always a chance that the applause was derisive. But Fontana's words proved otherwise and made the Maestro's shoulders relax a little.

'A masterpiece, Rondinelli! As long as it doesn't fit like a loose-slitted whore. Just jesting, just jesting! Now, let's see how it all looks. Come here, boy, I need your help.'

He was looking in my direction and, at first, I did not know what he wanted. It was only when I noticed the anguished look on the Maestro's face that I realised Fontana was asking me to help him undress. And why would he not? Even if Fontana hid his Baraccano molestations, he made no secret of his appetites; everyone knew he was no sodomite. I stepped forward and held out my arms, hoping that he would use me simply as a clothes carrier, but that was not his intention.

'Don't stand there like a fool waiting for alms, help me off with this doublet.'

He stood with his arms at his sides, not even attempting to undo the buttons, so I was compelled to stand close in front of him and ease each from its buttonhole. My fingers shook and I kept my head lowered; Annibale's charcoal did a good job of mimicking a new beard when seen at a distance but might not be so convincing up close. The smell of Fontana's hair oil made the bile rise in my throat but I took deep breaths and managed not to retch. He turned round and I slid the doublet off his shoulders before placing it on the Maestro's table. I forced myself to put on the mask of a smile before facing him again.

'Breeches next, Signore?'

I could have delayed this task – by far the worst. I could have wasted time on removing the undershirt from his bloated torso. But I had too many memories of Fontana deciding when his breeches came down; this time I would choose. He nodded and I started to grapple with the buttons down the front. It was so tempting to reach in, grasp his member through the linen undergarment and squeeze it until he squealed, yet I made myself think of the real target – not temporary pain but permanent disgrace. In a few moments, Fontana had stepped out of his breeches and I pulled his undershirt, voluminous as a tent, over his head. There was still the dressing to endure but at that moment the Maestro moved me aside.

'That is all, Cristoforo. I would prefer to dress Signor Fontana myself. If that pleases you, Signore?'

I shot him a grateful glance and busied myself with Fontana's discarded clothes, ensuring that they were neatly laid out, before joining the journeymen. Ulisse nudged me and, underneath the Maestro's patter, whispered in my ear.

'That must have filled you with joy.'

But the comment was not snide and it struck me, to my

surprise, that he was trying to lift my spirits. Fontana was parading around the workshop now, looking down to admire the cut and workmanship of his suit and twisting to get at least some view of the back.

'Perfect, Rondinelli. I will put every man there to shame.'

'If you could stand still for a moment, Signore. I just need to check the cuffs of the doublet.'

I held my breath. For my work to be found wanting now would be more than I could bear. But after adjusting the cuffs and the undershirt frills below, the Maestro walked around Fontana and gave a slow nod.

'My men have felt the honour of the task, Signore, and given you their best workmanship.'

'I see it, Rondinelli, I see it! Be assured that my recommendations to gentlemen of good taste will begin this very day.'

The Maestro made a low bow before allowing himself a grin in our direction.

After showering a prodigious number of coins onto our table, Fontana hurried off with the servant trotting along behind, almost hidden under his wrapped bundle. As soon as they were gone, there was back-slapping all round and Ulisse even dared a whoop, which went unreprimanded. The Maestro had to raise his voice to be heard.

'Go on then, lads. I can see we won't get anything more done today. Off to The Sun with you – but no late arrivals or sore heads tomorrow.'

Stefano scooped up the money and the journeymen jostled

each other out the door, bobbing their heads in thanks. The Maestro looked at me.

'Not going with them?'

'I don't think I am man enough for The Sun!'

The Maestro laughed.

'Then take the rest of the day for yourself. I am not expecting any customers but I will stay here and show my face at the counter.'

'Maestro, may I talk to you of an enterprise I have in mind?'

'Have you lost your senses, girl?' Rondinelli was staring at me, eyes wide. 'You could end up in the Torrone with your arms pulled out of their sockets. Don't think that being a woman could save you from the *strappado*.'

'But no crime will be committed.'

'You think that makes any difference to Fontana and his friends? They will come up with some charge, you can be certain.'

'But if my plan works, he will not dare.'

Rondinelli ran his hands through his hair.

'Even if you are right, you cannot expect me to sanction this. You have just seen how important his patronage is. I need to court the man, not enrage him.'

I glared back but said nothing.

'I am sorry, Elena. I have all sympathy for you and the other girls who have suffered at his hands . . .'

'And continue to do so. Possibly at this moment, since he left here in such an ebullient mood.'

'Yes, yes. And I regret it, but . . .'

'But you must put your workshop first.'

It was the answer I had expected.

'Indeed I must. This workshop gives three men their livelihoods. Not to mention my own. I thought you wanted it to provide yours too. Or are there tailors forming queues to give you work?'

That was intended to wound — and it did — but before I could reply there was the sound of a clearing throat, and we both turned to see Giorgio Malatesta standing in the doorway.

'Am I interrupting a wrangle?'

'Come in, Giorgio. Perhaps you can talk some sense into the girl. Tell him, Elena. Tell him your *plan*.'

The Maestro stamped off up the stairs to his quarters, and Signor Malatesta raised a questioning eyebrow.

'Shall we sit?'

We settled on stools on opposite sides of the Maestro's cutting-table and once again I went through the details of how I proposed obtaining justice for the girls of the Baraccano. I thought that I would also need to describe our sufferings, but those he already knew. What closeness must exist between the two men. Malatesta listened to my idea, nodding his head from time to time or asking a question. When I had finished, he sat in silence for the length of a few Ave Marias and then called out.

'Cecco, come down here, if you would!'

Though he descended into the room, the Maestro seemed unwilling to join us until Malatesta pulled up another stool and motioned to him to sit down.

'You need to listen to her, Cecco.'

'I *have* listened. But you both know that I cannot afford to anger Fontana. The workshop depends on him.'

I had to correct him.

'He is but one client, Maestro. And you heard him say that he will be singing your praises up to the church roof. More customers will come.'

'And will they trust a tailor who betrays his clients?'

Giorgio Malatesta put out his hand and placed it over the Maestro's.

'It is no betrayal to give justice to these girls, Cecco. You and I know only too well what it is like to be afraid – to feel that your body is not your own to do with as you wish.'

At that, the Maestro hung his head. For what seemed like a long time, a thick silence filled the room and I could hear the sound of my own breathing. Finally, he sighed.

'And how do I persuade the boys?'

I opened my mouth to speak but Malatesta shook his head.

'No, Elena. I will not have you describing such degradations to them. Francesco and I will tell them all they need to know when they arrive for work tomorrow. You must stay away until the afternoon. We will win them over.'

I did not know what to expect when I stepped into the workshop the following afternoon. All I could think of was the hostile welcome I had been given all those months before, when I sat alone every day, ignored by the three journeymen. Since then, I had earned at least a little of their respect, but now I was asking them to put themselves in danger for me, to turn against the client who brought them praise and money in equal measure. And all because of some evil doings which touched them not at all. It would not surprise me if they not only refused to help but sent me back to my cushion.

The workshop was silent, every man intent on the task in his hands. When he noticed my arrival, the Maestro paused his cutting but I could not divine an answer from his expression. It was Filippo who slipped down from the table and approached me first.

'Please accept my apologies, Elena.'

So, there it was; they would not help me. I could not lay blame on them for that, and at least Filippo was talking to me and recognised my disappointment. But he had not finished.

'I do not have the strength for the lifting task, my dear. These old limbs would not be able to take the strain. The bulletins, though.' He grinned. 'I am not so afflicted that I cannot scatter a few pieces of paper.'

I was confounded. What bulletins was he speaking of? I had never mentioned such a thing.

Ulisse joined us and slapped Filippo on the shoulders.

'Poor old man! He has not the strength of body, but we have, do we not, Stefano?'

Stefano shuffled over, eyes down.

'Of course,' he muttered. 'Pleased to help.'

I was unable to speak for fullness of heart, but I was saved from doing so by Giorgio Malatesta entering the workshop.

'Good morrow, boys – oh and Elena.'

The Maestro grunted.

'I do wish you would all stop calling her Elena when she is dressed as Cristoforo.'

Malatesta grinned.

'Yes, *Maestro*. Have they told you about the bulletins, Cristoforo?'

'My understanding is not complete.'

'I wanted to do my part so I will put my *cartoleria* to work. We will design something for the printing-press and Filippo can drop them from the Garisenda. That way, even more citizens will get to know what Fontana is really like.'

Chapter Twenty-Two

I slept poorly the night before Madalena's *nozze*, my thoughts as tightly wound as the silk thread on a cocoon, but I must have dozed off since I was roused by the Accursio clock tolling Prime. It sounded strangely muffled, but I thought little of it as I shivered under my blanket for an hour going over the plans once again, checking that there was nothing I had forgotten. It was only when I finally rose and opened my shutters that I discovered the reason for the bell's dull tone: the overhanging rooms opposite, though only a few *braccia* away from my own, had disappeared behind a chill shroud. A November fog had crept up from the canals during the night and wrapped itself around the city like a caul. I clenched my fists in frustration, though I knew that it would do me almost no good to rail against the weather. Instead, I sent up a prayer to San Francesco and threw in one to San Petronio for good measure; between them they could surely dissolve a Bologna fog. Meanwhile, I closed the shutters again and lit a candle before dressing. I had given much thought as to which person I would be that day: Cristoforo would have the freedoms granted by his sex and his clothing, and that could be an advantage, especially if things became parlous. But it was as Elena that I needed to denounce Fontana – if that were to be possible on this God-forsaken day. Our efforts would be in vain if the audience could not even see the spectacle. Once dressed, I pulled on my cloak, drew up the hood and set off for the Two Towers through the thick silence.

A stranger to the city would have become lost in moments that morning and even a resident could easily make a wrong turn into a canal. It was as though someone had poured fog into the narrow streets where it was swirling like curds in whey. My route into the city's centre was so familiar and yet I found myself taking tiny steps and keeping a hand against the wall at my left. When the wall ran out, I knew that I must turn a quarter to the right and go across the street where I should find the bridge. Yet I could see nothing at all except the greyish-white wall of fog. I kept my palms outstretched in front of me and walked straight ahead, testing each step as I went. It seemed much further than in the light and I was certain that any moment I would be sliding down the canal bank. The whole plan now seemed hopeless and I was at the point of turning back when a dark shape loomed out of the mist in front of me.

'You lost, dearie?'

The woman was large and shapeless under layers of dark *garbo* but she moved with a sure-footedness I envied.

'Could you tell me, please, where is the bridge over the canal?'

'You're on it! A few paces more and you'll be over the other side.'

She had slid away into the fog before I could thank her but she was right, and after a few steps, I stretched my hand to the left and felt the pillar of a portico.

Despite the weather, it was as though the whole city had agreed that the wedding of Antonio della Fontana's daughter would take on the mantle of their Lord's Day entertainment. If our plan went awry, everyone would be witness to it. My stomach knotted and I wiped damp palms down my skirt. The Asinelli loomed in front of me, its top hidden from view, but the fog seemed less dense here and I could make out spectators already lining Via Mercato di Mezzo, three or four deep on either side. The first ululations were rolling the length of it, announcing that Madalena had already set off from her father's house. Fontana's palazzo, as extravagant as the man himself, was situated near Porta Pia – the solid new gate which had made the wealthy feel safe in that corner of the city. Well, safe from invaders, at least; Fontana was about to find out that his enemies came from within the walls. I gave an almost imperceptible nod to Agostino and then to Annibale, who were lounging at opposite corners of the tower. Then I positioned myself between them, the rope just behind my heels, and took a deep breath. The Maestro and Signor Malatesta were standing nearby in the front row of the crowd, beside them Ulisse and Filippo. Filippo? At that moment he was supposed to be halfway up Garisenda ready to release Malatesta's leaflets to the four winds. Stefano was the fourth member of the carrying party – so where was he?

I did not notice at first that the fog was lifting, but when a lone outrider trotted towards us on a fine chestnut horse, its burnished coat was reflecting a weak sun. I looked up and saw a pale disc, settled over the Garisenda like a halo. I smiled – Fontana would be able to see every detail, as would everyone else. There were whoops and cheers from the crowd now, together with some traditional lewd suggestions, as more outriders filed down each side of the street, making sure the way was clear for the bride and her family. The groom's palazzo, just north of Mercato, was their destination but I had surmised correctly – Fontana would not allow the procession to creep off into side alleys before performing a circuit of the Piazza Ravegnana. The citizenry of Bologna knew it too and the throng was at its thickest beneath the Two Towers. When they saw the customary white horse approaching, the bride side-saddle on its back, the shouts rose to a crescendo. The gown Signora Ruffo had made for Madalena was in a deep burgundy velvet – its cut exquisite yet in proportion to her slight form. The bodice formed a tight V at her waist and was embellished with panels of embroidered ribbon. The tassels adorning the shoulders shivered as her mount trotted towards us. The bell-shaped skirt ended in a train which seemed to pour down the horse's flank. I could not imagine how many *braccia* of cloth must have been used in the gown's making, nor how many insects crushed to achieve that depth of dye. Madalena sat tall, her perfect posture keeping a gold crown inset with jewels perched on her head. On either side of her rode the male members of the family, led by Antonio della Fontana himself, clothed in our wedding suit and acknowledging the cheers with a regal wave. I had been right – the blue brocade looked very well against Madalena's gown. Behind her, four porters carried on their shoulders the two carved wooden *cassoni* packed with her dowry clothes and jewels. She was going to need those.

Fontana and Madalena were very close to the little piazza now, and at any moment, they would wheel their horses to the left and turn away from the Asinelli. I lifted my hand in the agreed signal to Agostino and Annibale, who pulled on the ropes hidden by their sides. Slowly the banner rose up the wall until it was stretched across the front of the tower, its message clear – even to those who had no letters. Agostino had painted on the canvas a story. It showed Fontana, his features unmistakeable, dressed in a favourite gaudy outfit, being greeted by the *portinara* as he entered the gate of the Baraccano. Next he was shown in the refectory, surrounded by meek girls in their uniforms seated at the tables. But it was the following scenes which caused the crowd to gasp, hold their hands to their mouths and, in some cases, even cross themselves to ward off the Devil. The background in each picture was the same – the gloomy boardroom of the confraternity – but in each a different girl, her face obscured, was being forced to endure Fontana's molestations. His member was depicted as huge and menacing, bearing down upon the girls in ways too obscene for words. His hands too were drawn so large that everyone could see exactly what they were doing. This was no common *pittura infamante*. They usually showed a man the law could not touch receiving the punishment he deserved: being hanged upside down was a favourite. But Agostino's shocking pictures depicted the crimes themselves. The crowd's gaze, and my own, now turned from the canvas to its subject. Fontana had pulled up his horse, forcing Madalena and the rest of the entourage to do likewise. Madalena's lip was curled in revulsion, even though I had prepared her; Fontana's arrogant smile remained fixed but his eyes widened as he understood what was being displayed for the whole city to see, and he had turned deathly pale. Even so, he was attempting an expression of amused indignation whilst glancing around at those who were part of the procession in a bid to gain their support. But they had all chosen that moment to attend to a horse's harness or stare at the nearest pretty girl.

As soon as the crowd had grasped the meaning of the canvas, Signora Ruffo set in motion the second part of our plan. She appeared from behind the Asinelli, where the meat market crouches in its shadow, at the head of a line of young women. Their ages ranged from scarcely ripe to about thirty summers and each wore the distinctive sky-blue uniform of the Baraccano as evidence of her suffering. And about halfway along, trembling but with head held high, walked Agnella. That column of women was proof that the justice we were meting out was not only for Laura, or for myself, but for Agnella and all the others like her. Once they had gathered in a group below the banner, it did not take long for the crowd to realise that these 'Baraccano girls' were bearing witness to what had been done to them by a man who had, a few moments before, preened and swaggered round the piazza on his caparisoned mount. At first there were just mutters and murmurs, but soon cries of 'Debaucher!' and 'Ravisher!' echoed off the surrounding buildings. The *sbirri* stationed on the crowd's edges were beginning to look restive, moving their cudgels from hand to hand. It was time.

Whilst looking straight at Madalena, I lifted my chin to signal that she should dismount. Nothing happened. Though

I was certain that she had seen me, she sat motionless, like a carved saint on a wooden altarpiece. A silence now hung over the crowd, which was waiting for the next scene in the play to unfold in front of them, but Madalena was unwilling to take on her role. At that moment, all seemed lost. It was clear to me that I had pushed this high-born young woman beyond what she could bear. She may have longed for the cloistered freedom of the convent, but her family was about to be swept away in a flood of shame and she could not bring herself to add to it. I was all ready to abandon the next part of our plan when Madalena slipped down from her horse and gathered her voluminous train over one arm. With the other hand, she took off her crown and threw it into the nearest group of onlookers, causing a tangle of bodies and raised voices. The perfect distraction. In a moment, I was beside her and Sofia joined us from behind a nearby pillar.

With Madalena between us, Sofia and I shouldered our way through the crowd and, as soon as we were clear, began to run south down Via Castiglione until we reached the point where the canal broke through from underground. We followed it for a short distance, ignoring the gawps of the late arrivals still making their way towards the towers, until we reached Via Sant'Isaia where it slices across the south of the city. It usually rumbles with carts piled high with sacks of grain and ripe vegetables, but on that day it was silent and empty. Once on the other side, we veered right and slipped in and out of the deserted alleys north of San Domenico. Madalena was gasping for breath now, her face flushed and damp; a combination of the heavy gown and her pampered life made her less able than a Baraccano orphan and an ex-slave to endure exertion. Sofia and I took an elbow each and we dipped into another maze of streets, still heading south towards Via Tagliapietre and the convent of Corpus Domini.

When I first noticed the running footsteps, they were far in the distance and I said nothing to the others; I was trying to convince myself that they were made by boys playing a game of *pallone*. But street games do not get closer, nor do they sound like several sets of determined adult feet pounding the ground. They were approaching from our left, in the direction of San Domenico, and my imagination conjured up a gang of armed *sbirri* sent by Fontana to reclaim his daughter. Sofia and I shared glances over Madalena's head. Though we tried to make her run faster, almost dragging her along the muddy street, the girl was exhausted and, as soon as we turned into Tagliapietre, she came to a halt and leant against a portico pillar, hands on her thighs, panting. We were so nearly there; the doorway of Corpus Domini was just visible on the right about a hundred *braccia* distant, but the footsteps were getting ever closer and, although the nuns were expecting us, there would likely be a delay after we had pulled on the bell. Sofia must have divined my thoughts, for she suddenly took off in the direction of the convent and, once there, tugged repeatedly on the rope before turning back towards us. It was too late. The footsteps were approaching along the alley to my left and I knew that we could not outrun our pursuers now. I turned in their direction to screen Madalena, though I still do not know what I hoped that would achieve, and in the next moment, four running men turned into Tagliapietre. My hand went to my mouth, but it was in relief rather than fear: staggering under the weight of the *cassoni* hoisted on their shoulders were two pairs of familiar figures – the Maestro and Signor Malatesta, and Ulisse and . . . Filippo. The dropped leaflets had performed their second function. While the citizens of Bologna leapt and scrabbled for the pieces of paper, the *cassoni* had been seized from under their noses. I had expected the four men to be far behind us, but they must have risked the wide-open precinct of San Domenico and so made up time. All were breathing heavily, their hair damp with sweat, despite the November chill. As they filled the narrow street beside us, it was the Maestro who was able to speak first.

'Quickly. They . . . are not . . . far behind.'

We must have made a strange sight as we struggled the short distance to the arched doorway of the convent: three young women, one of their number held up by the others, and four dishevelled men, out of step now, lumbering under the weight of the long wooden chests. The convent door swung open as we approached and an elderly nun, her face as deeply carved as the *cassoni*, fixed a gimlet eye on Madalena.

'We have been expecting you. Come in.'

Madalena clasped my hand briefly, then Sofia's, before a younger nun stepped forward and led her away to a life of seclusion. I have never seen her since.

The abbess was speaking again.

'I cannot allow you gentlemen to enter, but if you could put the dowry goods just inside the door . . .'

The four men lowered the *cassoni* to the ground and shoved them just far enough across the stone floor that the door could close. They stepped back, and Filippo slid down the wall onto his haunches, rubbing his arms and still panting. The rest of us stood in an awkward knot, uncertain how to take our leave; but the abbess made the decision for us.

'She will be safe now. Good day.'

And the door swung shut. It was Ulisse, of course, who broke the silence.

'A waste, I call it. She's a comely young miss. Why would she want to forfeit her life shut up in there with a gaggle of old hags?'

I blame my tiredness and the tribulations of the day. Whatever the reason, I swung round and hissed into his face.

'She will prosper far more in there without a husband than out in the world with one.'

Ulisse opened his mouth to reply but the Maestro laid a hand on his shoulder.

'We have no time for this wrangling. In a group we stand out like a carbuncle. We must split up and go our ways as fast as possible. Ulisse and Filippo, get yourselves home – by the back routes. And tell no Christian soul what you did today.' He fixed Ulisse with a glare. 'No one, you understand? Not even to gain a little glory.'

Ulisse nodded and Filippo pulled himself up to standing, ignoring Signor Malatesta's outstretched hand. His face was waxy and still slicked with sweat but he scurried after Ulisse down the nearest alley. The Maestro turned to Sofia and me.

'You two must make haste to Signora Ruffo's and meet her there. If anyone asks, you have never left your sewing.'

I bridled at this.

'So we are to get ourselves to safety. And meanwhile what will you be doing?'

Signor Malatesta clicked his tongue in an unusual show of irritation.

'Cecco and I will return to his lodgings. We *all* need to be safe indoors for the rest of the day.'

He was right, of course. In my mind, the day had always ended with Fontana's public shaming and Madalena's safe dispatch to the convent. I felt angry with myself that I had not considered the aftermath – and that a man had done so in my stead. But there was no time for self-reproach. I grabbed Sofia's hand and we ran down the first alley beyond the convent, dodging right, then left, east, then north, through the web of streets, never the direct route, until finally we had no choice but to cross the open space of the San Francesco precinct where the church now glittered in winter sunshine. Our eyes flicked this way and that, checking that we were not being followed, but the area was empty; even the beggars had abandoned the church porch in hope that a wedding would open purses. Ever since we left the Maestro and Malatesta, I had been turning a plan over in my mind, and the sight of small groups of people heading towards us along Mercato hardened my decision. They looked like families and friends returning home from the thwarted celebrations, but for me the day was not over. The door of the Signora's palazzo was opened by Agnella as soon as we knocked and I pushed Sofia inside, before turning and running towards the centre of the city.

I do not clearly know what I expected. A full-blown riot, though it would have been welcome, was unlikely and I saw no sign of one. Those citizens heading away from the Ravegnana were more disappointed than angry, judging by the scraps of conversation I could hear. As soon as the Two Towers came into view, it was clear that the crowd had already dispersed. The cobbles of the Piazza Ravegnana were littered with Signor Malatesta's bulletins and I bent down to pick one up. It denounced the 'Baraccano ravisher', without of course using his name, and was illustrated with a horned demon, a character familiar to all citizens of Bologna from the frescoes of Hell in San Petronio. A few beggars propped up the nearby walls but respectable citizens had already set off home – or to Mass. So much for Fontana's public disgrace. Even now that they knew about his secret vice, the Bolognesi cared little. I had arrived at the foot of the Asinelli and looked up at Agostino's canvas, which still hung for everyone to see. How could I have involved all those for whom I had regard in such a pointless display? And not just pointless. My friends were at that moment sheltering in their homes, fearing the results of their actions. I may well have led them into danger.

Instinctively, I turned away from the Ravegnana in the direction of Rondinelli's workshop but stopped in my tracks. If he and Signor Malatesta were hiding out there, as they had planned, I would be the last person they wished to see. I thought it wise to return to Signora Ruffo's palazzo to check that all was well but at that moment, I still do not know why, I decided to return by an indirect route. Instead of heading straight back along Mercato di Mezzo, I cut through the alleys of shuttered shops and came out onto Piazza Maggiore. A few children were scampering across the empty space, watched by indulgent parents who chatted in groups – a common scene on any Lord's Day in the city. I cut down the side of San Petronio where it blindly faces the fine portico of the Archiginnasio and then turned into Piazza dell'Accademia.

I didn't see them coming – they must have been waiting for me in the shadows of the basilica's back wall – but in a moment I was surrounded by five, perhaps six, *sbirri* swinging cudgels loosely in their fists. I took in neither faces nor bodies until one spoke. His draggles of dirty red hair and unkempt beard brought back that hateful evening in the workshop: it was the one who called himself Volpe.

'Good day, little bitch. What a surprise, eh boys? I thought you'd have the sense to be cowering behind closed doors like the rest of them, but here you are on the streets. Best place for a whore, wouldn't you say, boys?'

The others dutifully guffawed and one made a grab at my skirts. How I wished I had followed my first thought and gone out that day dressed as Cristoforo. But Volpe hadn't finished. He circled me, talking all the while, and I had to twist round to keep him in view.

'So . . . you and your friends spoilt Antonio della Fontana's day. We are not happy about that, are we, boys?' The gormless thugs grunted their agreement. 'Though we wouldn't have noticed you run off with the bride if it weren't for the Moorish whore with you. She stands out like a black sheep in a white flock. And we all know about their evil sorcery.'

One of the thugs crossed himself and another muttered, 'The Devil's creatures.' Volpe affected a shudder.

'Your difficulty is that we like Fontana. He's almost one of us – friendly, cheerful, generous. Especially generous. But he doesn't like being shown up and that's what happened today.' He stepped forward, his face thrust towards mine. I could smell the sour wine on his breath. 'So, which of those friends of yours was the ringleader? Whose idea was it? Just tell us and we'll let you go.'

One of the men gave an exaggerated sigh and Volpe stepped back, glancing in his direction.

'I know you want a bit of fun with her, Porco. You always do. I might let you give her a poke later but first we need her to tell us who set it all up. Because it was very clever, can't deny it.'

'It was me.'

The men responded with snorts of laughter that echoed around the empty piazza.

'Of course it was.' His tone was one you would use to a small child or a demented old crone. 'Just give us the name and no one need know it was you who blabbed.'

'The idea was mine. I dragged my friends into it. It is not their fault.'

'What a loyal little miss you are. She must be lusting after whoever dreamt it up, boys.' He slapped the cudgel against his thigh. 'So . . . this is what is going to happen. You will tell us who was really in charge. If not, we will take you to the Torrone. There's a nice little dungeon under the courthouse, did you know that? We'll let Porco do whatever he wants to you first – he likes a slut – while the rest of us get the *strappado* ready. I'm sure you know how it works but I'll just remind you.' I tried to keep my face impassive but I know that all colour left it as he detailed the torture, licking his lips from time to time. 'So... we tie your hands together behind your back. Then we attach a nice thick rope and throw it over the beam. We had that put up especially for this sort of thing. Very useful, it is. And we hoist you up by the wrists. You look quite light so it won't take too much muscle. After we have a couple of choices: we can leave you dangling there – awful pain in the shoulders, so I'm told. Or we can jerk you up and down from time to time. Now *that* is excruciating. Better yet, since you don't weigh much, we could put some weights on your feet. That will probably result in dislocation. You should hear the screams when we do that!' He smirked. 'Well, you will, of course, because you will be the one making them!'

More laughter from the rest of them, who were gradually closing in. I drew myself up tall.

'I'm telling the truth. I planned it all and told the others what to do. I can swear to it by any saint you choose.'

Volpe spat on the ground.

'An oath means nothing. Pain is the only way to extract truth. Take her, boys.'

They all closed in and my arms were twisted behind my back before a slab of a hand gripped both my wrists and squeezed them hard together. The bones felt ready to snap. Then one man shoved me forward and I was jostled among them, back along the side of San Petronio towards Maggiore. I turned my head this way and that, hoping a drunk student might be wandering through the university porticoes or a vagrant might be looking for a sheltered spot under the walls of the basilica. Perhaps some early worshippers might be climbing its steps. But the clock lacked an hour until evening Mass and even the priest would still be at home with a warmed wine. The falling dusk had emptied the square and there was no living soul who might try to help me. Straight across the piazza from the basilica stood the Palazzo Pubblico with its forbidding tower, known simply as Il Torrone – and that spoken in a whisper. Once the *sbirri* got me inside and its massive doors clanged shut, I would disappear from the city and the Quaranta would deny that I had ever existed. My friends would never find me – unless my corpse turned up on a rubbish heap somewhere beyond the city walls. The vast piazza seemed to have shrunk now and the forbidding doors of the Torrone loomed ever closer. I began to struggle, twisting this way and that, trying to wrench myself free, but that only resulted in more hands grasping my shoulders and neck.

The high-pitched scream bounced off the buildings that fronted onto the piazza, and for a moment I wondered if it came from me. Then I saw a figure running full pelt across the square from the direction of the alleys, mouth wide open, skirts hoisted. It was Sofia – no, Suhailah – and she was heading straight for us like a bird of prey with quarry in view. Volpe and his men came to a halt and began to mutter prayers, as though warding off a devil. As she came closer, I saw that she had a small cloth bag hanging round her neck, and when she was only a few steps away she thrust a hand into it and threw something in our direction, all the while yelling what sounded like curses in a foreign tongue. The substance seemed to be a powder, bright yellow-red in colour, like the gowns worn by women who trade themselves in the streets around the Guasto. The powder rose briefly in the still air and then settled on our heads and clothes, making the men cough and flap their hands so that they loosened their grip on me. I twisted my wrists free and pushed through the struggling bodies, their eyes still wide in horror as though they had seen some monstrous being. Sofia grabbed my hand and we ran – across the piazza and the length of Mercato di Mezzo, not even attempting to conceal our route by ducking down side streets.

Agnella must have been waiting behind the door of Signora Ruffo's palazzo and we tumbled inside before slumping at the foot of the stairs. Agnella slammed the bolt shut.

'Well done, Sofia. You have brought one back safe, at least. Did you see the Signora?'

I was puzzled.

'Is she not here yet?'

'She said she must make certain that all the Baraccano girls were safely on their way home first. But that was a long time ago.'

We plodded up to the workroom, where Sofia insisted on anointing my bruised wrists with some salve and Agnella warmed some wine. Then we all three sank onto sewing-chairs and stared at the floor. It was Sofia who asked it first.

'What you think will happen to Fontana?'

She was brushing powder off my hair and shoulders.

'I do not know, Sof. At best, he will lose some of that respect he cares so much about. At worst, the people of Bologna will decide they do not care that he molests girls.' I put my head in my hands. 'Perhaps it has all been to little avail. And now I have Volpe and his thugs after me. I cannot see them giving up just because you threw some powder at them. What is it, anyway?'

Sofia drew herself up, her face stern.

'Do not mock enchantment, Elena.' Then a smile crossed her lips and she giggled. 'It is pollen. But they think I am sorceress. They are very frightened now.'

Loud banging on the front door about an hour later jolted all three of us out of our exhausted silence. Agnella jumped up.

'The mistress at last!'

But the voices we heard when she had drawn back the bolt were male, and by the time heavy footsteps had reached the top of the stairs, I was cowering by the fabric shelves, certain of violent attack. If I had used my wits, I would have realised that the *sbirri* never entered anywhere without shouts and threats as their companions but, as it was, the appearance of Signors Rondinelli and Malatesta on the threshold caused my knees to weaken in relief. I ran towards them.

'Where is the Signora?'

The Maestro's brow furrowed.

'She is not with us. We thought she would be here long since.'

Chapter Twenty-Three

The two men looked awkward and ungainly standing in the middle of the workroom, but I was too anxious for news to invite them to sit.

'What has happened to Fontana?'

The Maestro shook his head and found it difficult to meet my eyes.

'No one seems to know. He sent others to pursue Madalena – in vain, of course – and he himself galloped away in the direction of his palazzo. The bridegroom slunk off home, and is probably closeted with his notary trying to find a way out of the marriage contract. Shouldn't be too hard.'

I had no patience with these details.

'But do the people not pay heed to what he has done? Why is there no mob banging at his portal?'

Rondinelli sighed.

'They pay heed, Elena. You saw how the pictures of his violations disgusted them. But there seems little appetite to do anything about it. We may have magnified—'

'So our endeavours have come to naught!'

'I did not say that. I think we must wait. At this moment, I am more concerned for the safety of Signora Ruffo.'

His words hit their mark. I was so entangled in the fate of Fontana that only then did I notice Sofia and Agnella lingering by the workroom door and wringing their hands, anxious for their mistress. Fortunately, Signor Malatesta was more considerate of their feelings than I and had engaged them both in conversation about the events of the day. He was even managing to raise a smile with his description of the exhausting run carrying the *cassoni*. I was reminded of something which had been puzzling me since we delivered Madalena to the convent, and I turned back to the Maestro.

'What happened to Stefano? I thought that he was meant to be one of the porters, rather than Filippo.'

'He was, and until yesterday he seemed eager to be one of our party. But he did not arrive at the workshop this morning and none of us have seen him since. Perhaps he is unwell – or fear set in.'

At that moment, we heard slow footsteps on the stairs and Sofia threw open the door just as Signora Ruffo reached the top. Her face was drawn with exhaustion but she was unharmed and waved away the arm Agnella offered, before sinking into one of the tapestry chairs.

'A cup of wine please, girls. I have never needed one so much.'

While Sofia went to fetch it, I took the Signora's shawl and loosened her leather boots. It was all I could do to hold back my questions, but a warning look from the Maestro made me bite my lip until Signora Ruffo had taken her first mouthful of wine.

'Where have you been, Signora? We were so concerned for you.'

'I found out that some of the women were more scared of their own husbands than the *sbirri*. They expected to be beaten on their return, so I accompanied each of them home to extract promises.' She sighed. 'I pray that they are kept.'

'And did you – I mean – are there any signs at all that our plan has worked?'

The Signora slipped off one of her boots and rubbed her foot, wincing as she did so.

'If it was mob justice you expected, Elena, then you will be disappointed – but there is one reason to be hopeful. The Carraccis' canvas is still in position.'

'I know. I saw it. But of what significance is that?'

It was the Maestro who answered.

'Of course! I should have noticed. It means that the Papal Legate has not given orders for it to be removed immediately. And that means . . .'

Signor Malatesta finished his sentence.

'The Church is not affording its protection to Fontana. If it were, the Legate would have made certain the painting was taken down as soon as possible.'

It was not the widespread outrage for which I had hoped, but Signor Malatesta was right. Without the backing of the Church, Fontana was like a man without his cloak on a freezing day.

So it was with a lighter heart that I set off for the workshop the following morning. I could not quite believe Sofia's claims that we were safe from the *sbirri* and I wore Cristoforo's clothes out of caution. But it was consoling to know that Fontana had been cut loose by the Church, like a sinking barge. As for Madalena, she was safely enclosed within Corpus Domini, where the closest Fontana could get to her was a conversation through a grille. And only if she so wished. I strode confidently into the city's centre, passing through Ravegnana to check on the Carracci canvas. It was still in position, flapping a little in the wind, its message as clear as when Agostino and the others painted it in their studio. I skipped my way down Calzolerie, dodging the leather-workers who were already lugging hides out onto their counters, and then sauntered into the workshop.

I did not expect there to be celebration that morning – as the Maestro had said, it was too early for that – but nor could I have anticipated the silence in the room or the despair on everyone's faces. The Maestro was sitting on a stool, hands on his knees, staring at the floor while Signor Malatesta stood as close to him as he dared, his expression all sympathy. Ulisse sat cross-legged in his usual place, head bowed over a piece of ribbon which he was interlacing through his fingers. Filippo was slumped on the wooden chest, his face still drawn in exhaustion. The smile slipped from my face.

'What has happened?'

The Maestro raised his head.

'It is Stefano. He is gone.'

I did not understand what he meant.

'Gone where?'

'Tell her, Ulisse.'

Ulisse gave the essence of the story, fiddling with his ribbon all the while. It was, he said, Stefano who had informed on the Maestro and Malatesta to the *sbirri*. They had come upon him one night with a stolen household icon tucked inside his tunic and offered him a choice: a severe beating or naming others to take his place. Terrified, Stefano had given them Rondinelli and Malatesta after receiving a promise that the two men would just get a little scare – nothing grave. The *sbirri* were lying, as Stefano should have known. The Maestro's pretence with me had put them off his track (most *sbirri* couldn't see a crow in a bowlful of milk) but Giorgio Malatesta had not been so fortunate. Stefano had been on the rack with guilt ever since, but the final screw was when we had asked him to take part in our action against Fontana. He knew the *sbirri* would be out in force and was frightened of being recognised. At first, I could not believe what Ulisse was saying – I had become so certain that *he* had been the informant.

'How did you learn this?'

Ulisse sighed.

'From the man himself. I went to his house to see if he was ailing and found the whole family packing their belongings onto a waggon. They are already on their way to Modena. He hopes to get work there, though without a letter of recommendation, he will find it hard.'

The Maestro twisted his head round and spat out a reply.

'If he expects one from me, he will be a long time waiting.'

Giorgio Malatesta touched his shoulder.

'He has children, Cecco.'

'I know, but I cannot forgive what nearly . . .' He shook his head as though to rid it of thoughts and stood up. 'So now we are a journeyman down and you are not at your best, Filippo. Time to get working.'

Filippo wheezed a laugh.

'Come, Maestro, I know that I am not in full health today but I can still sew a straight seam, and these two youngsters,' he gestured at me and Ulisse, 'have an abundance of skill. Let's get to it.'

Ulisse cast aside his ribbon and slipped off the table.

'Filippo is right. We can manage without Stefano.'

At that, the Maestro hurried Malatesta away and began handing out the day's work.

My first task of every day, before the shutters were even open, was to display on the counter the bolts of cloth that the Maestro wanted customers particularly to notice. His choice would depend on the season or festivals, but on that December day he told me to get down the most expensive and richly decorated brocades on the shelves, as though the Holy Father himself were due to visit the city and its foremost citizens urgently needed new outfits in which to greet him.

'It's probably the action of a madman. But just in case someone noticed Fontana's fine wedding outfit and wants something similar . . .'

Once the counter was ready, Ulisse raised the shutters and we joined Filippo on the journeymen's table. I was starting the first seams on a pair of black breeches for a notary and had swivelled towards the window as it was difficult work in winter light. But it was of little use. There was a crowd of jostling men just outside in Orefici who cared not a jot about blocking my sunlight. I clicked my tongue in irritation and at that moment, there was repeated banging on the counter, and from several hands. The Maestro looked up, startled.

'Be alert, boys. There may be trouble.'

He went out to the front of the shop, while we got off the table and stood ready – though for what, none of us knew. If the workshop was about to be breached, there was little two journeymen tailors and a girl dressed as a boy could do. We exchanged worried glances while straining to hear the voices from the street; at least there was no shouting or threats of violence. It was not long before the Maestro returned. He was smiling and followed by a gentleman whose leather gloves alone proclaimed his wealth. Behind him came another, and another – until the workshop buzzed with refined Bolognese accents and rich men lounged against every available patch of wall. The Maestro clapped his hands.

'Gentlemen, your attention, please. I know that you are all chafing to choose fabrics and tell me your requirements, but the appearance of any clothing, be it doublet or undershirt, depends on fit. We will begin by making a personal measuring strip for each one of you – my journeymen and apprentice are more than equal to this task. Please form a line.'

I went straight to the back beam and pulled down a set of blank strips, thankful that only the previous week I had spent an hour of the clock cutting a new supply. Soon the three of us were winding the strips around chests, waists, calves and wrists, and notching the answers on them before naming each strip after its client. One of them was not satisfied with being assigned to me and remonstrated with the Maestro.

'I don't want the apprentice, Rondinelli. He is no more than a boy. How do I know that he will make his measurements correctly?'

'Because, Signore, it was he who fitted and sewed the doublet worn by Signor Antonio della Fontana at his recent . . . public appearance. Oh, and he also suggested the fabric.'

At the mention of Fontana's name, several of our new customers made the sign of the horn to ward off evil. The client cleared his throat.

'Then I suppose I can trust myself to the young fellow.'

'You can, Signore.'

His broad wink could be seen only by me, and my customer was no trouble after that, meekly allowing me to take all the measurements I required. The Maestro meanwhile was jotting down orders for undershirts, jerkins, breeches, whole suits and assuring his new patrons that each would have an individual appointment to refine the details. I had thought that they would then slope off home to spend time doing . . . whatever it is they do, but they seemed inclined to stay, pulling bolts of fabric down from shelves to rub between their fingers or hold against their bodies, chatting amongst themselves all the while. Never had a seamstress, be she ever so skilled, earned such acclamation as we did that day.

By the time the last gentleman finally strolled out through the gap in the counter, the workshop looked as though a gang of *sbirri* had decided to give the Maestro a different kind of warning. There were half-unwound rolls of fabric everywhere and someone had even contrived to knock over the mannequin. At least we had kept charge of the measuring strips, which were now evenly spaced in a long row on the hanging beam. The

Maestro picked up his cutting shears and brandished them in the air. I had never seen him look so cheerful.

'It would seem, boys, that the great and the good of Bologna wish to have their clothes made by Francesco Rondinelli – and his assistants.'

Ulisse gave a cheer.

'And all because of Fontana's wedding suit?'

'The man was true to his word. He must have told every member of the Quaranta that the suit was made here, and once they saw it, they all wanted to use our services. For the first time he displayed good taste and our tailoring wasn't concealed by vivid colours and huge codpieces.'

Filippo was frowning.

'I know I said that the three of us could manage, Maestro, but that was before every man of wealth in the city required our workmanship – some in time for Christ's Nativity! What are we to do?'

'Time to get used to working by candlelight, boys.'

Chapter Twenty-Four

The Maestro had not lied. We all three got into the habit of arriving at the workshop long before dawn, to be greeted by him at his cutting-table where he was already hard at work. By the time the other tailors in Drapperie had raised their shutters, we were cross-legged on our table, 'the goose' warming on the brazier. Rondinelli had placed a notice on the counter to say that he could accept no new orders, but it did not stop men of quality trying to persuade him otherwise. Some even slid full purses across the counter as bribes but the Maestro pushed them straight back. He must have been tempted to accept – I would have been – yet he always refused, telling us that the good name of the workshop depended on fair dealings with its customers. It was a lesson I noted, hoping it would one day be of use. Our lunchtime pause was no more than a chance to walk around the workshop chewing at a hunk of bread or an onion and then we were back to our sewing, clawing as much light from the day as we could. Each afternoon at least one or two of our previously measured clients came to make their choices and when the Maestro wasn't jotting down their requirements, he was cutting the shape of a pair of sleeves from a figured velvet, or jerkin pieces from a glossy damask. When the shutters came down at the statutory time, we stayed on, huddled over an island of candles placed in the middle of our table. By the time we finished our eyes were sore, our fingers bleeding, but we all buckled to, tidying and sweeping ready for the following day.

Much as I wanted to see Sofia and visit the Carraccis' studio to give them thanks, by the time my work was ended for the day it was all I could do to stumble back to the canal and my lodgings before falling on my bed. Sometimes I was asleep before I had even changed out of Cristoforo's breeches, and Lord's Days were spent dozing and eating with no energy for company. More than anything I longed to know what had happened to Fontana, but no gossip was reaching us at the workshop and there was no time to seek it abroad. Despite my beseeching, the Maestro refused to ask direct questions of any of his clients, lest our part in Madalena's thwarted *nozze* was suspected, but there was one conversation which brought some enlightenment. Two of our new customers were clearly friends – perhaps more than friends – and arrived together to place their final orders. While the Maestro was searching the shelves for a fine scarlet wool, they chatted of this and that. Then they embarked on a theme which made my ears prick up.

'Has anything been heard of our city's chief debaucher?'

'Gone to ground. No one has seen him since he galloped away that day. Not even at Mass, despite all those loud claims to faith.'

'No doubt he has a pet priest who will shrive him at home. But there are few who would welcome his return to our piazzas.'

'May God give him a dog's life.' The voice fell to a whisper. 'He was keen enough to judge people like us.'

At that moment, the Maestro returned with a bolt of bright red cloth and the conversation turned to fashion once again.

So, Fontana was keeping within the thick walls of his palazzo – and it sounded as though he was not much missed. That was heartening news but I knew that he was not the sort of man who could live without public applause for long, nor was his docile wife likely to be offering much in the way of affection; her life, too, had been brought to ruin on a day which should have made her radiant with pride. I could imagine him, cloistered in his *studiolo*, pawing at his books of lewd prints and plotting a return to the city's favour. And what better time than the imminent celebration of Our Saviour's birth to buy forgiveness with gifts and jollity? A city's memory could be as short as a winter's day.

The two clients were leaving now and I returned my attention to the burgundy sleeve shaped across my thigh. There are some sewing jobs which allow thoughts to fly through the workshop shutters and wander where they may, but pleating a shoulder is not one of those. It is a task which demands a concentrated mind, for not only must the pleats be spaced with perfect evenness but each shoulder must be the twin of the other. For this reason, sewing sleeves is never a task to be split between journeymen. When I first began working for the Maestro, I would use short lengths of thread to measure the distances – a trick taught me by Signora Ruffo – but I had long since been able to judge them by eye every bit as well as Filippo or Ulisse. I was still, in name, though the name was Cristoforo, the apprentice at Rondinelli's – but it was a rare apprentice who was trusted to construct garments out of the most costly silks on the shelves. I was doing the work of a journeyman and the Maestro knew it, yet my remuneration remained as small as a pinhead. Meanwhile, his fear that the workshop relied on Fontana for its prosperity was proved baseless every time a new client emptied his purse onto the cutting-table. My natural inclination was to batter his dyed-in caution with demands for parity with Filippo and Ulisse, but something held me back. Perhaps it was the knowledge that the Maestro had risked all for me on the day of Madalena's *nozze*, though Sofia would say that I had simply grown up!

It was, as it turned out, Signora Ruffo who made my case to Rondinelli when she arrived at the workshop one afternoon without appointment. The Maestro had just bade farewell to one client and was jotting down notes before the arrival of another when the Signora stepped into the room. We all jumped to our feet and bowed low (even I), though the Maestro's greeting was less than warm.

'May I be of assistance, Signora?'

'Stop that nonsense, Rondinelli. You and I have known each other long enough for me to pay a visit without notice. Don't forget that my husband was a tailor in Drapperie when you were still playing with balls of lint.'

Ulisse snorted but a glare from the Maestro silenced him; we all three climbed back onto the table and resumed our work. He gestured to a stool and the Signora sank down on it, sounding somewhat breathless. She arranged her skirts before speaking.

'I am here to take you to task about young Elena here.' She nodded in my direction. 'Though I can scarce recognise the poor girl in that ridiculous clothing.'

'It is for her own protection, madam.'

'I do not need that explained, Rondinelli. But just look at her. She is exhausted. I do not know what hours you are requiring her to work but you forget that she is a young woman, not a tough lad. We, her friends' – the emphasis on the last word was heavy – 'have not seen her for weeks since.'

'We are extremely busy, madam, following the success of Fontana's wedding outfit.'

'For which Elena was, I believe, largely responsible. I trust you are paying her as a journeyman, even if obtaining registration would be burdensome?'

The Maestro avoided her eyes.

'It is difficult, madam. I already have two qualified journeymen.'

'And enough work for three, so I hear.'

She swung round towards us.

'You two – you would not object to Elena joining your ranks as paid journeyman, would you?'

To my surprise, it was Ulisse rather than Filippo who spoke up.

'She is as good as either of us, Signora.' He puffed out a breath. 'Better, perhaps.'

Filippo nodded his agreement and Signora Ruffo twisted back towards Rondinelli.

'There! You have no excuse but to pay what she deserves. And you will release her from here for the rest of the day so that she can take some repose with her friends. Come, Elena.'

I dared not move a finger but then Rondinelli dipped his head in agreement and I scurried out behind the Signora, who was already passing through the gap in the counter.

After a brief stop at my lodgings as I had no wish to see Agostino looking like a shabby apprentice, we reached the Carraccis' door just as Ludovico was hurrying out. The Signora smiled a greeting.

'I trust you are joining us, Ludovico?'

'Not I, Signora. Someone has to keep the commissions coming. It's about meeting people, knowing the city, that's what my cousins don't understand.' He nodded two quick bows. 'I wish you both a pleasant afternoon.'

Upstairs Sofia was in conversation with Maria, whose role as chaperone was obvious when she hurried back to the kitchen as soon as we arrived. It was thoughtful of Agostino – for it must have been he, rather than vague Annibale, who contrived it. I rushed across the room and clasped Sofia's hands.

'Sof! It has been too many weeks.'

'Again!' But her look was mischievous, not reproving. 'They say workshop of Signor Rondinelli is most favoured of all and work never stops.'

'It is true. We have so many new customers since Fontana paraded through the city in his wedding suit. And we are a journeyman short since Stefano left.'

'Why? He is good tailor, no?'

I lowered my voice, even though Signora Ruffo was loudly heaping praise on every piece of art in the room.

'It was he who betrayed the Maestro and Signor Malatesta. He has left the city.'

I had not noticed that Agostino was standing behind me until he broke in.

'He is not the only runaway.'

I turned, fearful of what he might have to tell me.

'You don't mean Fontana? Has the filthy coward fled the city to avoid disgrace?'

'Not he – his wife. Signora della Fontana joined her daughter in Corpus Domini five days since, and the word is that she intends to live out the rest of her days there.'

'I hope she finds peace. The poor woman must feel his fall from grace as her own, though she is blameless.'

Sofia muttered what sounded like a prayer before joining Annibale and Signora Ruffo in front of her portrait. I gabbled on, afraid of losing the rare opportunity of a private conversation with Agostino.

'I must thank you, sir – and Annibale and Ludovico, of course – for what you did for us. Without your canvas all our efforts would have been to no avail and Fontana would still be vaunting his charity around the city.'

'It gave me great diversion.' He grinned. 'My brother and cousin perhaps less so – but they were glad to be of assistance to you. As was I.'

'And do you know what has become of Fontana?'

'It is a mystery. He has not been seen in the city, but neither is there any reason to believe that he has left it. I do have other information. Two of the mistresses at the Baraccano have been dismissed for their hand in the whole loathsome business.'

He clicked his fingers in an attempt to remember their

names but I knew without being told.

'Mistress Giovanna and Mistress Serafina.'

'You have it exactly.' He studied my face. 'Is that good news?'

'It is indeed. Giovanna is – was – the *guardiana*. Her special skill was in not knowing about anything that happened in the orphanage. Serafina was worse. She knew all too well what Fontana did and it suited her to let him.'

Agostino's eyes widened.

'For payment?'

'Perhaps. Though I think she harboured some twisted affection for the man.'

Agostino shuddered. I would have wished to continue our conversation, and believed that perhaps he did too, but at that moment Signora Ruffo summoned us from the other side of the room. She was holding onto Annibale's arm for support but insisted that we join her in praising Sofia's portrait once again.

A few days later, Ulisse racketed into the workshop with news that the Yule Log was being prepared in Maggiore. It had been many years since I had seen it, most of them spent at the Baraccano where the approach of Christ's Nativity was marked by worse food than usual and more frequent Masses, and even the day of His birth itself brought no joy to those inside its walls. But when I was small, Mother and Father would take me to the piazza in the evening of the Vigilia to watch the Yule Log blaze and crackle while the circle of onlookers stamped their feet in its warmth and light. Afterwards, we would join the crowd thronging up the steps of San Petronio to visit the *presepe* in a side chapel, surrounded by banks of candles. The olive-wood figures of the nativity scene were each the length of a forearm and painted in rich colours, their gold-leaf haloes shimmering in the candlelight. Behind them a sky – formed of a swathe of dark blue silk with a jewelled star sewn on – hung from a beam above. But it was the Magi who interested Father most. He would lift me up so that I could see them, not yet arrived at the stable but placed as though they were descending a silken mound on the far side of the chapel. In place of paint, the models wore fabric costumes – new each year – made of rich brocades and velvets, ruffs around their necks, their legs clad in *perpignano* hose. Father and I would choose our favourites and in January my wooden doll always paraded a new outfit, thanks to the ideas I had stolen from the Magi. When we got home, I received the usual gift: my own little log which Mother had filled with sweets and fruits, decorated with spruce twigs and berries.

Talk in the workshop had turned to our own plans for the celebration of Christ's Nativity, but I added nothing to the conversation; without means to cook even a bean stew at my lodgings, I would have to forgo the customary fish dinner to mark the Vigilia. My best chance of eating well that evening would be to give the young food vendor on the corner a smile which promised everything and delivered nothing, in return for a flat loaf piled with vegetables. Ulisse's mother had, it seemed, been preparing for weeks for her boy's special meal and would be out at dawn to make sure the fish she took home was of the freshest. Filippo was hoping for an invitation to his son's house but so far it was not forthcoming. The Maestro was as silent as I and it seemed that he had nothing particular in mind for the celebrations.

But Giorgio Malatesta had different ideas. When he passed by the workshop later that day, grin wider than a cardinal's hat at the prospect of the festivities, he charmed the Maestro into agreeing to a Vigilia meal right there in the workshop.

'Come, Cecco. We have much to celebrate. Our safe deliverance from danger. Fontana getting the humiliation he deserved.'

'But the smell, oil on the fabric.'

'There would be no oil, would there boys – Elena? We will cover everything up – and open every window too, if that will set your mind at rest.'

But we never got to enjoy our Vigilia meal, and Christ's Nativity passed without our even noticing it.

Chapter Twenty-Five

My hopes of hearing what had become of Fontana were soon swept away by a great change which descended on the city. Bologna had been clamped in the grasp of bitter cold since the beginning of the month but one morning, when the calendar lacked but five days until the celebration of Our Saviour's birth, I awoke to a strange light filtering through the shutters. I could see my own breath without benefit of a candle and at first I feared that I had slept beyond my usual hour of waking. With a blanket round my shoulders, I went to the window and, with some effort, pushed one shutter open to find that I was dislodging snow onto the already thick covering beneath. Large, soft flakes were still falling and the roofs opposite were no more than a lumpy outline, white and formless. I stretched out a hand and scooped up some snow, chilling the tips of my fingers. I brought it to my lips and tasted. All at once, I was back with my mother and leaning out of our window above the workshop, the last time that the city had seen a fall of snow such as this.

'Put it in your mouth, Elena! Have you ever tasted anything so cold?'

I did so and shook my head, entranced by this wonderful substance and longing to join the children already careering down the alley in the direction of Piazza Maggiore. I hopped from foot to foot with impatience while Mother wrapped rags around my boots and pulled my hat down tight around my ears and Father fetched our thickest cloaks from the winter chest. When they were content that I was impregnable, the three of us tramped past closed shutters, the hem of my dress soon sodden and heavy. Though it was not the Lord's Day, the whole city seemed to have declared that no work would occur, and when Piazza Maggiore opened out before us it looked like the scene of a friendly battle.

The smooth surface of the snow was pockmarked with deep footprints, and everywhere children were scooping it up to form into rough balls before bombarding anyone who dared to come within reach. Balls of snow flew in all directions and most adults contrived to dodge out of the way, but one young man had made a neat pile of snow missiles and stood posing like some ancient statue, challenging the children to a fight. In no time a semicircle of small boys had gathered a few *braccia* away from him and the battle began. Though soon drenched from head to heels, the young man grinned and laughed as though no riches could buy anything better than that snowy day. I watched and clapped but did not ask my parents if I could join in; though I would not have been able then to put my understanding into words, I knew that as a girl – and sole surviving child – fighting with snowballs was not something I would ever enjoy.

Now I pulled my shutter closed and hurried to dress, grateful for Cristoforo's thick breeches and sturdy boots. It was likely that on this day too businesses would be closed, but we were still sewing our way through piles of cut-out pieces, and the Maestro would need us to work even if the shutters were down. As an unofficial journeyman now, thanks to Signora Ruffo, I was determined not to make him rue his decision.

By the time I reached the workshop my hat and shoulders carried a nap of snow and I had been caught by several well-aimed snowballs. Filippo had not yet arrived but Ulisse was standing close to the brazier rubbing his hands together, and I joined him there while the Maestro peered out of the window.

'I hope it lets up soon or the city might as well be under siege.'

He was right. Conditions were likely worse beyond the walls and the farmers would never even attempt to reach the gates with their carts; it would not take long for the hungry Bolognesi to reach the backs of their larders. At that moment, the Maestro let out a profanity and rushed to the workshop entrance. We followed and found Filippo struggling to stand up, clinging to the pillar of next door's portico. He tried to brush aside our help but eventually agreed to lean on Ulisse and the Maestro for the last few steps back to the workshop. He had found the walk from home through drifting snow exhausting and had stumbled at the last moment. Ulisse removed Filippo's cloak and tunic to reveal two more layers of woollen undershirts. His clothes had protected him from serious injury but a colourful bruise was already spreading across his shoulder where he had crashed into the pillar. I grabbed my hat and cloak.

'I'll get something from the apothecary for that bruise.'

'Will any be so foolish as to open today?'

'Surely one of them has to.'

Though the apothecary shops kept the same hours as all the others, the Quaranta ruled that one from among them had to remain open every Lord's Day and feast day; I was hoping that their rota also provided for the city's closure in an emergency. The morning was as dark as dusk and brooding clouds laden with more snow were rolling across from the Two Towers. At first, I thought that every shop in Clavature was shuttered but then I spotted, about halfway along, a thin yellow light reflecting off the snow in the alley. At that time of year, the apothecary shops usually glittered, their carefully placed lights showing off decorated jars and colourful packages to tempt customers with treats to celebrate Our Saviour's birth. But on that day cloths were spread over any luxuries and instead the assistants were busy weighing, mixing and grinding ingredients, while the handful of customers provided a background noise of coughs and sneezes. Once at the front of the queue, I put in my order for a large chamomile poultice. There was no need for me to describe Filippo's injuries – Mother had always put her trust in chamomile to draw the pain from a bruise. As soon as it was ready, I rushed back and positioned it over the tenderest spot on Filippo's shoulder, tying it on with a length of spare linen I found after rummaging in the *cavolo*. Meanwhile, Ulisse and the Maestro stood around with helpless expressions, putting their trust in the only woman in the room, despite her breeches, to tend the wounded.

Filippo was resolved that he could still work – as long as he was not required to lift any bolts of fabric – and once Ulisse had helped him onto the table, we all picked up our needles and began to sew by candlelight, as though night had already fallen. The Maestro was restless, one moment bent over his accounts, the next peering out at the weather through the gaps in the window shutters. We could hear no noises beyond the workshop walls – no chattering matrons or squealing children, not even the shouts of a drunken vagrant. Either the snow had muffled every sound – or there were none. But it was only when we stopped for the lunchtime pause that Ulisse shoved the shutters open and we all gasped. The relentless snowfall had filled up the alleys in every direction, even drifting under the porticoes and up against doors – and there was not one Christian soul to be seen on the streets. The Maestro shook his head.

'It is no use. The three of you must stay here until there is at least some sort of thaw. The city will have lost all its landmarks. One slip and you could be buried in snow or drowned in a canal.'

Unwelcome as the news was, he spoke the truth and arguing would be to no avail. Ulisse grumbled (out of the Maestro's earshot, of course) that his purpose was to squeeze from us every moment of work, but the complaint was made out of habit rather than true grievance. As it turned out, we were besieged in the workshop for three days and nights but the Maestro treated us exceeding well, providing food and wine every day and ensuring that we had blankets for warmth and water to wash. He even kept the stove lit beyond the working day and the men diced away their evenings huddled around it. The fug of stale sweat and woodsmoke in the workshop became thick enough to touch but I was given my own haven; the storeroom was set aside for me and I fell asleep each night cocooned among rolls of fabric. I do not think I have ever slept better.

The thaw, when it came, was swift. At dawn on the fourth morning, the cold inside the workshop struck less harshly against the skin and we could hear a steady drip-drip coming from somewhere close by. Before long, water was gurgling deep inside the walls and every so often large chunks of snow rumbled down the roof tiles and landed in the street below. Soon we could hear a hubbub of voices outside which sometimes exploded into shouting and blasphemies, as the shop-owners arrived to sort out whatever problems the thaw had brought them. The Maestro pushed open the windows first, letting in a chill blast to replace the fetid air we had become so used to. Once we were ready with mops, he pulled up the door-shutter and we chased out the freezing slush, greeting our neighbours who were doing the same. There were some broken tiles and the odd chunk of wood from a portico in Drapperie, but it was the goldsmith on the corner of Orefici who had fared the worst. Part of his roof had collapsed and water was now pouring down into the workshop. I saw the Maestro shiver; gold and gems would survive such an onslaught but a tailor with drenched stock would like be ruined. He was not the only one of the surrounding patrons who made a visit to the goldsmith that morning to offer whatever they had – ladders, a recommendation of a good builder, or just their rolled-up sleeves and goodwill. Our own workshop needed a thorough clean and airing, and since the pain in Filippo's shoulder kept him perched on a school, the Maestro helped Ulisse move the furniture while I swept and wiped. Through the open shutters we could hear matrons splashing past the shop on their way to the market in the hope of finding a stall or two selling fresh food.

When loud shouts came from the direction of Piazza Maggiore, we did not even raise our heads – tempers were jangling that day and, no doubt, new damage was being discovered in many a building. When Signor Malatesta burst into the workshop, breathless from running, we learnt that the noise marked something more serious.

'Come, come quickly. You will not believe what has happened.'

Signor Malatesta was half out the room again but the Maestro took his elbow to hold him back.

'What, Giorgio? Tell us.'

'You must see it for yourselves.' His hand went to his mouth. 'No, not you, Elena. It is too horrible.'

I bristled and pulled at the lower edge of my doublet.

'And what would people think if young Cristoforo were left behind – like a *girl*?'

'All right, all right – but prepare yourself for an ugly sight.'

In silence, we all took down our cloaks from the pegs and followed Signor Malatesta out of the workshop, the Maestro making it secure behind us; he knew well how a malefactor could take advantage when citizens and *sbirri* were distracted. Around us the goldsmiths of Via degli Orefici were doing the same and we joined a stream of people paddling through slush towards Maggiore, sharing snippets of rumour which were soon refashioned as facts. I heard Fontana's name mentioned more than once; the man was probably trying to regain the city's favour by taking control of whatever disaster had befallen us.

Citizens were entering the piazza from every direction, as though for a festival, but we all fell silent and footsteps slowed when we looked up at the balcony of the Palazzo d'Accursio. This was the same balcony from which the roasted pig had been tossed at La Porchetta, but it was not a pig which hung there. Instead, dangling from the balustrade, to which a thick rope had been attached, was a human body. It was well dressed in a poppy-red doublet and matching breeches, though a dark stain had recently crept down the cream hose. The rope had been formed into a noose which would have pulled tight when Fontana leapt from the top of the balustrade. Now his neck was bent at a strange angle and his tongue lolled while his feet swung level with the top of the arched entrance to the palazzo.

As if at a signal, the chatter around us began and, from the snatches I heard, people were at pains to make the city's former hero its archery target.

'May the Devil have him for a plaything. If a girl cannot be safe in an orphanage . . .'

I wondered if the speaker had ever been inside an orphanage.

'Had I known, I would never have sold him my best cuts of pork . . .'

Yes, you would, I thought. *Because he was a good customer and a regular payer.*

'It's those mistresses in charge I find fault with . . .'

Ah yes, at the final tally it would be women who took the blame.

In our group no one said anything until Ulisse broke the silence with a whoop of triumph before clapping Filippo on his injured shoulder, which made him wince. Malatesta and the Maestro congratulated each other with a careful embrace but I turned away, unable to share their joy. If I had been told weeks since that this would be the result of my stratagem – that Laura and all the rest of us would be avenged, that Fontana would suffer at his own hands rather than face the disgrace of remaining alive in Bologna – I would have felt that God had answered my prayers. Yet now it had come to pass, my overwhelming sentiment was anger. The man had outwitted us all. He had shut himself away in that massive palazzo, no doubt waiting to see if his company was still welcomed by his peers. Then when he found that it was not, and that his wife would no longer be the meek helpmeet he demanded, he had made his coward's choice. So much for his censure of Laura for the same act. I walked off, rage bubbling inside me, without any idea of where I was heading. Let the Maestro withhold my pay or mete out some other punishment, if he willed it – I could not work that afternoon.

The streets were soon empty once again; the brief excitement of Fontana's self-slaughter was not sufficient to entice people out of doors for long. Despite the thaw, there was still a chill wind and my feet were numb from treading through melting snow – conditions which matched my thoughts. Once again, I was back at the Baraccano: trying to thread a needle with fingers lumpy with chilblains; shivering under a thin blanket, unable to sleep; and worst of all being praised by Fontana for my hard nipples, as if desire were the cause rather than cold. There was – had been – no end to the man's self-delusion. When I finally came back to the present, I found that I was heading down Via Santo Stefano and there, on the right, the arches of the Baraccano formed a line of curves, like a lace edging, as far as I could see. This was the first time I had returned to the orphanage – to Via Santo Stefano, in fact – since the day I had fairly run with my bundle towards Signora Ruffo's palazzo. The Baraccano building still repelled me but I no longer feared that a mistress would step through the door and drag me back inside. In fact, it gave me grim pleasure to imagine how the remaining mistresses must be wringing their hands, wondering whether at any moment their casual cruelties would echo around the city's walls. In front of me a huge arch framed a view of the spindly columns of Santa Maria del Baraccano, the church where we knelt away the hours when we neither worked nor slept. Sometimes a girl's head would nod with exhaustion, her closed palms drooping, and her neighbour, if well disposed, would dispense a nudge. The punishment for a girl discovered dozing was to attempt sleep that night whilst sitting bolt upright in a hard chair – guaranteed to encourage a further offence. There were some girls, envious of Laura's beauty, who would have found pleasure in her loss of rest, but we made certain that we always sat side by side and kept each other awake.

I knew that I should have been rejoicing, perhaps calling out to Laura that I had avenged her – even whooping with glee, like Ulisse. Yet what I felt was a dull weight as though all the sadness and injustice of the city was pressing upon me. I trudged on towards the Santo Stefano Gate, where two guards were stamping their feet and clapping their arms to keep warm.

'Afternoon, lad.'

I nodded a response. I had forgotten that I was dressed as Cristoforo. At first, I had welcomed the freedom breeches gave, but now my masculine clothes seemed to confirm that Elena was not good enough and Bologna would only ever accept me as Cristoforo. I was tired of keeping a foot in both stirrups. I no longer had to hide my identity from Fontana, but how could I ever have believed that fine gentlemen would consent to have their chest, buttocks or inside thigh measured by a woman? The Maestro would be content to keep me as a journeyman, of that I was certain, but as for any greater ambition – I might as well aim at becoming a priest.

I knew that I should return to the workshop; a morning's work had been lost and the Maestro would be anxious to finish the orders required for Christmas. Yet I could not bear another afternoon playing the part of eager boy apprentice. I turned on my heel and ran back down Santo Stefano as though pursued by one of the demons in the frescoes of San Petronio. Once at the Two Towers, I slowed down and tramped through deep slush in the winding alleys that used to make up the Jewish quarter. The thaw was taking its time to reach these streets: no wider than a path and lined with buildings so tall they blocked out the sun. I did not pass another citizen (which was my aim) and soon reached the road that clung to the south side of the Reno.

With careful timing, I had avoided meeting my landlady while dressed as Cristoforo: hers was a rigid routine based around Masses and trips to the market. But on that day, I had forgot her pattern and longed only to be shut in my room, curled up on my pallet. I pushed open the front door to find myself face to face with her. She squealed.

'Get out, get out! What do you think you are about, young man?'

She had nothing to use as a weapon but looked quite ready to pummel me with knobbled fists. I pulled off my cap and yanked some pins from my hair so that it fell messily down.

'It's me, Signora. It's Elena. No need to be afraid.'

'Elena?' She peered at me with rheumy eyes. 'Why in the name of all the blessed saints are you dressed like that?'

'It is nothing, Signora. I was . . . I am just trying on a costume to wear for the revels on Epifania. I am sorry that I startled you.'

'A girl dressed as a man? The blasphemy.' She was crossing herself repeatedly. 'Never again under my roof, do you hear?'

'I do, Signora. I swear.'

And I meant it. I sidled past her and ran up the stairs. Once through the door, I tore off all my male clothes, throwing them across the room, and put on my undershift intending to lie down and hope to sleep. I was standing near my table when the weeping began. Since Laura's death, any tears I shed had been grudging and silent. But in a moment my body was shaking with guttural sobs, tears coursed down my face and I had to clutch the back of the chair, for fear that I would slump to the floor. I could not fathom the source of my tears; I was exhausted, yes, and perhaps that was grounds enough. And the sight of Fontana hanging by the neck had dragged me back into the confraternity boardroom and Laura's limp body. But as the tears began to subside and I sat with head in hands, I understood that I was mourning my failures: Fontana was dead but there were so many others ready to slip into his place; my hopes of becoming a tailor were thinning to nothing like one of Bologna's fogs. As for the Carraccis – as for Agostino – I could see no reason why I would ever see them again. It was time to accept the only future within my grasp. I would be the one female journeyman tailor in the city, though never to be registered as such. I would improve my skills until the Maestro and all his gentlemen could not deny them. And I would have Sofia as my friend. I went to my pallet and slept for twelve hours, only wakening with the mills.

Chapter Twenty-Six

It was as Elena that I arrived at the workshop the following morning and greeted the Maestro with a curtsey. He looked as though he might speak but instead chose to nod a greeting before setting us our tasks for the day.

We were each working on a different part of an extravagant purple brocade outfit with slashed breeches for a young gentleman with more money than taste: Filippo had the breeches, Ulisse the sleeves and I was sewing the doublet. We had all completed the construction of our pieces and were adding detail – in my case, a row of bound buttonholes. I clambered up on the table and arranged my skirts over crossed legs before measuring button against marking once, twice, thrice, as the Maestro insisted. The smallest error with the slashing tool and I would be making the whole of the left front again – wasting both time and fabric. Journeymen had lost their positions for less or, at the very least, had wages docked until the debt was repaid. I was concentrating so hard that I took little notice of the light tap on the counter outside and my head was still lowered when the Maestro led in our visitor. It was only Ulisse's nudge which caused me to look up; Sofia was standing in the middle of the workshop, brow furrowed and hands twisting at her waist. I slid off the table, scattering buttons.

'Sof! Is all well?'

'She said I must not tell you. But that is wrong.'

'The Signora? Tell me what?'

'She ill'

'How ill? Has she taken to her bed?'

'No. But she should. Agnella and I try to tell her. She does not listen.'

My first thought was to leave immediately and run all the way down Mercato, dragging Sofia behind me, but I had left the Maestro in the lurch only the day before and could not do so again.

'I will come straight after work.' Sofia's expression remained distraught. 'Do not worry. I will contrive a reason for my visit.'

Her head bobbed up and down repeatedly, as though she were trying to convince herself.

'I must go. She think I am at Ravegnana market.'

I took her hand and squeezed it.

'She will not know you have told me.'

She hurried out and I scoured the floor for my buttons before settling back to work. No one spoke for the length of an Our Father, and I feared that my life outside the workshop had forced itself past the counter once too often. It was Ulisse who broke the silence, without even looking up.

'I will clear up our mess today, Maestro.'

By the end of the day, twelve bound buttonholes were lined up like arrow slits on the Asinelli, and opposite each a pearl button. *Grazie Dio*, I had slashed none too loose. Clean-handed, I buttoned and unbuttoned – up and down, down and up until wrenching turned to securing. Then I took my work to the Maestro and he scrutinised it at the window, as always, before I earned a nod of approval and a shoo out the door.

She was in the wrong place: that is what I noticed first. For all of the three years I spent at the workroom, the Signora's embroidery table was positioned where light illuminated every stitch. But it had been moved – not just out of the sunshine but to a dim corner behind the painted screen. Agnella had led me up, and over her shoulder I caught brief sight of the Signora crumpled across the table, head held between her hands, back bowed. But as soon as she heard my greeting, she sat to attention like a cardinal's guard. I had to stop myself recoiling; her face was the yellow of *herba roccia* and her clothes hung from her like an empty garment on the beam.

'Elena. What brings you to see me?' She flashed an angry glance at Sofia who was arranging fabric bolts on the shelves. 'Or should I say "who"?'

'The thought was mine alone, mistress. I have not seen you since before the snow and I wondered how you had fared.' I took my gaze from her face and looked around the room. 'I see there is much work for the three of you.'

She sighed.

'Sit down, Elena. And let us do away with this pretence. Sofia has told you that I am ill. It is true.'

I pulled a chair behind the screen and sat opposite her.

'What ails you, Signora? Has a physician diagnosed the illness?'

'I will not be bothering any of them.'

'But why not? There is perhaps some medication they can offer – or even surgery. Where else but Bologna would you find a reputable surgeon?'

'I do not need a physician to tell me that it is some malignancy – and no surgeon will be slicing into me. The apothecary provides some relief with mandrake and hemlock – and ginger aids the vomiting.'

'Mandrake and hemlock are no cure!'

She reached across the table and clasped my hand.

'There is no cure, Elena.'

I wrenched my hand away.

'You cannot know that. Why will you not consult someone?'

'Look at me, my dear. I am approaching my end. All I pray for is that Our Lord does not send me much agony.'

'What of your friends? Of Sofia, Agnella – me? You must contrive to get well for us.'

A look of irritation passed across her face.

'I must do no such thing. All is arranged and I await God's time. Please do not make my last days more unpleasant than they need to be.'

I lowered my head.

'I am sorry, mistress. Tell me what I can do.'

'Please tell those who need to know – the Carracci boys, Rondinelli and Malatesta. They are all good men, Elena.' She smiled. 'As was my husband. Try not to forget that such men exist.'

She yawned and her eyelids were drooping.

'You should retire to your bed, Signora.'

'If I did so, there is much danger that I would never rise again. But I will rest on the couch. Give me your arm.'

I went around the table and she leant on me, her weight no more than that of a child. Sofia was already preparing the couch with the cushions and blanket which lay ready, and I thought it likely that Signora Ruffo spent most of her days and nights there. As soon as Sofia had pulled the blanket to her chin, the mistress was asleep, her breathing light and short. I pulled Sofia behind the screen and beckoned Agnella to join us.

'How long has she been like this?'

Sofia shrugged.

'No more than two weeks. It has been so fast.'

Agnella nodded.

'She had seemed tired and weak before that, but we thought it was just that we had lots of work.'

Agnella did not say it, but there was something else which had tired the mistress: all the arrangements for our unmasking of Fontana – and her tramping round the city to ensure the safety of those ex-Baraccano girls. How thoughtless I had been. I should have realised that the Signora was failing when the signs were there for all to see: her shortness of breath, the dark shadows beneath her eyes. Sofia touched my shoulder and spoke as though she had read my thoughts.

'It not your fault, Elena. No one's fault.'

'But is there nothing to be done?'

'You heard. She does not wish it. We will take care of her comfort. I promise.'

I longed to run to the Archiginnasio portico and drag a

university physician from his books to attend her. But the mistress had made it clear that such an action would bring her pain rather than relief. I felt powerless to help her.

I spent the next few days making up for all the licence given me by the Maestro over recent weeks. I was first under the shutters every morning and worked with furious attention all day until late December's early darkness filled the alleys, when either Filippo or Ulisse would accompany me home. Ulisse had lately begun to patch into every conversation the name of the barmaid at The Sun, and it suited him to escort me and then slip behind its counter on his way back to his own lodgings. Filippo teased him with questions about the need to summon a priest, but my guess was that the news she was with child would be sufficient ceremony for them.

When I had told the Maestro of Signora Ruffo's malady, he dispatched me to the apothecary at once with an order for a basket of medicinal herbs and roots to be sent to her. He and she resembled two pieces of fabric joined with pins – a barbed seam, but a seam nonetheless. Despite their attempts at concealment, I knew that each had great respect, maybe even liking, for the other. Giorgio Malatesta's gift of lavender-stuffed pillows with a kind note were a mark of the man. I had nothing to give except the task she had put upon me. With the workshop now told, I set off on the next Lord's Day for the Carracci studio.

Maria greeted me at the door and chattered her way loudly up the stairs. Ludovico and Annibale were out, she told me, working on the altarpiece at the church outside the walls. Agostino had to stay behind for a few hours to – she hesitated – deal with another commission. She was, I believe, giving Agostino a warning, for when we reached the studio, he was hurriedly covering up something he had been working on which lay flat on the table.

'Signora Elena.' He gave a deep bow. 'I am delighted to see you. Are you content for Maria to continue with her work?'

I had long felt safe in his company and nodded my agreement. As soon as she skittered down the stairs, I rushed out my message. Agostino sat down hard on the nearest chair.

'The poor woman. She has been good to us. She even buys our work from time to time.'

It was then I realised that something was missing from the room: Sofia's portrait was no longer on Annibale's easel and had been replaced by a fine Madonna and Child in progress, the fabric folds already roughed out.

'She has bought the portrait?'

'A gift for Sofia, perhaps?' He fiddled with the set of incising tools on the table. 'The Signora has achieved much in the life God gave her. Not least a happy marriage, I believe.'

'But it was as a widow that she became the most sought-after seamstress in the city.'

He got up and walked over to the window, his back turned to me.

'You think a married woman can have no success in her profession?'

'I am certain of it. Had her husband not died, she would still be tidying his workshop like an apprentice.'

He sighed and turned back to face me. Eager to change the

subject, I pulled at the cloth covering his work in progress, certain there would be something I could admire. It slid off revealing a metal plate – a partially complete engraving of another couple in congress. I bent close to it, admiring the incised lines, as fine as thread, that he had used to depict skin and drapery. The perfectly proportioned figures were both archetypes of human beauty – he muscled, she soft and rounded. They were immersed in each other and I felt like an intruder in the room, a peeper no less. My previous glimpses of Agostino's engravings had revolted me. In my imagination, I had seen a young woman being molested just as we Baraccano girls had been. But Fontana was right in one respect; the woman was welcoming her lover with a look of pleasurable anticipation as she guided his member with her hand. I almost envied her. How inconceivable it was to me that a woman should want to receive a man in that way, rather than endure his grappling hands. That was something Fontana had stolen from me. I looked up. Agostino's head was lowered, his hands twisting together.

'We are not all Fontana.'

'I know. But I could not ask any man to mend that particular tear.'

I left soon afterwards.

Chapter Twenty-Seven

Signora Ruffo died two days later, slipping away in her sleep so Sofia said, though I wonder still whether she told me the truth; the Signora's need for so many pain medicaments suggested otherwise. Agnella had run for a priest and the mistress managed to gasp out her final confession before her soul passed to Purgatory. I did not believe that her stay there would be long. With her customary foresight, the Signora had regularly handed over the necessary money to a confraternity so that her funeral service and burial place were already paid for. All was noted down in the back of her accounts book, its hiding-place at the back of a drawer in her embroidery table revealed to Sofia in her dying hours. Even in death, Properzia Ruffo would be taken for no man's fool. Together with the book was a small clay pot full of coins: for the candles, she said. They were to be of the finest beeswax – 'No tallow!' The woman had thought of everything.

Sofia and I removed her shawl and undershift and laid her

out on the cutting-table, which was her chosen bier. We washed her body with warm water, basins of which Agnella ferried back and forth from the Signora's living quarters, and patted it dry with pieces of the softest woollen cloth. The Signora had always been proud of her firm figure and stately height, yet now she appeared shrunken, her skin shrivelled away from her bones. Agnella was then dispatched to the best apothecary in the city, where priests of the finest churches placed their orders, to bring back eight of the best beeswax candles the little pot of money would buy. Meanwhile, Sofia and I forced the Signora's stiff limbs into her favourite dress which was made of a blue silk, its colour as deep as lapis lazuli.

We set up the candles around her body, two each at head and foot and two at either side of her waist, and settled in for our vigil with shutters closed against the dark. Once it was properly night, we took it in turns: two keeping watch while one attempted sleep on the Signora's couch, though the movements and sighs suggested that it was a wakeful night for us all. I could not stop brooding on the unfairness of the Signora's death. She was not young, that much was true – she must have completed five decades or near to it – but her workroom had, until the very end, been such an industrious place, and her mind so fertile with ideas to please her customers. That would have been sufficient to compass a life well spent, but Signora Ruffo had done so much more: sharing her skills and offering a home to many young women. Young women like me. I dared not imagine what my life could have been if I had ended up as little more than a slave to some rich couple careless of my humanity. I was reminded of Sofia – Suhailah – who truly had been a slave, forced to perform as Fontana's 'monkey' until Signora

Ruffo had freed her. And the mistress had clearly saved Agnella too, who had been in danger of losing her wits because of what she endured at the Baraccano. She had even helped some of the city's prostitutes to find safe work with Agostino. How many of us owed our safety from harm to her. The thought of Agostino took me back to our last meeting. It would be an embellishment to say that we parted friends – in fact, I do not believe that he even looked at me again after I rejected his tentative proposal. Agostino's handsome charm and easy manners attracted me – I would not deny it – but I could never take him for a husband. It was no longer his lewd engravings which caused me disquiet. If Fontana had not been salivating over them, he would have found a different spur for his visits to the Baraccano. There were greater obstacles to the marriage than that. My tailoring would never be able to compete for daylight with the Carraccis' art and I would end up resenting Agostino and being resented by his brothers and cousin – especially Ludovico. Nor could I envisage sharing Agostino's bed without Fontana also being present.

By the time the Accursio struck Prime, we were already blowing out the guttering candles, and soon after we began wrapping the Signora's body ready for burial. Though her station as an artisan – and a female one at that – demanded white linen or a sombre *monachino*, we chose a length of voided velvet in a deep burgundy, its pattern one of curlicues and teardrops, representing growing plants. The priest would, no doubt, curl his lip at the extravagance but our mistress deserved a shroud which reflected the glory of her profession. Soon afterwards, there was a knock on the outside door and Agnella went down to let in a whispering group, who turned out to be the Maestro together with Signor Malatesta, Filippo and Ulisse. Scarcely had she led them into the room than a further knock brought Annibale and Agostino Carracci. I nodded to each arrival and Agostino muttered an apology for his cousin's absence – as if any of us expected Ludovico to attend. Our mourning party was complete. After some discussion as to how it was to be managed, the six men raised the table to knee height and manoeuvred it through the door. *Grazie Dio*, the staircase from landing to front door is broad and they were able to shuffle down sideways keeping the bier level above the treads. We three women hung back until they reached the front door, when Agnella rushed forward and opened both leaves. Though custom required us to remain behind and take no part in the procession, slinking into church only as the priest intoned the opening words of the Mass, we three had no intention of allowing our mistress to travel to San Francesco without us. And it seemed that others had the same thought. As soon as the men raised the bier onto their shoulders and stepped through the door, I heard their gasps of surprise. Outside a crowd of women, one hundred or more, had been waiting to accompany their beloved seamstress, Signora Properzia Ruffo, to her final rest. They fell in behind us as a single bell tolled from the campanile of San Francesco and the sun rose through a fine drizzle. The slow walk began, around the low curved wall which enclosed the entrance to Santa Maria delle Laudi then taking a narrow way between tall houses, and left down a path which led straight to the entrance of the basilica. When the female procession trooped in, the priest's face spoke his discontent, but it was done now and his disapproving look counted for nothing with us. He droned through the Mass but, even so, Sofia and I clasped hands as our bodies shook with sobbing. When he had finished and finally turned to face us, the Signora's male friends once again lifted the cutting-table bier and we all trailed behind it around the outside of the church to the burial ground behind. The gravediggers were still hurrying to finish the hole, their blasphemies cut short by our approach, and we had to pause while the drizzle turned to steady rainfall, drenching our cloaks as we stood in silence, avoiding each other's eyes. Finally, the gravediggers shuffled off, dragging their tools behind them, the priest took his place at the head of the grave and our pall-bearers, with all the dignity they could manage, slid Signora Properzia Ruffo into it. The priest mumbled a few prayers, but my mind wandered from my dead mistress and I found myself imagining the gown which could have been made from the voided velvet, shrinking from the knowledge that it would soon be dirtied by the earth piled on top of her. I shook my head to banish the thought. The service complete, the mourning party moved as one towards the churchyard gate where it unravelled and small groups threaded their way in different directions. I was walking alone until the Maestro sidled up to me.

'I do not require you at the workshop today, Elena. It is always quiet after *Epifania*.' He gestured ahead to where Sofia and Agnella walked, their heads bent in urgent conversation. 'I think your friends need you. They are anxious.'

I did not grasp his meaning at once, so entangled was I in my own grief. Then I understood: Sofia and Agnella were trudging back towards the Signora's palazzo, a place where they no longer had work, nor even the right to live. They could both be earning their living on the streets within a few days and that thought had not been a whisper in my mind, even though I had known that fear myself not so long before. My own future was secure – the Maestro had made that clear weeks before – but, wrapped in my own distress, I had not considered what would happen to the Signora's two employees. No wonder they had been sleepless the previous night. I thanked the Maestro and hurried to catch up with them.

'Sofia, did the Signora talk of her plans for the workroom after her death?'

She shook her head.

'She say nothing. Only that will is with notary. I do not know how find him. What we do, Elena? No home, no work.' Sofia's Bolognese was deserting her.

'Do not worry. I know where to find the notary and no one has told you to leave the palazzo yet. You two go back and rest.'

'Yes, yes. Thank you. We will tidy up the workroom.'

I hid a smile. It was impossible to stop Sofia from working when she believed something required doing.

The Palazzo dei Notai might have been designed to discourage visitors. It was constructed as a solid, flat-faced fortress, on the same side of Piazza Maggiore as San Petronio but separated from it by a narrow alley. The Church and the Law displaying their joint power. Along the rooftop of the palazzo were mock battlements, as though to repel intruders, and above its door the goose-quill symbol of the legal profession was picked out in a stone relief. I took a deep breath and pushed at the heavy door, without any plan as to what I would do once I got inside.

The reception hallway resembled a huge ants' nest of notaries who scurried this way and that, up and down the broad staircase, each intent on whatever task he had to perform. A few looked askance at me – a young woman who had breached their citadel – but most did not even notice my presence, so much so that two barged into me. Finally, I saw a wooden construction, much like a confessional, tucked into one corner of the hallway. Inside it, a white-haired man, slumped in a chair, was nodding in sleep, jowls wobbling with every breath. My knock on the narrow counter was enough to rouse him and he peered at me through bleary eyes.

'What?'

'Please, Signore, I am looking for a notary.'

He waved his hand around the hall.

'Plenty to choose from.'

'I mean – that is – I am seeking a particular notary.'

'Name?'

'Elena Morandi, sir.'

'Not yours, you stupid girl. His.'

'I don't know.'

He heaved himself to his feet.

'Listen. If you have come here to waste my time, a couple of these young notaries will be more than happy to throw you out of the building. And give you a good grope on the way. Last chance, girlie. Who is it you want?'

I drew myself up.

'I need to see the notary of Signora Properzia Ruffo, who died just yesterday. I believe he has her will.'

His nods set his jowls moving once again.

'I heard she had left this world. A good woman, by all

accounts. The man you want is Cellini. First floor, third door on the left. But he will only tell you to send a man.'

I gave the shadow of a curtsey and hurried away.

The door of the room was open and inside five, perhaps six, desks were squashed together, each covered in toppling piles of documents. Only one chair was occupied.

'Signor Cellini?'

He didn't even look up, only continued flicking his quill across a page.

'I have sufficient business. No more clients required.'

'I am not a new client, sir. I am here to see the will of Signora Properzia Ruffo.'

At that, he laid down the quill and began scrabbling in a bundle of papers to his right. He pulled out a document and held it up to his narrowed eyes. Finally, he looked up.

'Elena Morandi? You are quick away from the mark.'

'Sir?'

'I will need a man of good standing to vouch for you, but then it is yours.'

I was confused.

'The will, Signore?'

'Not the will, girl. The palazzo, the business. That is what you wanted to know, was it not?'

'I – I just wanted to know what will happen to her employees, sir. I was concerned for Sofia and Agnella.'

He ran his forefinger down the written lines.

'Sofia . . . Agnella . . . Ah, yes. There is a condition that you give them employment for as long as they bring benefit to the workroom. Does that present difficulties?'

'Not at all. They are fine workers both. But is the Signora's business truly mine?'

He thrust the papers towards me.

'Can you read?'

'I can, sir.'

I took the papers to the nearest window, and read them by the sunlight carving sharp shadows onto the pavement of Piazza Maggiore below. The will was a simple one; the Signora had left a few small bequests to others (one of which would cause Sofia to rejoice) but the palazzo itself, including the workroom and all its contents, were to be mine. There were but three stipulations: that the workroom should 'continue to clothe the citizens of Bologna'; that the two seamstresses should be retained; and that I should offer up regular prayers to shorten the Signora's time in Purgatory and help lift her to Paradise. I don't know how long my silence lasted but the notary finally broke it.

'Is there a hindrance, girl?'

I shook my head.

'Then come back tomorrow. With a man. I assume you know a respectable one?'

I glared at him but made no reply. He cleared his throat.

'The legal matters will be straightforward. Tomorrow, no later than noon.'

I do not recall leaving the room, or even the building. I found that I had turned, out of habit, into the tangle of alleys alongside the piazza, but I was not ready to announce my news to anyone – neither the workshop nor my . . . employees. How strange it was to think of Sofia and Agnella thus! I needed solitude in which to think and so made once again for the church of San Matteo, tucked away behind Drapperie. I gave the door a gentle push and peeped inside to check that a Mass was not in progress. The censorious priest who officiated at Signora Ruffo's funeral had given me my fill of clergy for some time. There was no service taking place but this time I was not the only visitor; an elderly woman, a true worshipper judging by her conduct, was kneeling in the front row of pews, nearest to the altar. She did not turn as the door scraped shut, but maintained a constant mutter of prayer, her fingers never still as she worked them along her rosary. I took my seat in the back corner and lowered my head in feigned religious meditation, while my thoughts spun like a silk spindle.

I could not deny how generous the mistress had been. Though we shared no blood, she had bequeathed to me all that one might leave to a beloved son – or daughter. With one signature she had made me the gift not only of a business of my own, but also a comfortable home; these were things which had existed only in my reveries. She had trusted me too with her clients, women who would be eager to offer their loyalty and goodwill – as long as I proved myself worthy. The Signora must have believed it, and I was confident that I could soon earn their trust. It only takes a few well-sewn garments for a reputation to become shot through a workroom like the weft of a fine *cangiante*. The Signora had made provision for Sofia and Agnella too. How sweet it would be to tell them that they need have no fears for their futures: that they would never be bought or sold, and nor, as long as they made good choices, would they find themselves at a man's mercy. For all this, I should be grateful. And yet . . .

Signora Ruffo was forcing me to carry a burden I had not chosen. She knew full well that I longed to be a tailor, not a seamstress. She even praised the distance I had travelled along that road. Yet now it seemed that my once-mistress had wrenched me away from Rondinelli's austere workshop and put me back into a world of women. My thoughts returned to that morning when I crept out of her workroom with my bundle, determined never to return, because she had made a decision about my future without even a word to me. And the woman had done it again! She had decreed that I would become a seamstress and run a workroom, knowing that I could not reject the bequest when the threads of Sofia's and Agnella's happiness were so tightly twisted within it. I would be trapped in a welter of frills and furbelows! There was one certainty; I must return to Signor Cellini on the morrow with a 'respectable' man or risk throwing away the futures of two frightened young women. I needed to talk to the Maestro.

'You do not appear very pleased.'

Rondinelli had given the journeymen an early finish (The Sun their likely destination) and I was sitting across from him at his cutting-table.

'I am swaying like a tree in the wind. I am so happy that Sofia and Agnella can be safe and work as before. And I cannot deny that to live in that palazzo, to run my own workroom . . . it would be so very *comfortable*.'

'But?'

'I want to tailor. Even if that means I can never rise above unofficial journeyman.'

He stood up and walked to the window, staring out into the early dusk.

'I do not know anything of your skills as a seamstress, Elena, but I do know that you are a fine tailor. One I would be sorry to lose.' He turned to face me. 'I also know that you would never do anything which took security away from those two young women. You know only too well how important it is to feel safe from the whims of men. I think that you have already made your decision.'

I nodded. I could not refuse the bequest, nor sell the workroom to another, because to do so would leave Sofia and Agnella ever tiptoeing around a new mistress, fearful of offending. By accepting it, I would give two young women – or rather, three – a secure future. What more could I ask?

'Would you be so kind as to attend the notary with me tomorrow, Maestro?'

'With pleasure.'

'And, please, do not tell anyone of my doubts.'

I knew that my news would be welcome at Signora Ruffo's palazzo – I supposed that I must now call it my palazzo – but I did not expect to be whirled around the workshop by Sofia in a dance of joy, while Agnella alternated between sobs and smiles. Their gratitude seemed boundless, though I had to keep reminding them that it was owed to the Signora, not me. Finally, Agnella went to fetch some watered wine while Sofia and I slumped on the divan. She gave me a sideways look.

'You are happy, yes?'

'Of course! What a success we will be. Signora Ruffo will be proud of us. We will work so hard and sew such beautiful garments that her clients will not think of going elsewhere.' I attempted a laugh. 'But you will have to remind me how to gather a silk skirt onto a bodice. It has been nearly a year and I fear I have forgotten.'

Sofia laid a hand on my arm.

'Do not pretend, Elena. You are pleased for us, but a little sad for you.'

I stood up and strolled around the room. It was immaculate: not a speck of lint on the floor; every bolt of fabric neatly rolled on its correct shelf; equipment out of sight in the drawers, no doubt lined up in serried rows. Sofia and Agnella were honouring their mistress in the best way they knew. I pretended fascination with a roll of *rosato di grana*, rubbing the fine scarlet wool between my fingers.

'It matters not, Sof. The Signora was right – Bologna will never allow a woman to become a tailor. This,' I waved an arm to encompass the room, 'is the next best thing.'

Sofia's reply was little more than a whisper.

'For me – and for Agnella too, I think – it is the very best thing.'

Signor Cellini peered over the piles of documents on his desk as though trying to recall where he had seen me before.

'Yes?'

'Elena Morandi, Signore. You told me to return with a man to vouch for me.'

'Ah, yes. The main beneficiary of Signora Ruffo.' He gestured in the Maestro's direction. 'And you are . . . ?'

'Maestro Francesco Rondinelli. Tailor. And I can swear—'

'Hold fast.'

After some ferreting, he brought out the document I had read the day before and thrust it at Rondinelli. The Bible was on a shelf behind him and he heaved it onto the desk.

'Are you this woman's guardian? Husband?'

'Neither. I am her employer – for the present.'

'That will have to do.' He glanced up. 'There is no need of your reading it, Maestro. You are here only to swear that the girl is who she says she is.'

'Nevertheless . . . I wish to be certain that my friend – employee – does not mistake fireflies for lanterns. I would not want her to be misled.'

Cellini huffed his displeasure but did not interrupt the Maestro while he read to the end of the will. At one point, Rondinelli drew in a sharp breath and I wondered if he had found something amiss, but when he had finished reading, he gave me one of his rare smiles.

'All is in order, Elena.'

The rest of the business was over in moments; the Maestro placed his right hand on the Bible and swore to God that I was indeed Elena Morandi, the will's beneficiary. The notary then signed whatever it was he needed to sign before scrabbling about on his desk once more.

'I have had a copy made. This is yours.'

He tried to pass it to Rondinelli, but the Maestro took a

step back and Cellini was forced to place the will in my hands. I curtseyed my thanks and the notary's head was already buried in his papers before we left the room.

'Did you notice, Elena? Did you see what the Signora did?'

I had never seen the Maestro look excited and it was rather unsettling. He was running down the stairs of the palazzo and I had to raise my skirts in order to keep up with him.

'I don't understand, Maestro. Slow down, please.'

He didn't answer but strode off across the piazza and through the arch into Clavature. I assumed he was going straight back to the workshop but as we approached The Sun, he slowed down.

'Pretend to swoon.'

'What?'

'It's the only way we can sit and talk in peace. If he thinks you need help, the tavern-keeper will let us in and not mistake you for a prostitute.'

He was right, of course. There could be no private conversation at the workshop and an unchaperoned stroll would harm my reputation – even if it might be useful for his. Just as we reached the door of the tavern, I raised a hand to my forehead and stumbled, quite convincingly, I thought, against him. He offered an arm and led me across the threshold.

'Sir, we have a young woman in distress here. A seat in the corner and a jug of wine, if you please.'

The tavern-keeper gave me an appraising look but must have decided that my clothes did not mark me as a bawd touting for trade, because he nodded towards the far corner of the room. I made a good show of slumping onto a bench and the Maestro sat down opposite, shielding me from the door. Not that The

Sun's reputation was in much danger of being blighted, since the only other customer was a sleeping drunk who looked like he had been there since the previous night. Once the owner had brought us a jug of wine, one of water and a couple of beakers, the Maestro poured us both a well-watered wine. He kept his voice low, as though enquiring after my health.

'Tell me, Elena. What is the first stipulation of the will?'

'It says that I must clothe the women of Bologna . . .'

'No, it doesn't.'

I was becoming irritated. All this charade and the man had clearly not read the document properly. I pulled it out from beneath my apron and unrolled it on the table.

'Here. Look.' I prodded a finger at the words of the first stipulation before reading it out loud. '"The workroom under said beneficiary, Elena Morandi, must continue to clothe the citizens"—' I stopped and looked up, puzzled at my error. The Maestro's expression was gleeful.

'Do you not see? She has not limited you to being a seamstress at all. She knew full well that you wanted to become a tailor and she has tried to help.'

I rolled the will up again and stuffed it back under my apron.

'And how, by San Francesco, does that assist me? What gentleman will suddenly decide to abandon Drapperie and trudge halfway across the city to be dressed by three women?'

'But what if they do not go anywhere? What if you come to them? To my workshop, while their wives are being tended to by Sofia and . . . the other girl.'

'But who will run Signora Ruffo's workroom?'

'You will. Or rather, we both will. There will be two

establishments, run by us, where both men and women can buy fine garments. You will be both tailor and seamstress. I do not guarantee that I will find a new passion for frills and ruffles, but I am meticulous when it comes to keeping accounts and well versed in finding new custom. We will share the tasks. The details require attention but do you not think it could work, Elena?'

I fell silent, checking over the details of his idea as though it were a newly finished garment. To be both tailor and seamstress would be a hard undertaking indeed and would require all the stamina I had, especially if I was trotting daily between two workrooms. And though I had measured and cut for many a woman's outfit, I had still not yet done so for a man. I had much to learn, even assuming that the Maestro's clients would allow a young woman to measure so close to their codpieces. But . . . to be a proper tailor! Not just a journeyman who followed instructions. It was what I had always desired, and Rondinelli was suggesting a way to achieve it. My thoughts turned to Signora Ruffo's – that is, my – workroom. Sofia's skills had greatly improved in the past year; I had seen that for myself. She could now tackle a fitted gown that would satisfy the most thread-splitting of clients. And Agnella had taken Sofia's place as a useful workroom assistant who was able to make undershifts or sew long seams on gowns, as long as the fabric was tractable. Well supervised, they could manage the work without difficulty.

The Maestro had remained silent while I considered his proposal, and I was about to agree to it when I fell to imagining the daily comings and goings in the palazzo. All at once, I saw that it was impossible. While Signora Ruffo had been a constant presence in her workroom, Sofia was safe. She had no need to approach clients and risk being rebuffed – or worse. But if I were spending time as a tailor at Rondinelli's, she would need to talk to them, touch them as they tried on their gowns. I feared for her but also, I could not deny it, for the future of the workroom. How many would go elsewhere rather than permit a touch from Sofia's hands?

The Maestro interrupted my thoughts.

'If it is the cutting and fitting which concerns you, our lessons can begin today. Giorgio needs a new suit for those civic occasions he is forever being invited to, and I know he would be delighted to be your volunteer.'

'Would it were that simple.'

I laid out my concerns before him and he listened, nodding his head as I spoke but offering no pat answer. The tavern was filling up now as local artisans arrived to do deals over a jug of wine, and the owner was throwing anxious glances in our direction. It would only take an overzealous *sbirro* for him to be closed down for brothel-keeping. I stood up.

'We should return to work, Maestro. The others will be wondering where we are gone.'

'Indeed. But remember one thing, Elena. A good Maestro – or Maestra – persuades a client to choose the fabric and style which suits them. The clients do not make the choices, though they may think otherwise. In truth, we do.'

I had saved telling Sofia of Signora Ruffo's personal bequest to her and now it gave me good excuse to visit her again. Dark evenings meant that, dressed as Elena, I would not be safe out alone until the following Lord's Day. But that afternoon I returned home from work at dusk and pulled Cristoforo's clothes once more from their hiding-place under my pallet. By the time I arrived at the palazzo it was already dark, but those I had passed alongside the Reno paid no heed to a young man out alone at night. Agnella was all for closing the door on me, until I announced who I was, and she insisted on calling Sofia downstairs to check my identity. I had forgot that Sofia had never seen me dressed as Cristoforo and was unprepared for her burst of laughter, which prompted the same in Agnella. Even when we had settled in the workroom, Sofia could not resist an occasional snigger, but her mood changed when I told her of Annibale's portrait and how the Signora had bought it on purpose to bequeath to her. She clapped her hands in delight.

'It is so kind. I love the painting. I put it up in here.' She gave a cheeky grin. 'But only if my new mistress approves . . .'

I grinned back.

'In pride of place opposite the door, I think.'

Sofia's expression became serious.

'Do you think she knew she was dying?'

'I think she knew a long time ago. She spent many months organising everything.'

'It is true. Yesterday much fabric arrived. I was scared. How do I pay? But it was already paid.'

'She thought of everything.'

Agnella was busy piling up the new bolts of fabric on shelves and I took the opportunity to explain to Sofia the Maestro's idea for a joint workshop, serving both men and women, which would allow me to be both a seamstress and a tailor. I should have known that she would immediately spot the hindrance.

'So I would be here sometimes just with Agnella? With clients?'

'You are a fine seamstress now, Sof. You have the skills to dress any noblewoman.'

'Perhaps. But they have to wish it. And you know that they will not.'

I stood up and went to the window.

'That will be their choice.'

When she did not reply, I turned to find her staring at me, face set.

'You pretend it does not matter. It does. This' – she pointed at her face – 'will not go away. But the customers will. I will ruin both you and Maestro. Best I go.'

She stood up, seemingly intent on leaving that very moment and, for the first time, I stepped forward and held her in a tight embrace. I had lost one friend by letting go – it would not happen again.

'This is my workroom, Sof. I mean, Suhailah. I will decide who works here. Some customers may take their business elsewhere but I am certain that others will stay. They know the quality of our work.'

Epilogue

I will not lie; the first months saw a line of gentlewomen (or so they would call themselves) scuttling off down the stairway of the palazzo, swearing by every saint in the canon that they would never return while that 'abomination' or 'female devil' or whatever word they used for my friend was allowed near. I almost gave up and resigned myself to seamstress work alone so that Sofia could remain at a distance from them. The turning-point came when she created an especially fine wedding gown for a niece of the Papal Legate. It was in cloth of gold – a deep-red silk velvet with an added weft of gold thread – and became the main subject of conversation among ladies of fashion in the city for weeks. Our lost customers began to creep back up the stairs, each swearing that she personally had no issue with Sofia . . .

Via Mercato di Mezzo is well trod by me now. At least once a day I rush from tailor's workshop to seamstress's workroom, perhaps measuring and cutting a pair of breeches for a silk merchant at Francesco's, for that is the name I call him by now, and then returning to my palazzo to oversee the fitting of a gown for the man's wife. We have many married couples as our clients and we specialise in complementary garments: the slashes in a doublet revealing the same silk as the skirt of a gown; or the ribbons on a bodice matched with those on a shirt cuff. Many noble citizens of Bologna find the conceit pleasing – especially those whose marriage is based on love rather than money.

I myself have found no love. Agostino continued to pursue me for a while but the Carraccis are now renowned artists, and both he and Annibale spend much of their time in other cities. Only cautious Ludovico has remained in Bologna but he lacks neither work nor pupils, so they say. Sometimes Agostino will visit me when he is back in the city, but our meetings are becoming increasingly awkward and I would not be surprised if they cease soon. Suhailah – she bears her given name now – is married to a fine young man who comes from the same homeland. He is assistant to an apothecary and has such knowledge of plants as I have never before seen. I suspect that Agnella is being courted by a fruit-seller but she is giving nothing away. As for Giorgio Malatesta and Francesco Rondinelli – they relax only when among friends. Otherwise, they hold themselves aloof, always alert, constantly watching for possible spies who might report them whether for malice or gain.

Francesco has a new apprentice: a young man who keeps the workshop neat, despite his own dishevelled appearance. My former Maestro will soon smarten the boy up. Filippo is ageing and holds his work close to his eyes, just as Prospero did all that time ago. Ulisse married his barmaid and they have two brawling toddlers and another baby on the way. Sometimes Filippo and Ulisse make the journey along Mercato di Mezzo to view fabrics or escort a customer to approve his wife's gown. Signora Ruffo's workroom remains the preserve of seamstresses in the morning, but in the afternoons there are sometimes as many men as women bustling around. I had to buy more screens.

No one in the city mentions Antonio della Fontana these days; it is as though the man never existed. Though I am glad that he is not remembered as a public benefactor, I wish that his crimes were forever in people's minds. They certainly remain in the minds of his victims. After much searching, I found Laura's grave, though it was unmarked and beyond San Baraccano's churchyard wall, as is decreed for one who has committed self-slaughter. I cannot get it moved, the priest will never countenance such a thing, but he has allowed a small wooden cross with her name upon it. Laura will know that I did my best for her. Each Lord's Day, I visit the church of San Francesco to offer up prayers for Signora Ruffo so that her time in Purgatory is kept short. She was a good woman and I suspect she left that place long ago and resides where she deserves, but I continue to pray for her soul. I also offer up my own thanks to San Francesco. He is still my favourite saint and seems to have a special place in his heart for tailors – or this tailor, at least.

Author's Note

My first visit to Bologna was supposed to be a one-off short break to an unfamiliar city in a country I already loved. I did not expect to develop something of an obsession for the place and its history, which drove me to return again and again. Bologna today is a beautiful city famed for its porticoes, towers and red roofs, but in 1575 it was a noisy industrial hub criss-crossed with canals (think Birmingham, rather than Venice) which were lined with mills churning out flour, paper and – above all – silk. Outside its walls, fields and fields of mulberry trees fed the silkworms which, in turn, fed the silk industry. Like most Italian cities at the time, Bologna was home to many orphans who were swept away into institutions, such as Santa Maria del Baraccano. Once inside, children became invisible. Elena and her friend Laura are my inventions but they are typical of the girls who would find themselves in those orphanages. Antonio della Fontana also never existed. Except that he did: because, as we know too well, men very like him have always been lurking among us – no less now than in the sixteenth century.

The Bologna of 1575 was not as diverse a city as Genoa or Venice, for example, because of its inland position. However, the silk merchants would have been better travelled than most of its citizens and would have come across people from other countries. Some of those people were slaves from West Africa – a growing trade at the time. They were brought to Europe and forced to adopt European names (so Suhailah became Sofia). I have imagined that Fontana saw Suhailah and her mother in Genoa and bought them. Fortunately for Suhailah, in this period slavery was not always a life sentence.

When it came to creating the tailor in my story, I did not have to imagine what Francesco Rondinelli looked like. In the National Gallery in London there is a famous portrait by Giovanni Battista Moroni painted around 1570. Moroni was born just outside Bergamo and his subjects came from that city and the surrounding area, but I believe he would have felt at home in Bologna's streets. This particular portrait is called *Il Tagliapanni* and shows a well-dressed master tailor disturbed at his work by the viewer. He looks up with an expression of impatience and not a little disdain, as if to say, 'What are you doing here?' For me he became Francesco Rondinelli and that expression is the one I saw when Elena first dared to enter his workshop.

The only characters in *City of Silk* who actually existed are the Carraccis – Ludovico, Agostino and Annibale. Readers can also see the woman who inspired my Sofia / Suhailah in

Portrait of an African Woman Holding a Clock attributed to Annibale currently at the Louvre Abu Dhabi. The artists were at the very beginning of their careers at this time (Annibale just a teenager) and I have invented their personalities; but it is true that they collaborated on joint works, and Agostino is also known for some erotic engravings. Later Agostino and Annibale travelled, whereas Ludovico remained in Bologna and ran their Academy. History deems Annibale to be the greatest artist of the three and I like to imagine that Agostino was aware of that at an early stage.

I had just finished writing *City of Silk* in the spring of 2023 (it was sitting on my laptop, having a rest) when I saw the publicity for a new award: the Debut Writers Over 50 Award launched by Jenny Brown Associates. It was such an inspired idea that I had to enter – and I was thrilled to win it. Since then, Jenny and her Associate Agent Lisa Highton have nurtured me with their characteristic enthusiasm and kindness, always asking the right questions. Thanks to their expertise, the perfect publisher was found, and as soon as I met Lesley Crooks and Susie Dunlop at Allison & Busby, I knew that my book had been gently passed from one set of careful hands to the next.

Like most writers of historical fiction, I so much enjoyed the research for *City of Silk*, particularly since it demanded several more visits to Bologna. How could I resist? I did a lot of reading too, of course, and I am particularly indebted to the work of Professor Nicholas Terpstra of the University of Toronto. His books and articles on the social history of Bologna in this period have been utterly invaluable and are written in such an accessible style. I apologise for piggybacking on his extensive research in the Bologna archives and thank him for all the insights he provided and the orphans he brought back to life. I hope he may recognise the picture I have painted of the city.

I had kept *City of Silk* to myself for a long time. But there are a few people who knew of its existence and have never wavered in their support. Thanks to my sister, Hilary Booker, who has sent many an encouraging email from France; and to my dear friend Celia Jeffries, who has constantly cheered me on. But above all, thank you to my daughter, Isabel Virgo, who has championed my writing ever since she was a teenager and who drove all the way from Oxford to Edinburgh and back in a weekend to see me receive the Award. That says so much about her.

GLENNIS VIRGO started her career in education teaching classics before she became a primary school headteacher. Since her retirement, Virgo has spent her time improving her Italian, visiting Italy (especially Bologna) and writing. City of Silk is her first novel and it won the inaugural Debut Writers Over 50 Award. She lives in Essex.

@glennisvirgo